Playing
the
Air

Playing
the
Air

BILL DUNLOP

Matador
9 Priory Business Park
Kibworth Beauchamp
Leicestershire LE8 0RX, UK
Tel: (+44) 116 279 2299
Fax: (+44) 116 279 2277
Email: books@troubador.co.uk
Web: www.troubador.co.uk/matador

ISBN 978 1780885 469

British Library Cataloguing in Publication Data.
A catalogue record for this book is available from the British Library.

Typeset in 11pt Aldine by Troubador Publishing Ltd
Printed and bound in the UK by TJ International, Padstow, Cornwall

Matador is an imprint of Troubador Publishing Ltd

Offered to:

Nuala Kennedy

Katherine Nicol

Anna Wendy Stevenson

and

I. M.

Cameron Gaskell

Thank you for the music

THE SILVERY TAY

Dunpark House, Perthshire

Charlie Cameron rubbed his head. It still hurt. Having turned the key he began walking back to the house, puzzling over what to do next. The man couldn't be kept locked up forever, but it could be days before anyone turned up. Charlie knew he would have to wait till Katherine was better, which might be long enough. She'd looked a child when he'd carried her upstairs. What had the fellow wanted? There was hardly anything worth stealing. The family had never collected anything, except debts. Plenty other houses he might have picked on, so why Dunpark? What, in heaven's name, did he think he was going to find? Then Charlie remembered the piece in the paper about him lending great-great Uncle Archie to the National Galleries. The man must have thought there would be something else worth stealing. Sorry chum, Charlie wanted to say to the man he'd locked up, but there ain't. Whatever wealth there might once have been was pretty much all gone and if he didn't make a go of the new business, the bank would have more than a go at him.

Thinking like that turned his mind to Katherine once again. He wanted, needed her well, and his footsteps quickened the closer he came to the house. Near enough two hours ago, life had been simple, had felt sweet. Supper in the oven, he'd made his way toward Big Meddie, to tell Katherine it was time to get down off her high horse if she wanted fed. Silly wee joke, but she always laughed. The moment he'd swung past the gate into the field, he'd heard a scream like a seagull's. Then he saw Sugar Puff struggling up, putting feet nervously to the ground. Katherine was on her feet as well, lurching forward, hard hat clutched in one hand, moving as if she'd never put one foot in front of the other before. He'd managed to catch her as she collapsed, and they'd lain there, Charlie's jacket wrapped round her, while he wondered what to do. How long they'd stayed like that he'd no notion, but the next thing he knew – sensed – was someone standing over them. He'd got up then, to find he was staring into piercing eyes.

'Seems you're in a bit of trouble.'

Blinking into the slow-fading September sunlight, Charlie watched the face slowly emerge, so sharp and small it could have belonged to one of the Fairy Folk: the skin pale, the eyes sharp, fierce.

'How long have the two of you been here?'

He'd drawn a blank on that one, and knew he must have looked it.

'D' you think we should try and move her? It's getting cold.'

He'd nodded. He couldn't leave her here.

'Where to?'

'The house down there.'

'The big one?'

There was only themselves for miles either way, but this man didn't seem to know it. Charlie worried about moving her, but she'd lain so long it seemed the best thing. The two men were both breathing heavily by the time they'd reached the edge of the Loch, looking like a great flat saucer awaiting a giant cat. Glints of light caught ripples, flashed and were gone. The house grew into its size as they got nearer. Dunpark had once been a decent farmhouse, till Charlie's great-great-whatever grandfather had decided it was a wee thing wee for the Laird of Dunpark and turned his money into a long, low block of granite, its two storeys and warren of attic windows reflecting the last rays of sunlight, meditating the grandeur of a past the present couldn't match.

Charlie had thrust what was left of his strength against the door. In a moment they stood in the kitchen and he'd let Katherine down onto a chair. She'd been quiet enough till then; it was likely delayed shock made her sob like a child, impossible to comfort or console. When she'd seemed to calm a little, he'd lifted her up, carried her through into the hall and up the stairs. He'd near collapsed on the bed beside her; another kind of shock, he'd supposed. Later he'd remember saying something like:

'You're safe. It's all right now. You're home and you're safe.'

He'd no idea how long he stayed, once he'd wrapped her in an extra blanket and got the sheets and duvet near over her chin. He'd left a light on and gone back downstairs as softly as he could. The noise of his steps must have startled the man, who gave him a suspicious look as he walked back into the kitchen.

'She's sleeping.' Charlie had said, feeling desperately in need of sleep himself.

The man nodded at that, and carried on leaning against the row of kitchen cupboards.

'I ought to call the doctor.'

Charlie had said this as he slumped into one of the chairs, hand clutching the table edge, as if he needed to keep hold of something solid while previous certainties shifted. Ten years and a good deal older, he'd been sure he'd be the one to go first ...

'Pip! Pip! Pip! Pip! Peep!'

It was the radio alarm he'd rigged up. Better than a dinner gong, and they got the news.

'The eight o' clock news here on Radio Breadalbane. It's been announced that the Honourable James Cameron will become leader of his party in the Scottish Parliament, following the unexpected resignation of Neil Oliphant. We'll have full coverage of this development in our nine o' clock *'Holyrood Reporting'* programme. Elsewhere, police are searching for a former Northern Ireland terrorist believed to have evaded arrest on fresh charges and escaped to Scotland.'

The man had snapped off the radio and was staring at him.

'Enough of that nonsense.'

Charlie was still grappling with the idea of his younger brother as some sort of big noise in the Scottish Parliament. James, as far as his brother was concerned, couldn't organise a cheese and wine party, never mind a political one. Perhaps they were easier.

He'd got to his feet then, and was halfway to the door when the man had lurched toward him, barring the way. Charlie had kept himself fit. A point of pride when you share a bed with a woman more than ten years younger than yourself.

'I have to phone the doctor.' He'd said it as levelly as he could, though he could already feel the aggression coming off the man in waves.

'Course you do,' the man had said 'but when people are upset, they let their mouths run. Say things they don't need to. That they'll maybe regret saying.'

Charlie had glanced across the table to the plans he'd been working on before he'd decided to call Katherine in for supper. He'd been pleased when the idea of using the old ice house first came to him. When the distributors had told him they were going to cut the price they'd been paying for milk, it was the last straw. He'd been getting little enough as it was. Organic ice-cream had been Katherine's idea; he'd laughed at first, then thought about it, done a little research, scared himself when he realised what the regulations would mean, then gritted his teeth and decided that damn it, that was what they would do.

The ice house was supposed to have been a Masonic Lodge – you could see what looked like a square and pair of compasses on the lintel above the door, though inside it was bare to the stone. The last time he'd gone in, he had a sense someone had been there since his previous visit to the place. Nothing he could put his finger on, but something had been different. His eyes flicked to the plans again. Strange to have been sitting in the same chair a couple of hours ago, working out a future for the two of them and now wondering if either of them had any future at all.

He'd scarcely had time to realise what the man was doing till he'd ripped the phone line out. Charlie had been close enough to violence not to sense that he had to do something, and fast. The coffee pot was nearest to hand, and the stranger must've felt the full weight of it as he'd stumbled back, swinging blindly at Charlie before he'd crashed to the floor. The blow stung, but Charlie was still on his feet, breathing heavily as he worked out his next move. If he was the man spoken of in the news bulletin, the one who'd escaped, he'd have to be kept somewhere until ... He didn't have time to think that far ahead. He'd half-dragged, half-carried him to the ice house. There wasn't a soul within more than an hour's solid walking. With the phone dead, there was no-one he could call on. He'd no idea how long it might be before Katherine was better, and he certainly wasn't going to leave her alone with a possible murderer, even if he was locked up in the ice house. If he could only get Katherine through however long it took for someone to fetch up at Dunpark, he'd manage the rest well enough, and someone had to turn up, surely?

Edinburgh, the underground city

The underground city, that has more inhabitants than either the Old Town or the New, and all of them with so much time on their hands. Time and more, lying under the earth, to remember the questions that were never asked. To remember the night the dining room started to spin and to look as if all the stars in heaven were overhead, as the answers began to come, only there had been no time left to tell the scared and startled faces looking down, untying the cravat, listening for a heart beat where there was none. Whatever the answer might have been went fluttering out into the night. Twenty years before, when Revolution came to France, he had been forced to eat his dinners in other people's houses, hoping his hosts would not remind him how little he did to earn his meals. If your eating depends on the kindness of others, you don't contradict them, nor offer your own opinions. You know that's not wise. Easy to talk on a full stomach, when you're certain of always having one. Easy, too, to talk if your stomach's empty, and the only way to fill it is taking from others. Not so easy when it means listening to those who think what happens in another country more important than what happens in their own. Even after the King of France's head rolled from the guillotine, there were still folk who believed their own ideals were those of the French Revolution. One such was Thomas Muir of Huntershill. Such folk were watched, of course, but Muir made the mistake of letting people know his opinions. Because he made that mistake, Government decided to make an example of him. He was tried for the seditious crime of pressing radical books on people, and transported to Australia. Another with opinions was James Tytler, who had the good sense to flee before he came to trial. Tytler had been the first man in Scotland to fly in a balloon. Poor but educated, he kept himself and his family fed and himself in the air through writing much of the Encyclopedia Britannica. His fame, though, came about not because of what he wrote but what he did. As the first Scotsman to travel in a balloon, even supposing it had only gone a few yards, Tytler had ensured his name would be remembered. The government certainly remembered him for his dangerous opinions, not his appetite for danger, which seemed to evaporate when faced with being gaoled. Tytler decided discretion was wiser than valour, and took the first available ship for the United States, leaving his wife and children behind, and, it was rumoured, another, much larger and more air-worthy balloon. The man who imprisoned Thomas Muir and drove the likes of James Tytler from their homes was Henry Dundas. As Attorney General, he ruled Scotland for Westminster, making the work pay, with no time or patience for any who questioned his right to do so. When France supported reformers in other countries, whom the French imagined also wanted revolution, they gave frightened governments an opportunity to call reform treachery. Five years after the Bastille was stormed, Government in Britain seemed to be at war with those it governed. Before seventeen ninety seven was a few months old, a mutiny of sailors at the naval bases at Spithead and The Nore made demands Government had to agree to, even if it hung a couple of hotheads so as to seem in control. More luck than good soldiering made short work of a landing of French soldiers on the Welsh coast, though it could only be a matter of time before even more landed in Ireland,

which might mean the whole island would rise up. The year before
an expedition to Holland had to be evacuated after a dreadful defeat.
Henry Dundas, the Attorney General whose word was law in
Scotland, decided Scotland would come to the rescue. A militia
would be formed from every parish and corner of Scotland, ready
to defend it from the forces of revolution. Henry Dundas, however,
had reckoned without his fellow-countrymen.

Ann Street, Edinburgh

While Charlie Cameron was wondering what to do about a man who
had suddenly appeared, his brother James was wondering what to
do about a man who seemed to have disappeared.

'Tell me, Maurice, how do you think we ought to deal with this
little problem?'

The Honourable James Cameron proffered a glass containing a
measure of whisky clearly intended for a Free Kirk minister of
abstemious habits. Cameron beamed a photogenic smile somewhere
above Macquarie's head as he thrust out the glass.

'McIlwraith?'

Macquarie had known fine for long enough that diplomacy was a
game he'd never master the rules of, so didn't bother playing. Cameron
nodded sharply, as if Macquarie had intruded on private grief.

'He seems to have disappeared into the wide blue yonder.'

'We'll get him back, sir, dinnae you worry.'

'You will get him back, Maurice, or you will worry. Believe you
me.'

It had been a piece of luck, Macquarie had thought, to find
McIlwraith again when Macquarie had been seconded to Northern

Ireland. The bad luck, Macquarie reckoned, had been finding Cameron at the same time. McIlwraith had gone from breaking into the old Royal High School in Edinburgh to bigger and better things, from breaking into buildings with damn all in them to make political points, to breaking into country houses with valuable paintings and such, and making off with same.

Macquarie reckoned he ought to be sunning himself somewhere by this time, but here he was, still cleaning up Cameron's fine messes; Cameron, more charm than he knew what to do with, and nothing else. McIlwraith, his face like Peter Pan after a bad dream was a bad dream himself, when you thought about it, not that you'd want to. Twisted as fuck with one saving grace – McIlwraith knew more than was safe about what paintings were worth stealing and how to steal them.

It was only after McIlwraith had been pulled in while Macquarie was in Ulster that he'd had the idea for a bit of lucrative private enterprise. A somewhat noticeable spate of paintings had started to go missing from large country houses. Some of the paramilitaries had worked out that there was a living to be made from nicking the art work of the old country and selling the "masterpieces" to naively romantic ex-pats willing to part with more than the price of an Easter lily. A little bit of heritage could be theirs – for a price, of course.

When McIlwraith got a wee thing careless, and had been caught in possession of something he didn't have an auction receipt for, Macquarie had the idea and opportunity for his extra pension plan. McIlwraith quickly adapted to new circumstances and new management; it had all been going grand till one of James Cameron's pals got their house done over and Cameron had taken a considerable personal interest.

The sun faded across the windowpanes. Macquarie sighed inwardly. It had been quite simple. A wee word with Cameron, pointing out the considerable financial advantages, had eased Cameron into silence. Pointing out that since what they stole lined their own pockets and thus kept the profits out the hands of the paramilitaries, and that if Cameron was daft enough to mention any part of the scheme, not only could it be very messy, but also some of the mess could be Cameron in a bin bag, had clinched their deal. There were times when not being diplomatic saved a lot of bother.

Those had been no bad days. Then came the Peace Process, and Cameron was edged sideways to mind the leader of the Opposition in the new Scottish Parliament. Macquarie also found himself back in Scotland again. Bit of a come-down when you've had a nice wee earner turning over a good few thousand grand. Still, mustn't grumble. Neither Macquarie had, until he heard some of the paramilitaries had rumbled McIlwraith, and the wee nutter, caught in the middle of a turf war, had blown some innocent away. The authorities had picked up McIlwraith but not charged him. No mention of the case going to trial, but both Cameron and Macquarie knew fine that McIlwraith had more than enough information to leave them having to answer questions they'd sooner not.

James Cameron, meanwhile, was having his own breed of kittens. Oleg Vialysov had seemed such a pleasant person to do business with when he'd arrived as part of a Russian trade delegation. So pleasant they'd had several drinks together, and James had been introduced to Vialysov's even more charming Personal Assistant. His memory of the evening was blurred after that, but the photographs Vialysov presented to James the next day certainly weren't. It had seemed simple enough at the time; find a storage space for Vialysov's smuggled diamonds and collect a not-so-small reward for staying silent. He'd found Vialysov said suitable space and collected rather nicely, until the Russian trawler doing the smuggling had a going over from the boys in blue down at Leith Docks.

Macquarie had only been told there was something at Dunpark Cameron wanted moved quickly and with minimum fuss. He knew Cameron had a safe deposit box with the Bank of Caledonia and that Cameron would betray him as fast, if not faster, as he would Cameron. Which was why he'd talked Rob Ainslie into digging out an old passage of the South Bridge Vaults: the passage led straight to the basement of the Bank of Caledonia's headquarters building – to its safe deposit vaults, in fact. Macquarie was sure whatever Cameron had to hide was almost certain to be found in his deposit box.

McIlwraith had been supposed to be in touch by now, with whatever goods Macquarie wasn't supposed to know about, ready to hand them over in exchange for the passport Macquarie was holding. Only for some reason McIlwraith was unaccountably uncommunicative and nowhere to be found.

Macquarie had been the one who arrested Rob Ainslie when, along with McIlwraith, he'd been part of a daft plan to occupy the Royal High School building on Calton Hill. The idea had been one of the crazier notions of a bunch hanging onto the tail of Home Rule till they'd been scuffed off. Ainslie had gone straight ever since, but Macquarie would buy the odd bit of gossip off him for old times. You never knew when an auld acquaintance might come in handy.

Macquarie had given Rob a shovel and told him to start digging out one of the old passages in the South Bridge Vaults. He'd told Rob it was a hush-hush operation, and Rob hadn't asked what the hell Macquarie was wanting with a tunnel that seemed to be going nowhere. Then Macquarie learned that McIlwraith had disappeared into near enough thin air. Not disappeared, exactly, Macquarie told himself; only there wasn't a solitary clue as to where the hell

McIlwraith was. There had been agreed times when McIlwraith was supposed to communicate, but so far, not a cheep.

Strange sounds emerged as Cameron cleared his throat.

'I rather think, Maurice, that you'll have to go after our wandering boy.'

Cameron would now have to tell him where McIlwraith was supposed to be, and Macquarie had been hoping Cameron wouldn't. Macquarie was getting too old for cross-country runs with a tussle with a homicidal maniac at the end of them. A chance of an "excused games" note for this trip wasn't a possibility, especially when Cameron's jaw had set into an expression that wasn't going to take "no" for an answer. Cameron twirled to face the window and the lowering sun.

'I'm relying on you, Maurice. I know you won't let me – far less yourself – down.'

Macquarie didn't relish the prospect of one out-of-practice and out-of-condition investigating officer up against a younger, fitter, craftier hard case, most likely with a gun and probably no sentimental ties to old friends and past times. It was him that was past his time, not to mention his "sell by" date. "Sold" was exactly what he felt ought to be slapped on his furrowing brow.

Macquarie had wondered whose side the new leader of Scotland's Opposition was on. He knew the answer, of course: the same one as everyone else when the chips are down. The Hon. James Cameron would likely turn in his own granny for less than a fiver if it suited him, so was unlikely to be fussed if Macquarie got an early appointment with an undertaker. It dawned on Macquarie that with him out of the way, no-one would listen if McIlwraith came out with a story of a senior politician mixed up in art theft and God knew what else. Assuming McIlwraith was still alive. Macquarie needed fresh air, but he needed

Cameron to tell him where to find McIlwraith more. When the word "Dunpark" came from Cameron's lips, Macquarie decided it was time to talk to Rob Ainslie.

The ice house, Dunpark

McIlwraith's hands hurt near as much as his head. He'd been battering them against the door almost from the minute he'd regained consciousness. No-one was going to open it, of course. The guy that lamped him had heard the news broadcast the same as he had, and jumped to the right conclusion. Unless he could get out of wherever he was, the next people he was likely to see would be wearing blue uniforms. He turned away from the door with a quiet despair. His eyes were getting used to the dark, and as he looked around the space he was in, he began to make out a shape lying against the opposite wall from the door. Two shapes, big enough to be coffins. Chests, that was what they had to be, McIlwraith thought to himself. "In the ice house" – that was all he'd been told. Whatever Cameron was after had to be in one of the two muckle boxes facing him.

McIlwraith approached the one that was nearest and tried lifting the lid, but either it was too heavy or it was fixed somehow. He drew himself upright, and pulled with both arms and all his strength. Slowly, it began to lift, and at first all he could make out was the stour, till it cleared, and he watched as two plumes of what was surely only dust hanging in the air above the chest. McIlwraith stared until what he could see wasn't dust anymore; or if it was, it held a shape; two shapes, in fact. McIlwraith could barely stifle the scream fighting its way out of his throat as the dust slowly became two human bodies, and he could hear one of them speak.

'Airchie, we're still in the ice hoose! Yon uncle o yours cannae hiv pit us on the boat for Holland aifter aa!'

'I didn't trust him when he said he'd help us escape. Why should he have done me any favour, after all?'

'He was awful keen tae get his hands on Dunpark. Aabody said so. When we landed in the taigle we did, that was his chance, an it seems like he took it.'

'More fool me for trusting him to do right by us.'

One of the shapes disappeared back inside the chest then seemed to almost jump in the air.

'Here, Airchie! This is Uncle Neil's letter! Mind, the one he gied us tae gie tae Nathaniel, if we ever got back tae Scotland?'

'It's addressed to your cousin Nathaniel, but I wonder if we ought to read it?'

There was a sound as if something was being torn.

'I'm the one that opened it, Airchie, so it's no blame to you. Noo tell us whit it says.'

'My dear Nathaniel, your old father, Neil Gow, asks you with this letter to help the two men who bring it. They are Archibald Cameron, son of the old Laird of Dunpark, and Tam Linton, your Aunt Mary's laddie, from Edinburgh. They got taigled up in the trouble around Loch Tay a while ago. The old Laird's brother told me he would send them to the Low Countries to be out the way, but if they get that far, they'll win back to Scotland, I'm sure, and will come to you with this letter. Do however much you can for them, for my sake. It was not their fault they came to Loch Tay when they did, with folk ready to oppose the gentry and fearful what the new Militia Act might mean for them. Some still blame the trouble of that time on Angus Cameron, but he was as much caught up in what happened as any of the rest. Angus' father was the old Laird of Dunpark, though Angus wasn't his legitimate son.

I never told you about that when you were younger. The lad was educated at his father's expense, but they fell out, and the lad joined the army. Angus Cameron was sent to fight in the Low Countries, in that nonsense of a campaign against the French a few years back. He was captured, and some said he took to the opinions of his gaolers, the revolutionaries in France, which is maybe no surprise seeing aristocrats hadn't done as well by him as he thought he deserved. How Angus got released, I've no way of knowing. In any event, he found a way to get back to Scotland, taking passage on a ship sailing up the Tay to Perth. When word came that he had landed, I walked to Perth to meet him. If I'd known what fate had in store, I'd likely have stayed at home.'

The Forest, Edinburgh

Ninian Tulloch stared at the clock above the bar in The Forest. Nearly nine o' clock. He wished the man seated beside him would finish his drink, so they could both get the hell out of the pub and on their way. Eddie Corcoran didn't seem in much of a hurry, though. They made a very odd couple, Tulloch decided, clocking the two of them in the reflection from the mirror behind the gantry. Himself the thin, aquiline-intense specimen, set beside the generous proportion of Eddie's massive frame.

Meeting Eddie Corcoran, London-based comic and rising star of radio satire, wasn't the homecoming to Edinburgh Tulloch had expected, but then he hadn't known what kind of homecoming to expect. Nearly three years since he'd lived here. Only back once, for a few mad days after he'd had the phone call, and those days filled with lawyers and undertakers, floral tributes and memorial speeches to think about. They had been displacement activities to deaden the pain. He'd arranged to let the house, since selling would have been too final, and his brother Aiden was in near as much shock as he was. Losing both parents in one car crash was something that happened to other people, the ones you read about in newspapers. Aiden and he had never been really close. Not even the funeral had changed that. The last time Tulloch had heard from his brother was to learn he'd landed a short sabbatical in Prague. When Tulloch discovered that the US academic who was the latest tenant wanted to extend her lease for another three months, he decided he could doss down in the space over the garage – it was barely a room, until he sorted himself out. It was, to be honest, the only thing he could afford. Selling the business hadn't been hard – 'Theatre and Event Lighting Hire Company – thriving concern, potential to expand', the advertisement had read, but even when he'd got a far better offer than he'd expected, his bank didn't seem to want him solvent, even now he really was. He didn't regret the move, in spite of the temporary inconvenience. He couldn't bear living in London any longer, and the turn of the century – the millennium, he ought to have said – had propelled him into putting the business on the market. It had taken till June to find a buyer, and another couple of months to actually make the deal, but here he was, back in Edinburgh and glad to be so. There would, he'd been told, be a delay till the cheque cleared, and he hated overdrafts as much as banks. Solvent by the week's end, the bank had assured him, but he was decidedly skint today and already anxious to find something that paid money. He could have given the new woman in his brother's life a call, asked if she had a spare room, but he'd only met her the once and that had been briefly. Besides, Aiden had told him she'd a baby – trust Aiden to complicate his life. In any case, she (and the baby) were very likely in Prague with Aiden.

Instead of calling anyone, he'd walked toward The Forest, the great crossroads of Edinburgh's folk music scene, the place he'd first met Kit Barber and had his life changed in less time than it took to re-string a fiddle. It wasn't nostalgia that drew him back, so he told himself, far less some form of masochism. The Forest was a pub where theatre techies drank; he hoped one of the ones he knew would be in and able to tell him what work might be going. He'd somehow forgotten, in the busy, anxious time it took to move back, that the first days of September are not ones in which to look for tech work in Edinburgh. The Fringe and Official Festival are over or ending, the companies are leaving or have already left town.

A shy grin at a surprised Shug behind the bar was enough to get a pint pouring. Tulloch looked around. Nothing changes, everything changes. He'd half expected, if not Kit, then one of the others to be playing. The musicians huddled round the small table near the back of the bar were good enough players, but they weren't "John Knox's G Strings". Was it Kit or Heather who'd finally christened them?

He recalled being on the periphery of a long, boozy discussion over the name of the band Kit, Heather Inglis and Luce Cameron had decided to form. Each of the names they'd come up with had seemed to Tulloch sillier than the last, until someone – had it been Kit or Heather? – had cried out "John Knox's G Strings!" and silenced them all, till the other two had burst into fits of giggles. Whoever it was had been right, though. It had enough suggestion of naughtiness and "post-modern humour" – he'd read that in a Sunday newspaper supplement and had his own fit of post-modern humour when he had. It worked, pure and simple. It got them gigs, it stayed in people's minds and it sold records. He and Kit were barely an item then. Stay late enough at The Forest and you end up walking home with the musicians, walking the musicians home, walking home with one musician. Katherine 'Kit' Barber – five foot didn't matter in her stocking soles, and every centimetre damn near perfect in his eyes. So many Kits beneath her skin – breathless and glowing coming down off Schiehallion; disconcertingly elegant in a black silk trouser suit at a benefit gig; squealing protestingly as her wee bare feet pattered over chill bathroom tiles; warm and welcoming between smooth linen sheets on the only holiday they'd had together. So many Kits and none of them here.

A tap on his shoulder spun his head into the enquiring gaze of a man in a suit that looked too sharp even for its wearer.

'How much they get paid?'

Tulloch wasn't sure of either the nationality or the accent, but he recognised the unspoken assumption that, of course, everything and thereby everyone, has their price.

If you have to ask, you couldn't afford them were the words that formed in his head. Instead he simply said 'Nothing.'

He watched the disbelief in the enquiring man's eyes translate into a loud burst of language he didn't understand as the man gave his version of the inexplicable local habits to a gaggle of fellow countrypersons. Their excited responses suggested they didn't quite believe it either.

'It's called a session.' Tulloch didn't know if the group heard him, and scarcely cared if they had. A session. Not a bad one, either, though not as good as some of the many he'd heard over the years. Some imagined it was done for the drink – the traditional hospitality of the howff – but it only figured for some. A session was more than the craic or the drink or even the music. It was a conversation, with music the language. A civilised conversation, where the person who had held the floor minutes ago would be making noises to encourage someone more hesitant than they'd been. It was, perhaps, the last place where real democracy happened, where everyone got their very own kick at the ball, everyone else willing them on to make the best of their chance.

Tulloch turned his back before another question he didn't want to answer came his way. He could hear the whirr and click of cameras behind him, sense and see the flash bulbs popping. He'd never quite got used to the fact that what he and hundreds of others took for granted, and could listen to for nothing every night of the week if they chose, was something tourists imagined was laid on especially for them. 'Politics follows the culture. It has no option.' He couldn't remember who said that; probably Professor Roddy MacLennan, on one of his visits to see his niece, Luce Cameron, playing at The Forest, in the days before the band took over the lives of its three members. Whoever had said it, though, had said it exactly right. He'd known things were changing before he left Edinburgh. He'd missed most of what led to a Scottish Parliament at Holyrood, but he'd known fine the real struggle wasn't in any political back room, it had been in places such as this, and he'd been a witness to it, even if he'd barely noticed that he was. You had to have some sort of licence to sing in pubs in England. Somehow authority in Scotland missed that wise piece of legislation. So there was still the right of riotous assembly, the right of any one to get up on their hind legs and raise their voice against any authority, from the Queen to the toon cooncil. 'Freedom becomes people', someone else had said, and the other side of that coin is that people can become freedom, by doing what they want to do. Perhaps music isn't a bad place to start.

He slid from the bar stool and made for the door. Out in chilling September air, he quickly decided a bus home was the best option. If he stayed in town, he'd end up spending money he didn't have.

The Victorian gothic of the Royal Infirmary loomed ahead, a bus shelter standing empty beside its railings. Looked as if he might be in for a wait, then.

He was peering at the supposed arrival time of his next bus when he glimpsed something familiar in the figure walking toward the shelter. The outfit she was wearing had a faint echo of how some twentieth-century designer imagined a Victorian maid-servant, but the woman would have had to have worn a deeper disguise for Tulloch not to recognise her. Luce Cameron. She looked, if anything, better than he remembered. As if she'd grown inside in a way he couldn't describe, only admire. There was a cast to her face, holding some sorrow, trying not to let it go.

'Luce.'

She startled at her own name, then the words came in a rush.

'Tulloch! What brings you back to Edinburgh?'

'I decided to move back.'

'For good?'

'Don't know if it will be – good, that is, but I've decided to give it a try. It's good to see you, at any rate.'

He took a long look at her as her eyes drooped. Her skin had the same not quite copper sheen, and her hair the same rich blackness, but he could feel her withdraw even before he'd said the words

'Something's the matter, isn't it?'

'Uncle Roddy's dead!' she wailed, lost as a child in a suddenly frightening world. Uncle Roddy? Professor Roddy MacLennan, Luce's godfather.

Tulloch remembered how MacLennan would drop into The Forest whenever he knew Luce might be playing, and before long they'd be sitting in a corner, talking softly like a pair of lovers.

Tulloch wasn't the only one to wonder what was going on, but he came to realise they were simply too close to wish their affection otherwise. Folk still talked, of course, but Luce and her "Uncle Roddy" either didn't hear or paid no heed. Tulloch hadn't seen anything of Luce since he'd left Edinburgh, and here she was, and her uncle Roddy dead. She'd take it hard, Tulloch knew that much. There was a lot he wanted to ask and tell her, but a bus shelter on a main road was neither the time nor place.

'D' you want to go somewhere? Talk?'

Her response was to grab his hand and lead him in the direction of the warren of concrete accretions that had been added to the Infirmary over the years. He'd learnt about the plan to move the hospital to a new site out by Little France earlier in the day. Soon all the Victorian gingerbread would be sold off as luxury flats and the concrete bulldozed to make way for a shopping mall of chrome and glass cages. Suddenly Luce was whisking him through a set of double doors and along a corridor. At the end, there was another door.

Tulloch surveyed the battered metal cabinet and the narrow single bed. He wanted to ask Luce what she was doing with herself these days, and when she'd developed a taste for strange retro clothing, but she'd opened the cabinet and drawn out two pairs of boxing gloves before he'd a chance to frame those questions, let alone ask them. Quickly stripping off the skirt and blouse, Luce thrust a pair of gloves toward him.

'Billy and Dan – they're two hospital porters I know – come down here for a spar when it's not too busy. They say they do it for the exercise, but I'm not so sure about that.' She paused to tie the laces of her gloves, then flashed him a look that was anger, resentment and pain and Tulloch had no idea what else.

'Come on tiger, let's see what you can do.'

Tulloch decided he was having a very strange dream he really wanted to wake from. Then the first blow landed. It wasn't hard, but enough to rock him back on his heels. He yanked the gloves on, for protection as much as anything else, glad of their solid weight as Luce's blows beat against them. Now and again, she'd connect with his flesh, stinging more viciously than a bee. She danced round him, balletic one moment, threatening the next. A steady drizzle of blows tattooed against his chest, punctuated by more solid ones. At first, he tried brushing them aside with his gloves, and then let them fall, anger slowly building as he waited the opportunity to land the single punch that would end this foolishness.

It came, and he swung, but Luce half-parried the blow, catching its force on her eye. Tulloch hadn't meant that to happen; it only spurred Luce to another burst of punches. These were pop-gun soft, though, and slowed as her energy began to ebb, till finally her head sank against his chest and he could hear the frustrated grief in her sobs. He threw the gloves aside and cupped her face in his hands. She pulled away, then turned back to him, her defiance draining slowly.

'Fuck you' she managed, between deep, racking breaths.

Their lips faltered against each other, then connected.

Loch Tay

The water moves more slowly here, far beneath the Loch's surface. The less disturbance, the more time to recollect how it might have been, if … If you hadn't been in Edinburgh, year of grace seventeen hundred and ninety seven, and all the birds flown, or sent to Botany Bay, at the expense of his Majesty. You, Oliver Corcoran, a fraternal delegate from the United Irishmen across the water, unused to the ways of Edinburgh. You'd come to study medicine, but you spent the time between anatomy lessons trying to find folk willing to risk their lives for what they claimed to believe in. It had taken five years to build the United Irishmen; now Government was destroying them in far less time. Their agents had penetrated all the Irish Volunteer units, Masonic Lodges and Speculative Societies that had nurtured them. Morale was that low you'd have to dig for it. So you'd been sent across to Scotland, where United Scotsmen were supposed to be as ready to rise against oppression as United Irishmen were. Only Edinburgh wasn't Belfast, where being Presbyterian made it likely you'd be some class of a radical. In Edinburgh, being Presbyterian meant there was a good chance you'd prefer the apple cart of Government didn't get upset. There were always plenty who grumbled about the way their world was divided, but fewer that would risk so much as their little fingers to bring about change. Those who'd sent you hoped that Thomas Muir, transported to Australia on a charge of sedition, since escaped, and now in France, might be able to put some backbone into the United Scotsmen. Enough to make them distract His Majesty's forces for long enough to give a rising in Ireland a decent chance. Only Mister Muir had to be got to Scotland, and you learned that he was severely ill in any case. Though you thought the whole scheme mad as a cage of monkeys, you'd spent weeks trying to make contact with anyone that might be a United Scotsman, and found not a one who would admit to being any such thing. Precious little chance that any of those timid fellows would rise up and claim their freedom. You were getting that desperate to find at least one person that was a United Scotsman that you became careless as well. The day came that you made a mistake. You were lucky there was no one else you could incriminate, for you didn't know anybody else, but that only made it harder on you.

Sooner than swing at a rope end, you promised to find red-hot revolutionaries in Edinburgh, loose-tongued enough to blether what Government wanted to hear. You only had to keep on doing what you had been, finding no one, and both you and any revolutionaries there might be would both keep safe. Only the people you were now supposed to work for started to get impatient and suspicious. Which meant you had to find something or someone that would keep them occupied, off the scent and off your back. One day, you ran into Archibald Cameron on the South Bridge – or he into you. Apologising, he insisted on buying you a drink at the nearest tavern, and you didn't refuse. He was a talker, and no mistake. You had his life story out of him in half an hour. Soon as you heard about the balloon "Republica", the one James Tytler had been working on before Government caught up with him and he'd run off to America, you found a way to get an invitation to see the thing yourself. You already knew the French had used balloons for observation during their campaign in Holland. You wondered how they worked and if they had any other use. The two of you tottered down Blackfriars Wynd, in at a doorway that near bent you double, along narrow passageways until you came out in a great vault under the South Bridge itself. That was when you first saw it, and you knew this monstrous object and the half-crazy people that had it in their care might just be the saving of you.

Ann Street, Edinburgh

The Hon. James Cameron watched Macquarie close the gate and began the pech up the hill leading to Queensferry Road, the Dean Bridge and back to the centre of Edinburgh. The Bridge had been at one time a favoured choice of suicides. Cameron hoped Macquarie wasn't thinking of taking the plunge. The Vialysov business was becoming an even bigger worry than the missing McIlwraith. He'd gone along with Vialysov's scheme because generous cash donations to the party never came amiss when safe seats were being considered. Now he needed a new supply of sweetie money. With any luck, McIlwraith would see to that. As long as McIlwraith didn't make the sort of mistake he'd made in Northern Ireland, and James was sure he wouldn't, everything would work out fine.

All James wanted was the diamonds in his hands – for safe keeping, of course. All McIlwraith had to do was make sure he wasn't caught. James hadn't seen his brother Charles since James' departure for Northern Ireland. Charlie was still on his own as far as his brother knew, and Charlie's daughter, his niece Lucette, was in some sort of folk group the last he'd heard of her, so he hoped there wouldn't be any trouble from those quarters. If there should be, well, that was where Macquarie came in. Cameron sighed wistfully. The diamond smuggling operations had been as smooth as silk, only Vialysov had decided the internet was the way to sell diamonds. No great surprise "www.theicehouse.com" was a domain name that wasn't for sale; then James had read a story in the "Perthshire Advertiser" and understood why.

"Charlie Licks It Into Shape! Charles Cameron of Dunpark announces a new venture for the Dunpark Estate. The former ice house at Dunpark will shortly take on a role as centre of operations for his new venture, Dunpark Organic Ice-Cream". James couldn't believe the Dunpark Dunderhead, as he called his brother in company that didn't include him, had thought that one up alone. James, after all, was the one with brains. The one with a law degree, who'd spent years crawling up the greasy pole of Westminster politics, via a couple of unwinnable by-elections, to a seat he'd managed to win against the odds and the pundits' prophecies, and finally Under-Secretary of State for Northern Ireland. Then it began to unravel, when that chump had managed to lose the General Election, and James had to scramble back to Scotland, clinging to a wafer-thin majority. Even finding himself the new leader didn't mean much to James, who knew he was meant for better things than heading up a handful of incompetents in a talking-shop no one listened to, and he had every intention of being where he belonged toute bloody suite. They had to get the stuff out of the old ice house quickly. Remembering about McIlwraith had been a stroke of genius, James told himself, though he didn't really trust McIlwraith to stick to the script he'd been given, any more than he trusted Macquarie. He still remembered Macquarie telling him what kind of mince he'd be turned into if he blabbed about the art theft scam back in Northern Ireland. He'd have to keep a close eye on what both of them were up to: a very close eye.

Edinburgh, the underground city

He knew people called him "The Omnivore". He couldn't afford to eat every day, so he ate when he could, in other people's houses. He never passed up a meal, because he never knew when he might have another one. His habit, his necessity, of never refusing food placed before him got him his nickname – one who eats everything. Eating always in other people's houses put him in their debt. He knew he was in their debt, but saw no way out of it. One day, he would have to pay those debts. He knew that too, and the thought troubled him. When word had come that there was going to be a "British Convention" of the radicals, in imitation of the Convention that ruled in France in place of the King, and that it was to be held in Edinburgh, he'd been very afraid. It frightened him that he might be asked by one of the men who let him eat dinner to do … He wasn't sure what, but he had an imagination. He didn't want to be a spy. Edinburgh was full of spies. Only calling them spies made what they did sound grand and exciting. All they did was tell tales. Tell lies. About anyone they thought Government would like to hear ill of. Government, of course, was fool enough to listen to what it wanted to hear. There were plenty ready and eager to speak ill of their neighbours, employers, even friends. Plenty who were hungry enough to open their mouths so they could fill them. Scotland was governed by Henry Dundas, who had no wish that reform should break his hold on the two thousand voters who elected the handful of men Scotland sent to the Parliament at Westminster. Perhaps he ought not to have been surprised other men should become "United Scotsmen", in imitation of the "United Irishmen" across the North Channel. These United Scotsmen claimed they were ready to take up arms to free their countrymen from Dundas' government. Such things did not happen at once, of course. The man they called The Omnivore was not so much a fool as some chose to think him. His stomach might be empty, but his eyes were open. In fact, it was because his stomach was empty that his eyes had to be open. His ears, too. What came to him first, though, was the smell. Fear. He couldn't mistake it because it was so familiar to him. He'd lived with fear long enough to know how it smelt. Fear of having nothing to eat, nowhere to live, of the little world that was all he had to live in crashing around his ears. So he understood those who listened and watched. He knew these people would be the losers if their own little worlds were to crash – the butlers and valets, the sedan chair carriers, the caddies with their letters and parcels, who watched and listened because they wanted to have something to tell to those who paid them. Then there had been something to watch – the British Convention, where all the great names that opposed authority were to foregather, to be held in Edinburgh. It was a gift to Government, of course. All those eyes, all those ears, that had spent the past months watching and listening without knowing what or who it was they were to watch and listen for, now had somewhere to look, something with which to fill their ears. He'd tried not to do so, for the less he heard or saw, the less he could tell anyone who might ask. For all that, he'd watched and listened as Thomas Muir was tried and sentenced to transportation to Australia. Before that, he had watched the man Tytler take his balloon into the sky, and watched too, as he and it came down in the dubs of the Nor' Loch. He heard of Tytler's arrest on a charge of treason and of his flight to the United States, in a ship this time. He'd seen and heard much, perhaps too much, and knew that one day Government might ask him to be their eyes and ears instead of his own, and he waited that day with a dread he couldn't explain to anyone, and had no wish to explain to himself.

Upper Bow, Edinburgh

Unsteadily, Maurice Macquarie heaved from the close-head, his gasps like racking sobs. Any casual observer might have wondered if he was mourning a lost friend. Rob Ainslie was no friend according to Macquarie, certainly not when he'd pushed past him, havering about ghosts and refusing point blank to go back down the tunnel he'd been digging for the past couple of hours. Macquarie needed the dozy bugger's panic attack less than a bad dose, and he needed Rob's muscle if he was going to get anywhere near the Caledonian Bank and its Safe Deposit room. He'd nearly got his hands on the wee nyaff while he was running down the Cowgate, as if all the fiends in hell were after him. Macquarie had never thought of Rob as in any way athletic, but he'd fair looked as if he'd taken up training for a marathon. He might have caught up with him, all the same, Macquarie told himself, if it hadn't been for yon eejits with the car.

It seemed to come out of nowhere, turning sharply out of an underground car-park, narrowly missing the ample bulk of one Robert Ainslie. The two blokes in the car caught Macquarie's professional eye. One of them was on the very large side, wrapped in what looked like one of Macquarie's Auntie Jean's best curtains, the other a skinny bloke in a long coat and hat that had both seen better days. They pulled up beside Rob and began talking to him. Next thing Macquarie knew, Rob was in the back seat of the car and it was driving off along the Cowgate, heading west. Macquarie tried clocking the number plate, then realised the car was plastered with what looked like posters. He could make out "Eddie" something or other – "The Entire Political"… never mind, can't be many of them about, he told himself.

He clutched again at the stone at the head of the close. He needed more than its solid support. He needed … he wasn't sure what, but it would have to terrify yon muckle sumph, Rob Ainslie back to doing what he was supposed to. If something had put the wind up Rob, chances were he'd gab about it to anyone who'd listen. Macquarie didn't relish the prospect of Rob telling his tales to any Tom, Dick or Harry, especially if they were police, far less talking to the two weirdoes it seemed he was travelling with. Macquarie reviewed his situation and decided he didn't like it one bit. Maurice, you are well and truly gubbed if McIlwraith gets you before you get him. You're also very near gubbed if Rob Ainslie blabbers about what he was doing in the South Bridge vaults, even if he doesn't have a clue what you're up to.

'When you know the how, you know the who'. That's what John McGrath always said. The realisation leaped across Macquarie's consciousness like a lightening flash. McGrath. Selling fishing books in wildest Perthshire these days. Likely to still be subsidising slow horses and fast women, in need of cash and possibly a wee thing bored. McGrath was all the help he was likely to get, supposing he got him. Make a phone call, Maurice. See if you can tempt the bugger out of retirement. Macquarie began to feel better than he had before. It was almost like the old days. He felt almost happy.

the ice house, Dunpark

What had gone wrong? McIlwraith, you eejit, you opened the wrong flaming box, that was what went wrong. The only thing stopping him opening the right one were the two shapes between him and the other chest. Maybe they were that wrapped up in what they were doing, they'd no notice him. He lay down, flat as he could on the bare earth floor, and began crawling toward the chest that still had its lid closed.

'The harbour at Perth was a busy place, and it took a while to find Angus Cameron. I wonder how much you remember of him, Nathaniel? As a laddie, he was more a handful than you ever were, and he was near as much when a grown man. I could see his time in the army had given him confidence and there was the same spirit in him that he'd had as a laddie, that wouldn't be easy tamed. It turned out his notion to come home wasn't only to take up a trade, but also to be among his own again, getting from them the credit and respect he thought he ought to have. For all his time in a red coat, Angus Cameron considered himself a gentleman who deserved better from life than it had given him so far. If he'd

been born the right side of the blanket, he might have been the Laird of Dunpark in the place of Archibald Cameron, who was learning to be a lawyer in Edinburgh. Why Angus asked me so particularly to be the one to meet him off the ship, I didn't know. I could see that he looked taller, stronger and as I told you before, with more confidence in himself. There was a cast to his eye, though, a way of looking as if no one else mattered as much as he did.'

McIlwraith was a foot from the chest when he saw it had a padlock, held by a chain running from the lid to the front panel. He near wept when he saw it. There was nothing he could use to bust the lid, and anything he did was sure to attract attention.

'I said that I could help set him up as a weaver, like myself, but he told me he had an idea of going into the timber trade. He settled to that well enough at first, renting a cottage and working like a very devil to make a success of his venture. Then I heard he'd been over at Appin, talking about something cried the United Scotsmen, and saying less than two thousand folk in Scotland voted for the men who sat in Parliament, and it was time more honest folk and fewer fools decided things. Seeing you live in Edinburgh now, Nathaniel, among grand folk, you'll maybe have your own thoughts about such talk. His Grace the Duke of Atholl still pays me, and it's best I keep my own counsel, but whatever I might have thought, I did begin to worry what else Angus Cameron might say and what trouble he might cause. I decided to ask him about the United Scotsmen.'

He felt the floor, till his hand touched on metal. Picking it up, he discovered it was long enough for what he had in mind. A spike with a bar at its end that looked as if it were meant to be a handle. If he put one hand on either end of the bar, then twisted, maybe he could pull the padlock off. The wood was likely dry as old bones.

He slid the spike into the hoop of the padlock and began to pull. It was going to take time but it was the only way. In any case, he'd nothing else to do.

High Street, Edinburgh

Tulloch watched as Luce picked at a plate of garishly bright peppers and scraps of rocket. He tried to remember how long it was since he had last seen Kit. Here he was, sitting opposite someone who knew her almost as well as he did, but there was no way Tulloch could think of to bring Kit into the conversation. She paced his mind though, even after the last hour and all it had contained. How long had he known Kit Barber? If he'd ever known her at all? He kept drifting to those days when "John Knox's G Strings" had been what dictated his time with Kit, when ceilidh dates figured largely in the band member's diaries, along with more coming-of-ages, twenty firsts and weddings than any three women had a right to, even on a professional basis. "Strings and Bows" was the first album, out within the year. Tulloch had all of them, autographed on the sleeve notes, the "Kit" followed by a barbed wire entanglement of kisses. Tulloch would have stayed in that time that had never really been, if the restaurant hadn't been so obviously about to close for the night. He couldn't imagine why Luce had picked the gaff, its plastic umbrellas colour coordinated and coded for each table, its predictable selection of "mezze" proffered by uninterested student waiters. True, they'd agreed to accept her credit card, when he'd been forced to explain to her that the sale of a thriving business meant he was temporarily, well, skint. Only till the bank cleared his cheque, of course.

'You mean you're broke?'

Luce concised his situation to its barest boards, forcing him to admit, in public, that he was one hundred per cent borasic. He might have no more than a fiver to his name, but trying to draw attention from the waiter who persisted in staring into the middle distance three feet above his head caused Tulloch to wonder what other social misdemeanour he'd committed. He loved watching her eat, though. The second sexiest overbite in Scotland. No prizes for guessing the first. They had got as far as "Byzantine coffee", the only Byzantine aspect of which appeared to be obtaining two cups from a waiter engrossed in watching his own image in a mirror.

'So,' Tulloch gambited, reckoning that securing coffee entitled him to make the opening move.

'Uncle Roddy told me before he...'

There was an awkward pause, in which Luce ferreted fruitlessly in her bag for a handkerchief.

'He talked about Neil Gow.' she managed finally. 'He'd this idea that he'd found a lost Neil Gow manuscript.'

Neil Gow? Hang around folk musicians – Scottish folk musicians – long enough and the name has a habit of cropping up. Perthshire weaver, self-taught (mostly) and the finest composer of fiddle tunes for near enough two hundred years. That much he knew. A lost Neil Gow tune? One no-one had ever known about? Somewhere in Dunpark House?

'Luce, what the hell is all this about?'

She told him what Professor MacLennan had tried to explain to her. Tulloch digested this with as much difficulty as he had the mezze. According to the recently deceased Professor Roderick MacLennan, a manuscript by Neil Gow lay somewhere in Dunpark House, Luce's family home. A place she seemed very reluctant to go.

'So you will help?'

Luce's question had hung in the air like heavy tobacco smoke, leaving Tulloch puzzling his way through the screen of evasion. He'd not been able to work out what, but had no doubt there was something he'd not discover from her, no matter how persistently or patiently he probed.

Tulloch had tried looking beyond her, continually drawn as he'd been by the two pale blue pupils that complemented her sandal-wood complexion. He had felt himself trying to deny they had been so intimate such a short time ago. The burgeoning, almost purple blemish above Luce's left eye forced him to admit the truth of their encounter and gave him a greater sense of unease. He had heard the story almost twice by then. One way, he supposed, of keeping Roderick MacLennan's memory alive a little longer.

'You will, won't you?'

Her voice was a pleading, cajoling child's. Tulloch had known from her first broaching that he wouldn't be able to refuse. It seemed entirely fantastic, nonetheless. Travel all the way to Dunpark House, ask Luce's father to let him rummage in the library and return triumphant with a previously unknown Neil Gow manuscript, which by some miracle he'd easily find despite it being overlooked for nearly two hundred years.

He wondered who, apart from Luce Cameron, could have spun him this yarn and made him even half believe it. He knew perfectly well that this sort of belief begins with the eyes. It always does. What you see is what you get. A trick of the light, a catch in the voice and the rest follows, but the eyes always start it. Clear as the evening light streaming through the windows that Luce would accept no refusal from him. In as long as it had taken them to drink down the bad coffee, his steps had been marked, from there to Loch Tay.

Out in the September chill of Princes Street, she'd kissed him. No hint of passion, but the warmth had enveloped him for a moment, and he knew the strength that was in it would carry him as far as he needed. Further that that, maybe. Luce flashed him her best and bravest smile.

'Good luck, Tulloch.'

The smile flickered briefly before she'd turned to walk off in the direction of Marchmont.

'Bye, Luce' he'd murmured after her, turning on his heel, determined not to look back until he'd decided what he was going to do with this particular weight of expectation he wasn't the least sure he could fulfill.

Loch Tay

You, Oliver Corcoran, remembering again the day you encountered Archibald Cameron on the South Bridge. After he tells you a load of nonsense you don't believe at first, you follow him down the brae of Blackfriars Wynd, then in by a little door and along snaking passages to come out in the hugeness of the vault. You were amazed by the size, the width and height of it. Hanging there, above the middle of the vault, like a great black bat asleep upside down, was "Republica", James Tytler's last unfinished project. It was suspended from some sort of hook set in the dome far above you. The bag, if that was what you called it, was huge. Near enough high as a house and about as wide. That was when you began to wonder what might be done with it, and you'd fancied for a moment that Thomas Muir could be carried in it all the way across Scotland. It was a foolish notion even than, for Muir was almost certainly too ill to travel.

Though you didn't own it and couldn't afford to pay for it, you already thought of "Republica" as yours in some way. You look up again, gape-mouthed, at a balloon no one else would have dared build, as Tam Linton, the lad who was James Tytler's assistant, and in a manner of speaking, his heir and successor, tells you he intends to make an ascent in her. He tells you he's worked out a way of concentrating the heat, so she'll stay in the air for hours at a stretch instead of minutes. You don't believe a word, and turn away, only to find yourself looking into the eyes of a slip of a girl Archie Cameron introduces as Matilda Tytler, James Tytler's daughter, and the one the balloon properly belongs to. At once you can tell she doesn't trust you. It's like she's diagnosed the disease that's in you and is going to make sure you infect no-one else. You're going to have to watch her, for it's clear you won't win her round. The balloon is a monster, sure enough. It scares you, simply looking at it. Tam Linton looks at this mass of silk and rope and God knows what with something close to love. You can't believe it will ever fly, but Tam and Archie tell you it will, so you nod agreement, if only to be polite. They tell you it'll take time to get the thing into shape. The problem, they say, is money. They need money to buy the ropes and the silk and all the other stuff they tell you they need. You see a way of tempting them into a position of owing you a favour. Make them owe you something – owe you money they'd find it hard to repay. Tam has practically none and Archie's told you how much his uncle grudges every penny that's his by rights. So put them in your debt and make whatever use you can of the bargain. Tell them you can get as much as they need. Soon as you'd said it, you regret it, but Tam carries on explaining every bit of rope and canvas, as if he owned the thing, and you were some investor. Which is what they want you to be. They never ask where the money comes from, or what you might want in return. Even Mattie stays quiet, for the sake of the balloon and the two men who work on it. All they have on their mind is making "Republica" fly. Tam because he loves balloons, and Archie because he loves Mattie. Your problem now is that having opened your mouth and your pocket, you have to find a use for what you've bought. While others are making all sorts of plans for Mister Thomas Muir, he is slowly going where no scheme can touch him. Yet the work goes on, while you write the kind of fiction that will keep two sets of masters happy, and as you do that, you envy Archie Cameron and Tam Linton. They know what they're doing and why they're doing it. You no longer do, since you don't even know which master you serve when you do their work. You've stopped keeping a looking glass in your room. You're frightened what you may see in it.

The Forest, Edinburgh

Tulloch was still considering a request he didn't know how to refuse when a shape loomed out of the descending gloom

'Edinburgh welcomes careful pedestrians.'

The irony of the observation was lost on Tulloch as he quickly shifted gear to avoid the kind of bulk even Goliath might have swerved.

'Good God! It's Ninian Tulloch!'

Tulloch allowed himself almost as deep an inward groan as he'd given the last time Scotland was knocked out of the World Cup. Eddie Corcoran. After years of careful avoidance in a strange city, he'd been caught off guard on home turf.

'Great to see you, man!'

Tulloch nodded mutely.

'Eddie.' He managed, after a deep breath.

'Last I heard, you were staying in a shoe box not a million miles from Vauxhall Bridge Road. Funny we've never run into each other. Anyway, are you visiting old haunts? Or is it old flames you're fanning?'

Eddie Corcoran sometimes gave the impression of having the mind of an eight year old child, but a remarkably perceptive eight year old.

'What brings you to Edinburgh?' Stupid question, but Tulloch had to ask it.

'Oh, the usual nonsense. Little show called "Eddie Corcoran – The Entire Political Plectrum". Closed at the Assembly Rooms last night. If I'd known you were in town I'd have made sure you got a comp.'

Coming from Eddie, Tulloch had known this to be the height of generosity. He even managed to look impressed.

'Let me buy you a drink and tell you about a little job that might interest you.' Eddie continued, his generosity apparently unabated.

Eddie had uttered the magic word Tulloch had waited all evening to hear. Nonetheless, some dark memories of Eddie Corcoran continued to be remarkably fresh in his memory.

'What sort of job?' Tulloch asked.

'Why don't I buy you that drink?'

Even with a drink inside him, Eddie felt nervous. Suggesting to Tulloch he might have a job for him meant telling him what the job was. Where the heck was he supposed to start? 'Tulloch, once upon a time there was this fat comedian, whose agent got him a gig in Belfast...' It had been a benefit gig, and his agent hadn't secured it, the Secretary to the Student Union had rung him up – how he got the number Eddie had never discovered, but he succeeded in persuading him to do a benefit for the student helpline in less time than it took Eddie to remember the words to "Danny Boy", which he hoped he'd get away with as an encore, supposing there was one, supposing they let him live that long ... He'd spotted the three young women, along with their instrument cases, and wanted to ask if they were on their way to a gig, but it seemed too obvious a chat-up line. Then he'd found his taxi was following theirs along University Avenue.

"John Knox's G Strings" they were called, and they came from Edinburgh, which tickled him no end, since they had to have been around in his student days, though he'd not followed the folk scene much.

The gig had gone okay, then suddenly it was over and Eddie found himself following the three women again, back toward the city centre and a taxi rank. He'd offered to carry their music cases, and encumbered with three fiddles, attempted conversation. The slim dark one was called "Luce", short for Lucette, her more solid friend was Heather Inglis, and the one Eddie could only think of as sex on legs was Kit Barber. He'd liked the name "John Knox's G Strings", and told them so. They'd still been laughing when they reached the taxi rank, where a couple of drunk men clung to consciousness as they clutched at the stanchions, while a pair of teenagers fumbled and gasped into one another's faces. As the tiny queue crawled and slithered into one cab after another, Eddie flagged down the upcoming taxi. The driver slowed to a halt, and seeing the three women and their luggage, jumped out and ran to open the passenger door. For a moment, Eddie had thought an engine had backfired, or some partygoer popped a balloon. The scream was loud enough to change his mind, and the sudden spray of wetness across his face real enough to turn his eyes to the figure on the ground, a large hole where his forehead had been, staring up at him as if asking a question Eddie had no answer for. Eddie's father, the late Regimental Sergeant Major Corcoran, had managed to lead a sheltered life for a man in the military, which was the way he'd liked it. That meant the only dead people Eddie had ever clapped eyes on until the night in Belfast had lain peacefully "asleep" in chapels of rest. The sight of dead flesh in a cheap suit with its eyes still full of questions was turning the contents of Eddie's stomach into something very nasty.

It was only one of the girls yelling, 'Stop him!' that made Eddie turn as a small dark figure ran toward a canyon of tenement streets. The urge to vomit swept away as Eddie instinctively obeyed.

For sixteen going on eighteen stone, Eddie Corcoran was surprisingly fast, but as he realised, pounding after the receding figure, not as fast as the man he was pursuing. The small shape had turned down a side street. Eddie quickened his pace, knowing how easily he could lose his man in a warren like this. A blank wall ahead told him he already had.

They were very good at the police station, Eddie had to give them that. Thorough but considerate, in the way doctors and lawyers are expected to be. All the questions you might expect, a few you hadn't, sympathy for the shock of being in close proximity to someone having their head blown off, and, of course, a cup of tea. When question time was over there wasn't going to be a flight out of Belfast till the next morning. The ladies had decided to wait at the airport. Eddie decided to take his time. Violence was a thing he'd managed to avoid till now. His father had, by good luck or good judgment, never seen combat. Any visits the family made to these shores had been peaceful, avoiding the "marching season" or any other potentially troubled times. What he'd witnessed would have shocked him at any time, but for some reason the memory stayed fresh. He'd found out which church the funeral was to be in, went along and found a seat at the back behind a pillar. He got one or two suspicious looks when he missed the congregation's responses to the priest, but the strangest looks came from the eyes of two children in the front pew.

They kept turning round to look at him until Eddie wondered if it was more then sixteen plus stone and a weird haircut that sparked their curiosity. Afterward, he found he couldn't get them out of his mind. He'd felt an urge to explain something to them. What that was, he could hardly explain to himself. Hesitantly at first, he began buying books on subjects he'd have dismissed before. The history of how two groups of people came to be at each other's throats rapidly consumed all his spare time and spare cash. He tried not to talk about his new-found interest, but sometimes the compulsion became too great and he'd hear the word "anorak" used by friends when they thought he was out of earshot. He was sure they weren't suggesting an addition to his wardrobe. As Eddie's bookshelves bowed beneath the weight of fresh acquisitions, he stumbled on Oliver Corcoran. Eddie couldn't be sure the man was a relation, since Oliver had disappeared in 1797. He'd disappeared in Scotland, which was unusual for a United Irishman. The United Irishmen were the ones who wanted an independent Ireland and had tried talking the French into doing more than cheering from the sidelines. There had been United Scotsmen as well, though in the end the Irish had taken the faint chance of French help seriously and the Scotsmen hadn't. Oliver Corcoran had studied medicine at Edinburgh for a time, and got to know a young lawyer called Archibald Cameron, who also seemed to have disappeared around the same time. Eddie was sure there was a connection if only he could work out what it was. Then, a day or two before the end of his Fringe show, marking time before curtain up, he'd wandered into the bar at the Assembly Rooms and found himself in the company of an attractive researcher for the BBC.

He'd met Anne Enderby a couple of times in London. They'd gone for drinks once or twice and Eddie was on the point of inviting her out for dinner when a post in Edinburgh came up and Anne took it. Now she was looking for someone to "do something" for a Radio Scotland series entitled *Scotland's Forgotten Patriots*, of whom it seemed Archibald Cameron was one, on the dubious strength of a loose attachment to the United Scotsmen and a portrait on loan from Dunpark House, which had been his home as a child. Eddie could have kissed Anne, and not simply for old times. She was clearly keen Eddie took the job, though Eddie suspected desperation at least as much as residual affection. He'd hesitated long enough to convince Anne he wasn't desperate, then jumped with both feet. Eddie's plumiest "luvvie" accent had assured her 'Anything for you, dear heart, bar arson or murder.'

He was ready to do almost anything that would keep him out of sweaty basements, packed with punters high on alcohol and their own egos and all too ready to have a go at anyone who had the temerity to stand on stage and dare to entertain them. Truth to tell, age was creeping up on him faster than he cared to admit. Late night adrenalin rushes no longer held as much attraction as eight hours uninterrupted sleep. Anne's offer, on the other hand, held out the prospect of a subtle career shift into what he would once have sneered at – "serious" broadcasting. Eddie already had a fantasy career shaping in his head – a single half-hour documentary catapulting him into national consciousness, from interviewing some present day Cameron to grilling Cabinet ministers in all but a single bound. Eddie Corcoran would become the natural presenter of choice and defining voice of the BBC. Anne, of course, couldn't offer Eddie any support, technical or otherwise, for this trip to Loch Tay, and he'd thanked his lucky stars they were near the end of Edinburgh's month of artistic indulgence, when it was going to be a wee bit easier to get hold of the kit he reckoned he'd need. He would, of course, also need a technician. Which was how it had come about that after inveigling Tulloch into The Forest, Eddie was delighted, if a little surprised, to find Tulloch remarkably willing to jump at the prospect of a trip to Dunpark House. Eddie offered only the barest outline of his motives, particularly as Tulloch didn't offer any reason of his own. Eddie assumed money was a large one and left it at that. By now, they were sipping second pints of Eddie's purchase, winding toward departure from The Forest.

'Bit quiet, but then, end of the Festival, what' d' you expect?' Eddie observed. 'Been doing anything yourself?' he continued, clearly expecting tales of late-night fit-ups and desperate attempts to acquire additional lamps from sundry sources.

'Moving back up here. Permanently' Tulloch had responded, watching as Eddie's eyebrows rose a quarter of an inch.

'Takes all sorts. I love this place.' Eddie had gestured beyond the windows of The Forest, which reflected the lights of late evening traffic. 'I had some great times here. Nearly cried when I left. But I've lived in The Smoke too long, that's the trouble. Which is full of too many people trying to do too many things and all of it at once. I'd miss the buzz, though. Good luck to you, all the same, if it's what you want.'

Eddie rocked gently on his stool. He'd been doing the standard stint of comedians on the Edinburgh Festival Fringe; a show every night, and as many radio spots and other interviews as his agent could arrange and his diary cope with. He'd been looking forward to a few days off when Archibald Cameron's name had crept into a certain conversation. He was looking forward to meeting Archie's descendants. Come to think of it, wasn't the leader of one of the parties in the new Scottish Parliament a bloke called Cameron?

'You know, I'm damn glad you're coming along.'

Tulloch tried to look suitably flattered.

'No, I am. It isn't only that you're a first class techie, but the thing is, I went and hired meself some top of the range gear. I want this to be a little bit special and you're the very one to bring it off. I need someone who'll fit all those gadget things together and get them working without losing their temper and taking it out on me.'

Tulloch tried not to choke. Eddie Corcoran was capable of driving any theatre technician to drink and recreational drugs in less time than it took to wire a plug, though Eddie always became defensive when it appeared his relations with stage management were becoming strained. Tulloch remembered the times he'd been called on to pour oil on water Eddie had unwittingly troubled.

In prospect, nonetheless, was a journey to Loch Tay in far less time than he'd have made, left to the use of his thumb and the whims of the motoring public. Also in prospect, however, was the likelihood of several almighty rows before they got there. Tulloch remembered a cartoon from the First World War in his school history book – two soldiers shelter in a crater from the bombardment going on all around them. One is saying to the other "If you knows a better 'ole, go to it". He didn't know a better hole.

First prize, a night out with Eddie Corcoran, second prize, a trip to the shores of Loch Tay with Eddie Corcoran. He picked up the pint glass, ready to drain it, reckoning if he'd swallowed his pride for the sake of a grieving woman he scarcely, if he were honest, knew a damn thing about, he probably deserved whatever was coming.

Edinburgh, the underground city

The Omnivore had eaten well that evening; now, watching the port travel down the table, he heard someone whisper a name. He listened more carefully as rumour grew to speculation, theory into fact. Thomas Muir of Huntershill, sentenced to transportation, was no longer a prisoner in a far-off land. He had escaped, taken ship for America and then France, and was even now advising the French on how to invade. Then someone else said that if Dundas' scheme for militias were to go ahead, there was every chance that desperate men, armed with British weapons, might turn those same weapons on those they once obeyed. The Omnivore thought little enough of such dramatics, but decided it would be impolite to say so. Another voice said that if Dundas couldn't be persuaded to abandon such a half-baked scheme, its operation would need to be watched. The first man that had spoken pointed out that if Government were determined to carry on with such foolishness, there would be sure to be resistance. The highlanders had never been tamed, not even after Culloden and all that followed after. Someone else laughed, saying the second coming of Jesus Christ was more likely than a rush to the colours for England, home and Henry Dundas. But suppose there was, said another, could there be any doubt those who might enlist would have their own reasons for doing so? Would they not, in all probability, do so only at the bidding of Thomas Muir, or perhaps of the French themselves?

The Omnivore began to feel afraid. He didn't know where the talk would lead, but already he felt he was being looked at. Appraised as if he were a horse, or a piece of furniture. He suddenly felt chill, then uncomfortably hot, as nausea began to rise from the pit of his stomach. He wanted to get up from the table, but couldn't. Some force held him in his chair as if it were pressing him down. He tried to open his mouth; found words didn't come, and sank back. Heads were turning toward him. The Omnivore stared back at them, wondering why he should be the object of anyone's curiosity. One of the men spoke, but he didn't hear all the words spoken, except the one he'd waited so long to hear that he couldn't believe someone had said the word "commission". He couldn't understand why anyone would utter that word and look toward him. It was surely someone else they spoke of. He heard the words "Dunpark" and "Perthshire", but didn't know why they were repeated. He couldn't work out what it all meant, even when the proposal was put to him. Only it wasn't a proposal, it was a series of demands. The kind of demands he'd known might one day be made of him, the kind he'd always dreaded. As the words were spoken a feeling he couldn't describe, a mix of fear and revulsion, churned his stomach. Go north to Perthshire, to a place called Dunpark House. The laird there had an old Masonic lodge on his estate. He wanted it made into an ice house and The Omnivore, it had been decided, was the man to do it. "Remember what we've said. It may be a while till everything can be arranged, but be ready to travel as soon as it has. We need someone we can rely on to keep their eye on how things are turning out. I'm sure we can rely on you." The Omnivore listened, but did not speak. It had all happened so suddenly, but must have been planned for days, even weeks, before. Wait until he was invited to dine in a certain house. Set the other guests talking about Thomas Muir and on to the danger of sedition and arming those who might rise against the gentry. Not so great a step from there to wondering who might be sent to watch and listen, and then the great revelation that the very person who might do this was sitting amongst them. It had been so very simple after all.

Queensferry Road, Edinburgh

Rob Ainslie could feel his stomach churning, with everything in it ready to come back on him at any minute. The candy floss, toffee apple and the "hot dog" that had been no more than an ordinary sausage dribbling grease from both sides of the bap. Rob was six years old again, on the dodgem cars, feeling his stomach lurch and tighten with every flick his dad gave the steering wheel, till he was ready to chuck the whole lot up across the dashboard of the tiny car. That had been near thirty year ago, but Rob was sure it was going to be the same this time. At least he'd managed not to scream out loud. Bad enough to be scared shitless without letting the poncy pair up front know he was. Not every day you're in a car with the driver going doolally, so the next thing you're that close to a dirty great artic going the other way you can see the driver's copy of "The Sun" on the dashboard. Rob swallowed hard. Tell yourself you're not going to be sick and you won't be, simple as that. He flashed a glance at the two in the front seats. He must have been desperate to take a lift off the fat one behind the wheel, with his daft caftan and hair halfway down his back; the other one looked about as weird, with a leather coat near enough to his ankles and a hat with a brim the size of a dinner plate. Not what Rob would've described as inconspicuous, but neither was the car, with "Eddie Corcoran – the Entire Political Plectrum" posters plastered all over it. Just his luck to get in a car driven by somebody almost famous. It wouldn't have been so bad if he was almost a driver instead of almost famous. Mind you, that was his luck these days, and today a bit more so. Rob clutched his knees in an attempt to keep in touch with reality, and being the nearest to comfort he was likely to get. Who did these two think they were, anyway? Whatever they were on, Rob wished they'd share it, then decided he was glad they hadn't offered. The car lurched back into the right lane; the one marked "Forth Road Bridge". Rob was thankful to be getting out of Edinburgh. Near enough anywhere had to be better than where he'd been. Anywhere, even a car driven by a maniac, was better than yon hole he'd run away from, the cellar where daft Maurice Macquarie had had him digging his way to Australia an hour or so ago.

It hadn't sounded that bad when Macquarie had first put it to him; dig out one of the tunnels in the vaults under the South Bridge as far as it would take him, for cash money. Rob wasn't in a position to say "no" and Macquarie knew that fine. So he'd grabbed the spade with open arms and set to. He'd aye been happier working with his hands than anything else, and shifting the muck hadn't been as hard as he'd thought it might be. Then slowly he'd started feeling he was being watched. Nothing he could have explained in a way that would have made him seem anything bar crazy, but there was something he couldn't put his finger on, something he was sure he didn't want to put his finger on, but that would likely finger him if he stayed there long enough. So when Macquarie came strolling in, complaining he'd no been working hard enough, it was near enough the last straw. Then, bang on cue, the last straw tapped him on the shoulder. Not exactly tapped, mark you, more brushed against him. That was enough, however. Rob all but leapt in the air, with a scream that would have justified a triple "X" rating. Macquarie jumped at that himself, inconveniently barring Rob's otherwise clear run for the opening at the head of the tunnel.

'Not so fast!' he heard Macquarie yell, like a voice from a bad thriller. Rob reacted by lamping Macquarie a thing harder than he needed, shoving past the slumping detective, and making for the exit as if the demons of hell were after him, which as far as Rob was concerned, could well be the case.

He was breathing hard by the time the fresh air hit him, and he took a good lungful before hurling himself through the opening and out onto the deserted street. It was either a fair pech up toward the Royal Mile or a quick bowl down to the Cowgate. Rob chose what he reckoned was the quicker and easier option. Then he saw a car moving out of an underground car park. If you don't try, you don't get, he decided. Seconds later Rob was parallel to the vehicle, banging hard on the side window till the driver began to roll it down.

Eddie was unsure how to react to a large bloke in jogging bottoms and flip-flops trying to hitch a lift. Tulloch felt his jaw slacken as the panting hulk banged on the window, thumb thrusting upward in a clear gesture. Having rolled down the window, Eddie twisted to face the man, who was by now holding onto the car as if it might disappear at any moment. A swift turn of the rear door handle and a large blue mass was stumbling onto the back seat.

'You guys leavin Edinbury?' A short pause for breath, then 'Any chance o a lift?'

'Right on the first question. Not sure about the second.'

Tulloch squinted at the figure on the seat behind him.

'We're heading north. Perth's the next stop. Any good?'

'That'll dae.'

If Tulloch had thought to carry his mobile, he'd have been able to phone the police and request assistance with a demented nutter who had commandeered the rear seat. Instead, he let Eddie lead the conversation.

'You seem in a bit of a hurry to leave town. None too fussy about the company you leave in, either.'

'You're no the cops, are you?'

'Make any difference if we were?' Eddie asked.

'My friend asks the sensible questions,' Tulloch intervened. 'I ask the stupid ones. You're not trying to escape from anywhere, are you?'

'Only the same loony bin youse two are gettin out o.'

'The other escaped lunatic is Ninian Tulloch, who prefers you call him by his last name. I'm Eddie Corcoran.'

'Rob.' A pause while he gathered what breath he had left. 'Rob Ainslie.'

'Three for the road then, which is Perthshire way.'

'Long as it's oot o here, I dinnae mind.'

The car picked up speed and headed westward.

the ice house, Dunpark

It wasn't as easy as he'd hoped it was going to be. McIlwraith's arm muscles ached from twisting the iron back and forth. The padlock remained obstinately in place, while the wood wasn't as dry or brittle as he'd expected. He pulled away from the chest, looked down at his hands, raw and beginning to bled from the effort of trying to break the padlock free of the chest. Every muscle in his body was telling him he needed a break, but the prospect of Macquarie or Cameron or worse still, the police pitching up meant he needed to keep at it more than he needed a rest. Getting the chest open had become a kind of obsession to him. McIlwraith knew that even if it was, it was keeping him going, and he was determined not to stop until he knew what was inside the mysterious chest.

'I had no idea who, or what the United Scotsmen were. I'd heard that there were United Irishmen over the water, and it was said that they were a desperate band, ready to slit throats and do all manner of things. But in Scotland, Nathaniel, there were plenty at that time that owed what they had to Henry Dundas and other great folk. For all that, it was said the United Scotsmen were in some kind of league with the United Irishmen, and if that was true I didn't want to be mixed up with them. I went to see Angus Cameron, over in his cottage, to ask him what he knew. He didn't seem to know much; he was the same as he'd been as a laddie, caught out in some ploy that he ought to feel guilty about but wouldn't own up to. Instead, he asked me what I thought about a few men in Scotland being able to lord it over the rest of us. He knew fine I was the Duke's man, so why he asked me that I didn't understand. I wondered if maybe he was some sort of spy, for there were plenty rumours about folk that would set innocent folk talking and then make out to the Government men that they'd said all manner of nonsense. He wouldn't deny being acquainted with the United Scotsmen, nor did he admit to being one of them. In the end I gave up trying to prise the truth from him, and when he saw that I wasn't going to press him further, he shook my hand, so we parted as good friends. For all that, I made up my mind not to tell him anything more than I needed to in future; for one thing, I knew that you were moving among gentlemen and ladies in Edinburgh, grander, some of them, even than the Duke of Atholl was used to entertaining. I'd no wish to jeopardise your position, Nathaniel, any more than I wished to jeopardise mine. Walking back to Inver, I thought over what Angus Cameron had said, or, in fact, had not said. All I knew of the United Scotsmen was that they had some notions the United Irishmen had likely put in their heads, but very probably lacked either the drive or the devilry to do more than talk about any of it. It seemed to me that Henry Dundas and the rest of those set over us had little to fear from such men. Nonetheless, the times being as they were, I was pretty certain Angus Cameron and anyone fool enough to listen to him would be watched. The thought caused me much anxiety on my way home, for it seemed to me that whether or not he knew more than he told me, Angus Cameron had put all the folk of the valley under suspicion. No-one anxious to earn their informer's money would make much distinction between honest folk and those who were suspect when it came to claiming their reward. Whatever might be the truth would count for very little if even a scrap of it proved to be true. I became anxious for myself, for you, for the folk of the valley. I thought about my nephew, another of your cousins, Nathaniel, Tam Linton, who had been an assistant to James Tytler. Him you'll have heard of, on account of his going into the air in a thing cried a balloon. It was your cousin Tam helped him with that. But Tytler did a lot of other things, including ones some of the great folk didn't like, and he had to get out of the country for that, leaving his wife and bairns behind. So I worried about Tam and the rest of us on account of that. Then I heard something else that worried me; talk of a thing called the Militia Act.'

Forth Road Bridge

The lights on the bridge flicked by, a parade line of illuminated salutes. Eddie ruminated in silence about the mysterious Archibald Cameron. Memory took him back to his encounter with Ann Enderby. He never ought to have gone into the bar at the venue, but he liked watching the scenery go by. Edinburgh in Fringe time was always good for the eyes. Occasionally someone would ask that loaded question – 'You're not that fellow from the telly, are you?' and he'd have to be careful in case they meant that awful "Funky Chicken" advert. Very occasionally he'd get chatted up, which hardly ever led anywhere Eddie might have wanted to go, but didn't do his ego any harm. The evening he re-encountered Ann, Eddie had found himself trying to impress her with his knowledge of the life and times of Archibald Cameron. When the phone broke in on next morning's hangover, Eddie picked it up to discover Anne had sold her boss on Eddie contributing to a radio documentary on a forgotten Scottish patriot. That, at least, was how Archibald Cameron was going to be presented.

Hung over, missing the beauty sleep he clearly needed, judging by the image staring back at him from the bathroom mirror, Eddie had been too stunned to say more than "yes" and "thank you". Tea and toast brought a smile back to his face. He'd been looking for a way out of doing more late night gigs than a man past thirty ought to be taking on, and of avoiding the nastier sort of heckling drunk. He needed to be more than a satirical songwriter, each carefully crafted pastiche with a "sing by" date that set him on a continuous treadmill of racking his brains for fresh material. Radio documentaries, that was the way forward for a man of his abilities. Once he'd begun to feel better, Eddie began to panic. He knew a bit about Archibald Cameron, but not enough to fill half an hour of talk radio. That's nearly five thousand words. Eddie hadn't tried writing five thousand words since university. Five hundred were the most he'd ever needed, and he'd sweated blood over every one of them. It couldn't be that hard. He thought about the books stacked shoulder high in his Vauxhall flat. There were probably more than five thousand words in the shortest of them. Other people could obviously manage to churn out words, and what else had he ever done, for God's sake? A bit more of them than you usually get away with, Eddie, that's all. A drop of the midnight oil for you, son.

Good job he was in Edinburgh, with its National Library and Record Office, though if he'd not been in Edinburgh, he wouldn't have got the job in the first place, so there you are. Handy, all the same, having the class of an institution like the National Library of

Scotland less than ten minutes' walk down the road. Guess where he'd be spending all the mornings till the run ended? No sessions in the bar after the show, either. Sorry, got to get an early night, I've a hot date with a dusty tome in the morning. Ah well, saves a bit of money. Does the waistline a bit of good and all.

Eddie stared ahead if him. Against the darkening sky he could barely make out the shape, but it looked like a balloon. In the middle of Fife, in the middle of the night, he was watching as a damn great hot air balloon flew what looked like yards ahead of them. He steered the car away from the verge they were approaching. Careful, Eddie, you'll be in a ditch next, and try explaining to an insurance investigator that you'd seen a bloody big balloon before you put the vehicle arse over gear box. Eddie swerved the wheel violently to avoid a white minibus. Its horn blared angrily at him. He was tired, Eddie told himself. The get-out had been a late one, he'd wanted to sort out the takings before heading north, and of course there had been a bit of a party. The balloon had now disappeared as suddenly as it had arrived, but Eddie had an uncomfortable feeling that he hadn't seen the last of it.

Loch Tay

Silk was the problem. That was what Tam Linton told you, and Mattie backed him up with nods of her head. They needed silk to finish "Republica" which was how it came to be hanging in the South Bridge vaults, waiting for some fool with money to buy it a new dress. Silk was hard to come by these days, said Tam, and expensive when it could be got. A rumour came along that a French smuggler was lying in the Firth, with bales of silk as well as other goods such as brandy the folk of Edinburgh had scarcely seen since the war with France began. It was the devil's own job getting enough money together. The three of them seemed to think you only had to fish in your pocket and pull out the needful. But you, Oliver Corcoran, knew better than that. You had to find the right card game and the right drunk playing in it, and even that was barely the start. You had the money in a couple of days, all the same, which was as well, since the smuggler's boat could leave at any time, and would, if they thought the Excise were anywhere near. You tied your winnings in a kerchief and let Mattie hold it, like some token of good faith, and you and she, with Tam Linton looking a bit sideways at you, went down to Newhaven and hired a fisherman's boat to take you out to where the smuggler was supposed to be. For all he might be brave in the air, Tam looked white as a sheet as the little boat pitched and tossed its way toward where the smuggler lay. They threw out a rope and you scrambled up, your feet sliding this way and that against the wet, pitching ship's side. They let down a tackle arrangement and Mattie slid her foot between the ropes and came up like a queen, though when Tam's turn came, he clung to the ropes like they were his dearest possessions. On deck there wasn't as much gear as you'd imagined, and Tam muttered that the best stuff had likely gone already. There was one bale, though, and since it was lying in the middle of the deck, it had to be something of worth, and that was likely silk. Mattie was on it in an instant, and some fellow jabbering in French at her that fast you hadn't a notion what he might be saying. Mattie caught herself on quick enough, though. You saw yourself he was demanding more for the bale than Mattie knew was in the kerchief, and she was beating him down in a mixture of sign language and pidgin French, adding as much charm as she could bestow on the creature. In the end she emptied the kerchief onto the bale and gestured to the man to count it. He scowled at her, not used to females who tell him to take it or leave it, and knowing that the ship couldn't stay close to land much longer, nodded and scooped the coins into his hand. You and Tam grabbed the bale and lowered it over the side to the waiting fisherman, who complained loudly that it'd capsize his vessel long before it reached Newhaven. But it didn't.

Within the hour you're all on land again, in a wagon making its way toward the city. It takes the three of you – yourself, Tam and Archie, to struggle the bale along the passages and into the vault. It's only then you start to unwrap it and realise the silk is black. "Black as a pair of whore's drawers" says Tam, and Mattie asks him how he comes to know the colour, and Tam blushes redder than his hair while you and Archie laugh. Then Archie picks up a fold of it in his hand and says; 'Well, at least it's silk and good enough, by the feel of it'. Mattie takes it from him and you can tell she likes the feel of it, and you almost think it worth all the effort to see that smile of hers, only she catches you looking and her gaze near freezes you on the spot. The talk turns to how it's going to get used and whether they've enough of it and it's clear you're out of the picture till they need you again. You're not upset, for you know the time will come when they do need you, and when it does, you'll make sure you're the one holding the cards.

The A9

'Okay back there?' Eddie's voice sounded almost solicitous.

Rob nodded and tried to smile. When you're in the same car as a pair of nutters, no sense being unpleasant.

Eddie turned his attention back to the road ahead. A question lingered in his mind, however, from his earlier conversation with Tulloch.

'What's in this for you, Tulloch?'

'A few quid and the pleasure of your company, Eddie. I thought I'd like to take a look at Loch Tay. I've never been there.'

'Well, you'll have a chance to do that. Dunpark House is right on the shore, I'm told.'

A strange look drifted across Tulloch's face, but Eddie decided that if Tulloch wanted to keep a secret, then let him. None of his business what it might be, so long as Tulloch did what Eddie needed him to do.

Tulloch was not about to divulge the reason for his sudden urge to visit Loch Tay to Eddie or whatever class of nutter was occupying the rear seats. Eddie might try to prise more out of him at some point, but Tulloch decided to ignore the possibility for the moment. What couldn't be ignored was the rattling noise coming from somewhere beneath the car's bonnet. Increasing in level, it caught Eddie unawares, and his hands clawed the steering wheel as the vehicle slewed, till he fought it back into the right lane and edged it slowly toward the verge. Tooting, honking horns sounded past while Eddie swayed over the wheel, breathing with the relief of one who knows they've got away with about as much as Fate allows at one time.

They could still see the lights of the Forth Road Bridge, tucked away at the end of the incline, the traffic a broken ribbon of lights beckoning them back to Edinburgh. Rob and Tulloch stood awkwardly aside, like relatives at the bedside of the gravely ill, while Eddie, oil-grimed and cursing, probed the mysteries of the car's engine. Looking like one of the living dead and giving Rob an awful fleg, Eddie's head rose slowly above the line of the car's bonnet, briefly illuminated by a passing lorry.

'That ought to get us as far as Perth' he announced, as if holding out the possibility of a further six months' existence.

'What the hang are we goin tae dae if it doesnae?' Rob wailed in response to Eddie's pronouncement.

'Walk, I shouldn't wonder.' Tulloch muttered, confirming Rob's worst fears.

'There's bound to be a car we can hire in Perth.' Eddie tried smiling a reassurance he didn't feel.

'It's no Edinbury, though. There'll maybe no be as many places ...'

Tulloch let the pair of them argue the toss, drifting in his mind to where he wasn't sure he wanted to go. Dunpark House. Not that he'd ever been there in the first place. He knew it was Luce's family home, the place she'd brought the "G Strings" to rehearse, recuperate from *that* tour and "chill" as she'd put it at the time.

He'd never seen Kit since. What had happened, Tulloch never knew. Not so much as a "Dear Tulloch" postcard to mark their severance. He'd wondered long enough if they were severed, sleepwalking through a life he didn't much care about. Work was a great cure, it was said. It wasn't in his case. London had seemed a good bet at the time. More work, new faces, different bars. The faces blurred, the bars slid into meaningless repetition, the work kept him halfway sane and usually solvent. It hadn't always kept him sober. He'd never found the right hole to fall through, though. He discovered a talent for business he never suspected he had. Making deals and arranging contracts came quickly and surprisingly easily to him. Then he got bored, so he'd sold up and come home ... what had prompted him to make his promise to Luce? He tried telling himself he didn't need to do a damn thing about it. MacLennan had been quite capable of firing you up with his latest enthusiasm, then within twenty-four hours denying he'd ever thought any such thing. Let it rest, Luce. Let him rest.

'Planet Earth calling Ninian Tulloch.'

Tulloch gave Eddie a look that might have drawn tears from a gargoyle, but Eddie simply smiled back, apparently oblivious.

'Tenner says we're eating breakfast in Perth.'

Somehow Eddie's confident assertions always sounded to Tulloch as convincing as a Friday night drunk's estimation of a barmaid's morals. He knew from past encounters there was no point telling Eddie Corcoran anything Eddie didn't want to hear. The annoying ego that was Edward Osnabruck Corcoran would simply smile and nod at any amount of protest and carry on doing what he was going to do anyway. Which was how they came to be staring into the waters of Loch Leven as pre-dawn light began to glint reflections across its surface. Eddie knew he ought to have listened when Rob and Tulloch told him loud and lengthily he was going in the wrong direction.

'Not that far off.'

Eddie's voice betrayed more than a hint of defensiveness as a careful study of the map revealed the distance between where they were and where they ought to be. Mercifully, he didn't realise how close refusal to realise his error had taken him to playing the great comedy gig in the sky. Rob glowered darkly from the back seat, while Tulloch fumed in silence beside Eddie's bulk, indulging a homicidal fantasy in which Eddie, strangled with a convenient microphone lead, swayed gently from one of the telephone poles flitting past. The car's complaining engine punctured the pre-dawn quiet of the village they coasted into. Eddie eased the car to a halt outside a shuttered Chinese take-away.

'Too late for Special Fried Rice' he mourned.

Tulloch sighed. The mezze of hours ago no longer filled his stomach. Images of glistening bacon, eggs shining with fat and sausages grilled until their skins gleamed almost black flitted before him. He knew nothing the place could offer would match such cardiac-arresting dreams, but he couldn't stop his mind running in the direction of carnivorous forms of satisfaction.

Rob would've settled for a comfy bed, preferably his own. When he'd got that phone call from Macquarie, he'd given in, said 'Ay, fine, I'll dae your bit diggin for you, Mister Macquarie, no questions asked'. He ought to have asked questions. You didn't need a PhD in smelling fish to know something strange was going on inside Macquarie's devious wee brain.

The night he'd been collared trying to break into the Royal High School, and the psycho that had been with him had done a runner, he'd been scared witless of Macquarie. It was only later he realised he'd been scared witless of doing time. Familiarity breeds contempt, or something. In Rob's case it wasn't so much contempt for Macquarie, more a sort of pity for the sad wee git. Macquarie thought he was the bee's knees. A couple of years being Macquarie's stool pigeon had made Rob see the man barely had enough brains to bless himself. Which didn't mean he couldn't scare the hell out of Rob at times. For all that, Rob had done no bad out of Macquarie. He could always bet on the wee nyaff seeing him right when needed. There had to be a reckoning, he'd aye known that. A favour for a favour given. Rob had aye been an optimist, which was his trouble. He'd always believed something would turn up.

What had turned up was Macquarie, putting a shovel in Rob's hands and telling him to dig a tunnel and not ask where it was supposed to go. Rob didn't need a sense of direction to work out it would lead straight to the vaults of the Royal Bank of Caledonia. Talking to Macquarie about eejits with fantasies was one thing; robbing a major Scottish bank something else. That had to be what Macquarie was up to. Whatever he'd seen, or thought he had, was the best excuse he could have to get the hell out before he ended up doing more time than he was likely to have left on the planet. He'd legged it down the vennel to the High Street as if his life depended on it, and maybe it had. Thank God for Eddie Corcoran, whoever he was. All the same, he wouldn't have minded being somewhere that wasn't the back seat of a car with a pair of nutters up front pretending they were asleep. But then Rob had aye been closer to trouble of one sort or another than he'd wanted to be. His Granny was aye telling him that he was born with a nose that smelt trouble, supposing it was ten mile away, and that he liked the smell of it too much. It wasn't his fault, though, most of the time. He'd fell into it that often it had become a habit, and harder to break than most. Stupid, most of it, like yon time McIlwraith the psychopath – that was what folk called him, though not if he could hear you – had got Rob climbing up the drainpipe of the old Royal High School on Calton Hill. Which was how come he'd fallen into the hands of Inspector Macquarie– literally, near enough, seeing as Macquarie was at the foot of the drainpipe where McIlwraith ought to have been. An experience like that can scar a person for life, and Rob hadn't healed yet. He turned as far over as the narrowness of the car seat would let him, and tried for sleep. It still didn't come. For one thing, he'd no idea what he was going to do next. Rob had been that glad to see the vehicle he was now in that he'd not worried what his next move was going to be, bar get away from Macquarie and whatever he'd seen in the vaults as fast as he could and as far as possible. Well, he was a fair bit away now, and with peace to think, he began to wonder if he'd done the right thing. Of course he had – getting out of Macquarie's clutches was his smartest move in a long time, but what the hang was he going to do now, further from Edinburgh than he'd been in years, stuck with two weirdoes he'd body-swerve sharpish in any other circumstances? Make the best of your chances, Rob. All you can dae, son. Relax and let them worry about how they get this car back on the road and wherever the hell they want to go. Not your problem. Your only problem is if Macquarie decides to come after you.

Edinburgh, the underground city

Angus Cameron. The Omnivore had never heard the name before. Little wonder, since he lived, or eked out an existence more like, in Edinburgh, while Angus Cameron, it seemed, was a timber merchant in a Perthshire village called Dull. Why Government should be suddenly interested in a Perthshire timber merchant wasn't clear, although Government was interested in a great many people. It had even taken an interest in a simple soul who asked only to draw plans of houses that would never be built and carry on eating his dinners without having to pay for them. The night when the talk had been about Henry Dundas raising Highland militia and what else those Highlanders might do, he'd not realised at first what would be expected of him. He ought to have paid more attention. Suddenly, he had a visitor. He never had visitors. There was no room for visitors. They disturbed his papers and drawings by picking them up and looking at them. This one didn't bother picking anything up, even if only to make space enough to sit down. He stood, and spoke the name Angus Cameron. The visitor went on, talking about this person who was a merchant and lived near Dull, which sounded a suitable place for a simple merchant. Only it seemed Angus Cameron wasn't simple, or simply a timber merchant. He had been wild in his youth, the illegitimate son of a Perthshire laird, sent to the army for his better discipline, had fought in the Netherlands campaign, been captured by the French and became, it was said, much taken with revolutionary notions. He had got back to Scotland and set up as a timber merchant in this place called Dull. Cameron became a man of some interest to those who added to the few pennies they earned by keeping Government informed of what it might like to know. The United Scotsmen were still a bogey to frighten those who feared handfuls of the starving could overthrow the powerful. It was clear the visitor had no more belief in such a possibility than The Omnivore had, but that, of course, was not the point. If Dundas' scheme for a highland militia was to succeed, opposition had to be eliminated. That it was likely to be unpopular was certain. That some might actively oppose it very likely. Those voices needed to be silenced. A show of strength might be necessary. It could even be that such a thing would be for the good, if it meant United Scotsmen and those in sympathy with them were identified, and other troublesome individuals cowed. Government could only use force if it could be justified, of course. If there were such a need, it would have to be communicated. What was needed was someone who could do that. Someone with a reason to be talking with all manner of people. The visitor said The Omnivore would receive an invitation to visit Dunpark House, on the shores of Loch Tay, to look at the building the Laird wanted turned into an ice house. The visitor made it clear he had no choice but go to Dunpark and wait for someone to make contact with him. The United Scotsmen had over two thousand members scattered across the country. Roughly the same number elected the Members of Parliament for Scotland. 'United' the discontented might believe themselves to be, but their organisation was not. Government did not always need to buy its information. There are always those desperate in different ways. 'Spy' is not a pleasant word. Still less, 'informer'. Anyone brave or foolish enough to be either risks revenge or justified wrath, leaving the same bloody mess, foul smells and unfinished business. To pay for his dinners The Omnivore was going to have to pry, wheedle and if needs be lie, and hope he would not be found out doing any of those things.

Wester Balgedie, Fife

Eddie stared into the lessening darkness as light slowly spread from the hilltops down and across the Loch. He'd managed to discover the least uncomfortable position for his bulk. For all the growing daylight, he couldn't make the memory of the balloon disappear from his thoughts. It wasn't a cloud. Rationalising what you couldn't explain only made it safe for as long as it took to clamber out from behind one's own mental sofa and pretend it had only been the imagination on overdrive. Bollocks. He'd seen a balloon sweep its way ahead of them. He couldn't make sense of what he'd seen or why he'd seen it. Even though Eddie decided to stop trying, the image kept returning to interrupt his dozing.

Rob tried turning over, but found the back seat was too narrow for any such ambitious manoeuvre. Just his luck, he reckoned, lying back as far as he could against the seat. He still wasn't sure what had been in yon tunnel, but he knew there had been something there; his imagination didn't often get the better of him, and he was sure it hadn't. He could get a fleg as easy as anyone else, but he didn't scare easily, and whatever had been in the tunnel had near scared him out of his wits. For a moment, Rob was glad he was less than comfy on the back seat of a car in the middle of nowhere. It beat the hell out of being stuck in a tunnel with God alone knew what.

Tulloch tried for a more comfortable position, only to end up in a less comfortable one. Now fully awake, he tried re-composing the poem he'd written and never sent, having nowhere to send it. It had got lost among all the bits and pieces he'd packed before the move, but he still remembered the words.

'For walks over mountains,
A hand in my hand, holding back the fears,
Pointing to circling seabirds, bursts of blossom,
Marking every house you made a home,
Then left with smiles and no regrets,
For boxes of music left like man-traps
On curving stair-cases. Postcards from nowhere,
The sound of your key in our latch,
For an ocean of time spent with impatience,
For every furtive, quirky kiss snatched
Between eternities of silence,
For every sweet, impossible moment,
Spent believing we belonged to each other,
For all that we are worth,
For auld lang syne, my jo,
For no particular reason,
Except the most obvious one.'

It had lain in a drawer in Pimlico long enough to get lost in the frantic flitting northward. He ought to have forgotten it by now, and Kit along with it, but he hadn't. What had they ever really known of each other? What made them pin so much hope on another frail, uncertain human being? Expect so much of them?

He'd know Kit was Kit the moment he'd met her, but he'd forgotten that, somehow. It had got overlooked in the romance of loving her. Had he ever loved Kit? Of course he had. Had. Past tense, future uncertain and likely to be imperfect. And Luce? He didn't know. Knowing was an illusion. You could never say you knew someone, only imagine that you did. Every so often a domestic murder, suddenly revealed affair or unexplained disappearance claimed headlines and reminded you that most of the time we sleep-walk our way through what we laughingly refer to as "reality", heedless of the people around us. Not long after he'd started going to The Forest, Tulloch had come to the conclusion that music was the only thing you could rely on; the only thing that managed to stay the same, yet always change, without leaving you feeling as if you'd been cheated. People, though, were another matter. People could lie to you, cheat on you, do anything and still manage to justify it to themselves. He understood that; the need to feel we're in the right, neither wicked nor selfish nor foolish. That we are, after all, good people. But then only good people feel the prick of their consciences, the difficulty of embarrassment, or chide themselves for their mistakes. You have to be hellishly naive to have no problems in life.

Tulloch wasn't used to speculation this early in the morning. Normally, he'd still be asleep, or busy assembling the lamps and rig needed for the day's exhibition or the evening's gig. Memories of those early mornings nudged his stomach, which performed a definite rumble. Philosophy had made him hungry. He wished breakfast was cooking and he had someone to share it with who wasn't overweight, a comedian, or on the run.

the ice house, Dunpark

McIlwraith lay exhausted on the ice house floor. He couldn't remember when he'd worked that hard, or for as long. The chest he'd been trying to open was still resisting all his efforts to separate hasp from padlock. Somehow he would, though. He wanted to find out what Cameron was so anxious to get his hands on. Whatever it was, it was sure to be worth money. Knowing Cameron, it would be worth very serious money. Exactly what had got him into trouble in the first place, McIlwraith thought to himself. He'd always liked beautiful things. Even when he was wee he'd an eye for what he wanted, and never a problem about taking what he wanted, either. Kids grow out of sweets and toys, but he'd never got out the habit of seeing something and spending the next few days, or weeks, however long it took, working out how he was going to get it. He'd got a bit sophisticated over the years. Art and antiques were more his thing than turning over a bookie's for pennies and ending up behind bars with nothing to show. Find a niche market and stick to it. So he had, until he'd got taigled into yon daft nonsense at the Royal High School. He'd been stupid enough to think there was going to be some money in being patriotic, but the whole pack of them were daft as so many certifiable monkeys. He must have been drunk when he and yon Rob what was his name? Oh ay, Ainslie, had broken into the old Royal High School in Edinburgh. He'd near enough been caught, but he'd got away while Rob was the one who'd ended up being arrested. He'd tried his chances in Ulster after that, only to find yon toe-rag Macquarie on his case and ready to shove him in gaol for long enough. He'd sweet-talked Macquarie and his softheaded superior Cameron round, though. It had all been going great until he'd been leant on to do that wee job for one of the godfathers. Shot the wrong man, it turns out. Typical. Then Cameron gets in touch to say he has his own wee job with a "get out of gaol free" card attached ... So here he was, trapped in the middle of wildest Perthshire with the cops likely to turn up at any minute, his only chance being to find out what Cameron's wee job was really all about. He sighed heavily and turned back to the chest.

'I'd hoped, Nathaniel, Angus Cameron would settle to his work, but then the Militia Act came into law and folk worried what it might mean for them. The Government wanted to take young men from all the parishes into a militia and put the great folk over them as officers. According to Angus Cameron, the army that went to the Low Countries had been led by vain old fools and inexperienced young ones, an opinion he often let slip when he drank in the howff kept by John Maclaggan. When the folk around the Loch began to hear that lads might be taken from their looms and off the fields, they grew fearful, for who would be left to do the work apart from bairns and old men? There was another thing, though, that stirred the gossip; the Laird of Dunpark decided to turn the old Mason's Lodge into an ice house to store salmon from the Loch till they could be sold in Perth. He hired a man from Edinburgh to oversee the work. This man arrived one day, and it was soon clear he was more used to a drawing room than a building site. Though I saw little enough of him, I could tell he was fearful of something or someone. Maclaggan managed to wind him around his little finger, and got himself and his crony, James Menzies, the one they called "The East Indian", put in charge of the workmen. So you had the Duke of Lennox, which you'll mind was what John

Maclaggan called himself, on account of believing he was some relation of the Lennoxes, and "The East Indian" making out they were the grand factotums of the Laird of Dunpark, which might have been comical if hadn't been pathetic. The wee man from Edinburgh let them alone much of the time, though they only obeyed his orders when the notion took them. It was soon clear that building this ice house would take more time than the Laird had thought. Maclaggan let the men doing the work have plenty slack time, so they could spend it in his howff. The man from Edinburgh said nothing of this, and seemed as much in awe of Maclaggan and Menzies as the men drinking in the howff were of Angus Cameron.'

Wester Balgedie

Cars, Eddie decided, were not designed to be slept in. They certainly didn't make sleep easy when the mind was racing, as Eddie's now was. He was going to be a day late reaching Dunpark, as the vehicle clearly needed a proper repair. Then there were the two unknown quantities beside and behind him. Tulloch, in Eddie's opinion, could be a temperamental nightmare to work with. He knew Tulloch felt much the same about him, but he'd needed a techie and Tulloch had happened to be in town. He could hardly regret making so obvious a decision. Rob, if that was his real name, was a very different sort of problem. He could be a serial killer for all Eddie knew. Unlikely, but it's the quiet ones you have to watch. One wrong move and Eddie's promising career could end very prematurely. He decided to stop speculating and concentrate on how he was going to get the car back on the road. Even if the place didn't have a garage, he wasn't going to let that be the end of his trip to see the Cameron family. Something or someone, he felt sure, would turn up. As the light began to colour the horizon, he tried finding the joke Will Shakespeare had missed … "Rosy fingered Dawn, if she's up in time". Dawn Blackwood had caused Eddie to lose sleep before, and thoughts of her now might have kept other ones away, if only Eddie's conscience would stop bothering him. Giving Tulloch the blah the previous night was one thing, but he wondered if he should tell him what was really taking him on this probable wild goose chase to Dunpark House. How to explain it? Where could he start? With the blood trickling down his leg as if he'd peed himself? The gunshot? The screams of the three girls?

What kept coming back to Eddie in the days afterward were the kids, the wee soft eyes he could imagine turning hard as marbles in a few years, hiding behind cheap dark glasses, minds trying to turn harder still. Excuses, all of it. He was doing this because he wanted to; it was his own daft notion and pretending altruism didn't get you anywhere except laughed at. For the first time in years he thought of Miss Paterson, who taught Primary Two and had set his infant feet walking the way they had, to fetch up miles off course for a rendezvous no-one else gave a damn about. Go to the kind of schools he'd grown up in and myths are what you pick up along with the germs. Learning that myths are mostly nonsense is part of growing up. Coming to disbelieve what the Ma and Pa want you to believe is part of growing up too; no teenage rebellion without rejection of the household gods. All myths have some morsel of truth clinging to them, though, or at least we want them to. Even if they are a load of old cobblers, they're ours, and that's what makes the difference.

'Remember you're a comedian, son, not a philosopher. Doesn't say "philosopher" on the programme, does it?'

The voice of the late Regimental Sergeant Major Corcoran frequently intruded on Eddie's inner musings, as hard to ignore in imagination as he had been in life. As when Eddie had done that radio interview a few weeks back.

'The Comedy Cafe near Camden Lock re-opens tonight, after a six-month refurbishment. Topping the bill is Eddie Corcoran, nominated as "Most Promising Comedian of the Year" Looking forward to tonight, Eddie, or do you get nervous before you go on stage?'

Ignoring the off-stage comment of Corcoran *pere* that Eddie had been nominated "Most Promising" two years in a row and wasn't it time he was nominated for something else, Eddie tried to work out how to tell the interviewer he'd never been nervous of going on stage until he started getting visits from two smiling children.

He wasn't psychotic (unless someone tried to play a James Blunt track), but the two kids were hard to ignore. He'd ended up laughing the question off by saying he only got nervous if he could tell no-one else was, then he really did start to worry. The interviewer had bowled through his early days. Edward Osnabruck Corcoran because that's where he was born, Osnabruck having been a British Forces overseas posting at the time. Schools many and various, owing to his father's career. Discovering that he could make people laugh had been a revelation that had kept the bullies at arm's length and come in very handy at other times. It had helped when work was as boring and repetitive as checking the expenses claims of Cheesy Delight salespersons. He lasted a week there, he told the interviewer. Lie. He'd stuck it for three months, to be able to buy the most expensive Fender guitar in "Frets and Scales" on the High Street.

The interviewer made no mention of Eddie's time in Edinburgh. No interest to a London audience, he supposed, though he owed the city a lot. He'd arrived confused, clutching an acceptance from the University, and left four years later knowing exactly what he wanted to do with his life, if not how he was going to do it. He'd scraped second-class honours, enough to make his Mum think it was worth her while buying a new outfit for the graduation, after all. As the train pulled out of Waverley Station that last time, Eddie knew he was going to be back one day. He owed the place something, more particularly he owed the University's Drama Society for showing him what his real mission in life ought to be.

They'd had this late-night comedy thing on a Friday, and one half-cut evening, Eddie had staggered out of his seat, announcing he could do at least as well as the bloke on stage. He'd not been booed or dried up, and, apart from a couple of slurred pauses no-one seemed to notice because they were still laughing at the one about explaining to the landlord how the bed had got broken, it went okay. The next week Eddie brought his guitar along, pastiched a couple of popular numbers with lines based on the week's news headlines, almost brought the house down and scarcely looked back. That was when he'd met Tulloch, a mere techie in those days, fitting up lighting rigs and running the cues. He'd always liked Tulloch, for all his dour moodiness, and despite Tulloch's apparent inability to reciprocate Eddie's appreciation.

The interviewer clearly wanted to wrap up and get on to the next record, which wasn't one of Eddie's. At least they hadn't asked if "there was anyone in his life at the moment", as he might have been tempted to announce on air that if a Dawn Blackwood was listening, and was still interested in a date with a promising comedian, he'd be delighted to hear from her. Dawn had been Assistant Stage Manager at a gig he'd done in Barnet, whose number he had lost the night his wallet was nicked off the bar of the "Duke of Albany".

He'd ferried the drinks over to the table, turned back to pay for them and found only French-polished mahogany where his wallet ought to have been. Highly embarrassing and disastrous when it came to getting back in touch with Dawn. She was far too good for him anyway, he reckoned, not that it was any consolation. These thoughts were rudely interrupted by a sound very similar to the rapping of a wooden umbrella on the windscreen of a car. Eddie looked up to see a purple-faced man in a tweed jacket gazing down at him. Eddie might have been easily convinced the apparition was part of a bizarre dream, only the figure indicated to him to roll down the window.

'Good morning to you, gentlemen.'

The accent could almost have been one of his uncles, if any of the family had stayed in Scotland for the best part of twenty years.

'Morning.'

Eddie's response was guarded. You never knew what some dubious individuals might do to get a lift. Take one Robert Ainslie, snoring on the back seat, as a prime example.

At least half Eddie's mind was still on Dawn Blackwood, and he wasn't the least grateful to a stranger reminding him he was dossed down in a barely functioning vehicle with two charmless companions and very little likelihood of ever seeing the delectable Dawn again.

'I was wondering if you might be able to help me?'

The enquiry was polite, but Eddie remained non-committal. Tulloch was by now pulling himself upright on the seat next to Eddie's. Rob was making a sound, neither yawn, snore nor anything yet recognised by science as he came to on the back seat.

'You see, I've had a wee bit of a breakdown.'

This revelation didn't surprise Eddie. He looked at the stranger, waiting a fuller explanation, which didn't seem forthcoming.

'What sort of a breakdown?' Eddie enquired, hoping he wasn't the feed to the stranger's punch line.

'It's the old jalopy' the man wailed, making it sound a medical condition instead of a quaint term for a motor vehicle. 'Missus McGrath told me it'd break down on me if I tried to force it, but do I ever listen to her?'

Eddie's early life had immunised him against blackmail disguised as Irish charm.

'Where is she now?'

'Likely getting the toast on, I shouldn't wonder ...'

The voice trailed off, a small smile breaking then freezing as the speaker noticed a pair of eyes staring at him from the back seat of the car, suspicion clearly deep and active.

'Eddie Corcoran's the name. We seem to have broken down as well.'

'Pleased to meet you. McGrath, John McGrath.' A pause, then 'You've broken down as well, you say? Here was me, wondering if you fellows could help me out with a lift.'

''Fraid not.' A bit terser than he'd meant, but no point raising the man's hopes. McGrath cast an appraising eye over the vehicle.

'Funny thing, mine's the same model as yours. Same year, I wouldn't be surprised. D' you think it might be some sort of design fault?' He went on. 'Wouldn't you say it was a bit coincidental, the pair of us with the same vehicle, same year, and both of us broken down? You know, seeing as how they're both the same car, in a manner of speaking, why don't we see if yer man at the foot of the brae there, can't do something for at least one of us?'

John McGrath beamed on all of them, though he could feel Rob's eyes still intent on him from the safety of the rear seat,

'I was on my way there when I spotted yourselves' he added.

Rob began to feel a lot less safe than he had with Eddie at the wheel. You are up to something, Mister whoever-the-hell-you-are, and whatever it is, I know fine well I'm no going to like it.

Eddie, meanwhile, quietly speculated on what any motor mechanic, supposing the place possessed such a person, was likely to make of an old bloke in a tweed jacket and a fat geezer in a caftan seeking their assistance.

'Where did you say you were heading?'

'I don't recollect mentioning that.' A short pause. 'Not that it's any great secret. What about yourselves?'

Eddie didn't much care for the sharply questioning eyes suddenly turned on him. 'Loch Tay' he responded, hoping that would be enough to discourage any attempt to cadge a lift.

'Are you now?' McGrath beamed delight. 'It looks as if I might have to change my plans, the way the old jalopy is. I'm not that far from Perth, myself, so I wouldn't be much out of your way, would I?'

You wouldn't, Eddie had to admit to himself.

'You know, there might be enough of yours and mine put together to get us where we all want to go.'

Eddie wasn't sure if this was some oblique sexual approach or a truncated "Thought For The Day". Either way, he definitely wasn't interested. Eddie's blank stare only seemed to encourage McGrath. As he gently persuaded Eddie toward the scatter of buildings ahead, he began explaining his way out of their predicaments. If Eddie's car was the more easily repaired, McGrath would leave his at the garage and Eddie give him a lift to his home. If McGrath's proved the easier vehicle to deal with, Eddie would drive him home, where they could phone to arrange a hire car to take them north. As he explained his idea to Eddie, Rob, walking a little behind them, speculated on the package McGrath carried as if it were a small, delicate baby. He held it firmly but gently in his large, pink hands. Tulloch couldn't work out why Eddie seemed to be going along with the other man's daft scheme. Rob tapped his arm and whispered confidingly.

'See yon John McGrath? Watch him. He's Special.'

'His mother might have thought so, but I've my doubts.'

'Special like in Special Branch' Rob explained patiently.

'Away you go!'

'Bet you any money.'

John McGrath allowed himself a moment of self-congratulation. When he'd taken that call from Macquarie, asking him to track down a car almost exactly the same as his own, he'd wanted to tell Macquarie it would be about as easy as finding a live turkey on Boxing Day. He'd set off nonetheless, heart in boots and with about as much optimism as a terminally ill undertaker. Macquarie's mention of posters on the car with the words "Eddie Somebody" had been enough to mark it out for McGrath. Spotting the car as it came off the approach road to the Bridge had been his best piece of luck for a long while. Eddie was an erratic driver, to be fairly polite about it, but McGrath had managed to keep up the tail until Eddie's vehicle had pitched up by Wester Balgedie. He still couldn't believe his luck. Maybe it was coincidence, but McGrath preferred to think not. He'd quickly put into practice his training for disabling a motor vehicle, then settled down to watch and wait. He hadn't needed to wait long. For all that it had been smooth so far, he smelt trouble with a capital T. When Macquarie had first got in touch, it had sounded fine. There was a debate coming up on expenses in the Scottish Parliament. Specifically about security. Cameron was all for security as long as the taxpayer didn't have to pay for it; he needed persuading security costs money and folk have to get used to that. With luck, Macquarie had told him (though he hadn't explained how), McGrath could be back out of retirement and finished selling books to Americans who haggled the price and didn't appreciate what they were getting. He'd be able to set Jinty up in something. Lingerie, maybe. He might even be able to escape from Mrs. McGrath, and the thought of that possibility gave him particular pleasure.

Business before pleasure, all the same. "Surveillance", Macquarie had said, that was all. McGrath hoped it was all, as he struggled to keep up with Eddie's long strides. He flung a glance at the two figures behind him. It was the one Macquarie had said was called Rob Ainslie he ought to be keeping an eye on. Seemingly this Ainslie had been pals with McIlwraith before McIlwraith went to Ireland and got into even more trouble. Now McIlwraith was back in Scotland and hadn't been heard from for a couple of days. McGrath hoped he'd died of something very nasty, but somehow doubted it. He knew fine that Macquarie was up to something with McIlwraith, but he didn't know what. Whether it was best not to know or know and at least be ready when solids hit the air conditioning, he wasn't sure. The thought of getting closer to McIlwraith than he cared to imagine was doing unpleasant things to his digestion.

Sandy Lennox was flicking through one of the more pictorial dailies as Eddie and McGrath wandered into the corrugated shed with a sign reading "Lennox Motors" in blistered black paint above the wide open doors. Sandy stuffed the paper away as if it was top secret rather than top shelf and stared at Eddie.

'Morning.'

It was a statement rather than a greeting. Tulloch watched at a distance, remembering you don't get many six-foot blokes wearing caftans in Fife.

'It's the car!' Corcoran and McGrath chorused, adding an additional element of confusion to the opening of their dealings with Lennox Motors

It took some time to explain what they, or rather McGrath, had in mind; namely the repair of one car from what functioned in either vehicle, leaving the other to be repaired when further spares could arrive. Sandy listened without comment. Apart from the implied slur on the resources of his establishment, there was a mad logic at work. Whether Sandy wanted to work for it was another matter.

Wester Balgedie, after all, wasn't the back of beyond, some place where you sent a native bearer off in search of a missing piece of white man's magic no-one had ever heard of. Let the pair in front of him blether till they got tired. He'd all day. In the spaces between listening to the Colonel expand on his notion, Sandy created a fantasy football team drawn entirely from retired East Fife players. The team complete down to the subs, Sandy flashed Eddie and McGrath the kind of obliging smile that added twenty quid to the bill.

'I'll take a wee look.'

Neither car was up to much, and both had seen the best of their days, being run to destruction by blokes who ought not to have been let loose with a clapped out bogie. Nothing new in that, only it made the job that bit harder, so that bit more expensive. Sandy Lennox eyed up his two customers and decided it was time to quote.

'Reckon you're lookin at a ton at least.'

'A hundred pounds? It's a repair we want, not a new car!' McGrath roared.

'Could be a bit more.'

It certainly will be, the more you blether, you old goat, Sandy thought to himself, as he swung over to the workbench and became occupied in finding a set of spanners. Meanwhile, Rob and Tulloch were giving Eddie and John McGrath stares that would have plumbed depths undreamed of in any of Fife's deserted coalmines.

Two hours later, their tempers shortening, their stomachs still empty, they were on the point of mutiny, when a sudden whizzing sound accompanied Sandy out from beneath the vehicle. Clambering off the dolly, Sandy Lennox beamed in Eddie and the Colonel's direction.

'Well, I've done my best for ye.'

Eddie pulled himself away from the bench he was leaning against and looked hard at a machine that now seemed as dodgy as about half the contracts he'd ever signed. He'd never been killed driving a contract, though.

'D' you think this'll get us as far as Loch Tay?' he asked.

'I'd say it might' came Sandy's reply 'Then again, I'm no the one drivin it.'

Tulloch almost grinned. Trust a Scot to put it in a nutshell and you in your place along with it. Eddie nodded toward Sandy. That was the trouble with life; it never came with a guarantee. McGrath sighed. He'd agreed the big eejit could borrow the car for his trip to Loch Tay, on the understanding he was dropped at home, from where he could phone the insurance and get them to send a replacement vehicle until his was returned to him. Eddie's car would remain with Lennox Motors to be picked up on his way back. Everybody happy.

McGrath had already decided he'd give Macquarie a call on his mobile when he could do it safely, and tell him to get someone else. They could watch out for his car heading for Loch Tay if Macquarie was that keen. Even selling salmon books to Yanks was better than trying to find McIlwraith. Let some other bastard sweat. He'd get them to take him over to Perth, and give Jinty a wee surprise before he went home.

'How much do we owe you?' Eddie asked.

'I'd say a hell of a lot, considerin yon machine's back on the road.'

Tulloch hid another smile. There'd been times in the last few weeks he'd questioned his sanity, selling up to come back to he'd no idea what kind of future. This morning, listening to Sandy Lennox, he knew damn well why he had.

'Cry it a ton' Sandy relented.

Rob and Tulloch watched as McGrath gave a stand-out impression of a man taken with a fit of apoplexy. Eddie was glad – or at least relieved – that he'd had the foresight to hit a cash machine the previous evening. He counted half of the entire contents of his wallet into Sandy Lennox's waiting hand. Having done so, Eddie opened the nearside door for McGrath, who gave him a smile that a Borgia cardinal might have shone on his deadliest rival.

'I'll be fine sitting in the back with this gentleman.'

The gentleman referred to was about to have his own peculiar fit when the steely grip of John McGrath attached itself to his elbow and propelled him onto the back seat, wedging him into place with the good-sized parcel McGrath still clutched as if it contained his entire personal fortune.

'Slight change of plan, if you don't mind' McGrath announced.

'What's that?' Eddie's reply was guarded; he had his suspicions, and wasn't going to abandon them lightly.

'I'd be obliged if we could make a stop in Perth'

'Any particular reason?'

'This parcel I have here. It's for a friend of mine.'

'Where does he live?'

'The address is Auchterless Terrace.'

'Auchterless Terrace it is, then.'

As they wound across Fife toward Glenfarg and the road to

Perth, McGrath tried thinking things through, which didn't prove easy. McIlwraith back in Scotland and Macquarie mixed up with him hadn't been news he'd wanted to hear. Macquarie asking him to do a wee job for him would've been about the last offer he'd have taken up, only he'd been losing quite a bit on the nags lately, and now he'd landed himself here. Well, no further. He'd made up his mind, even suppose it meant tightening the belt for a while. He'd talk to Jinty. Maybe she'd have a notion. Not that he really expected one from her, with her wee head full of daft ideas about opening a boutique or a sanctuary for stray cats, or both at once. Anything was better, though, than Macquarie bleating in his ear about McIlwraith the Psychopath. He'd phone Macquarie and tell him he'd have to do his own missing person searches from now on. He wasn't looking forward to that conversation, so best do it sooner rather than later.

'Could you stop, please?'

'Something up?'

'I need a pee.'

Eddie sighed, slowed into an approaching lay-by, with tall bushes beyond a wire fence. McGrath got out and stumbled toward the fence, over it and out of sight.

'Reckon I need one an aa' Rob announced, clambering out the back of the car and following McGrath. As soon as he'd climbed the fence, Rob took his shoes off and crouching low, established the direction taken by McGrath. He moved silently, listening carefully and watching his own every move.

'The person you are calling is unable to take your call at present. Please leave your message after the tone.'

McGrath wanted to let out a sigh of relief, but anxious it might be picked up along with his message, breathed in and began.

'Maurice, this is John. To let you know things haven't worked out the way we hoped. My car is now being driven by a fellow called Eddie Corcoran, who's going to drive it to Loch Tay. There's a man called Rob Ainslie with him who's probably the one you mentioned. So it's my car you should be looking for. Sorry I can't help you any more. If you call me at home about this message, I probably won't be in.'

So McGrath did have something to do with Macquarie. Rob hadn't a clue what the something was, however, and even if the two of them did know each other, what the hang had that to do with the price of fish? He'd need more to convince the pair back in the car there was something going on, and he'd need to get them on their own to even start that, in any case. Fat chance of that so long as they had McGrath on the back seat. McGrath was making his way back to the car. Rob had to move fast to get ahead of him, so McGrath wouldn't put his need for relief down to curiosity. He was going to need to be careful all the way to Perth now.

Eddie drove more slowly, sticking to minor roads. Tulloch watched McGrath, sitting on the back seat, his eyes flicking rapidly left and right. It made him wonder whether Rob's notion that McGrath was a Special Branch officer made any sense. If he was, what the hell was he doing begging lifts from clearly certifiable lunatics? If he really was Special Branch, surely he could commandeer any passing police car that happened along? There was something strange about the man. He was keeping a secret. Tulloch wasn't sure he wanted to know what it might be, except that he might figure in it somewhere.

Less than half an hour into the drive, Eddie started seeing it again. They were cruising along with a tall beech hedge on Eddie's right when a white ball emerged from behind the hedge. At first, Eddie had kidded himself it was some sort of agricultural machine, the grass bag for a gigantic hedge trimmer. Piece of nonsense, of course. It was a balloon, only this was broad daylight and Eddie couldn't excuse what he was seeing as a trick of the light or the onset of exhaustion.

Morning quiet on country roads kept things safe. There weren't any buses or fully laden lorries to worry about and swerve to avoid, but Eddie's silent companion was now drifting above them in the middle of the road, every now and then bobbing earthward to left or right, until it became a dance as Eddie veered in the opposite direction, only for the balloon to ascend before coming down right in front of him again. Each time it came down, the balloon was close to the bonnet of the car, and Eddie would find himself yanking the steering wheel like a nervous learner driver as he fought the vehicle away from contact.

'What the hell's got into you?' Tulloch screamed in Eddie's ear as the car made another swerve 'St Vitus' bloody Dance?'

The balloon was disappearing over the hedge again. Eddie slowed the motor into the side of the road and switched off.

'I think we should all take a little break' Eddie suggested, when his heart had stopped pounding as if it were in training for a coronary.

A little break is exactly what I feel like giving you, Tulloch wanted to say, somewhere that'll hurt.

On the back seat Rob and John McGrath had been briefly, silently united by fear. Rob let out a breath so long he thought he might not stop till he died from lack of oxygen. McGrath now knew he'd made the right decision. He'd come about as close to death as he could have if he'd been daft enough to chase after McIlwraith. To hell with dicing with mortality, it was life he wanted. All he had to do was get himself to Auchterless Terrace in one piece. Which, it seemed, wasn't going to be as easy as he'd thought.

Eddie was walking up and down the grass verge, while Tulloch dished out verbal GBH to Eddie's inner ear and Eddie discovered reserves of patience he never knew he had. Tulloch was right, Eddie admitted to himself. The state his nerves were in, he wasn't fit to be in charge of a skateboard. He turned to face Tulloch.

'Okay, my driving is crap, but unless you've got yourself a licence in the past two years, which I'm pretty sure you haven't, how else do you suggest we get to Loch Tay?'

The argument was irrefutable, unless Tulloch was daft enough to suggest walking some forty miles across open country, carrying Eddie's precious kit into the bargain. Tulloch raised his hands in mock surrender and let them fall.

'All right, Eddie, you've made your point.'

Eddie swung back into his seat, pretending he hadn't heard Tulloch's despairing 'God help us all.'

Eddie watched and waited for the next signpost to Perth to appear, while Tulloch, desperate to escape thoughts of death in a freak road accident – with Eddie driving, any accident was certain to be freak – turned Rob's suspicions over in his mind once more. There was undeniably something strange about McGrath, Tulloch admitted, though he wasn't sure what made him suspicious. According to McGrath's own account, he'd retired a few years ago and set up in business selling antiquarian sporting books. Why was a bookseller giving him the creeps? Roll on Perth and seeing the back of him.

Uppermost in Eddie's mind was his awareness that time wasn't on his side. At this rate it could be Wednesday before they got to Loch Tay and he'd still have to persuade the Camerons at Dunpark that a radio documentary about their long-deceased relative was more important than milking the cows or whatever they did for entertainment. Eddie wondered about that; they might even be sitting round the radio at that very moment.

Loch Tay

A few weeks after Mattie had bought the silk and it had been brought back to the vault, you asked what state 'Republica' was in. Tam said that she'd be able to go for a trial fairly soon, so you asked how soon. Tam replied 'soon enough'. You asked again how soon that was. Tam went over everything that was still needed, Archie backing him up on every item, till you could see that what was needed was a good hand of cards. More than one good hand. A good hand of cards wasn't always easy to find, and even harder to keep, but you were desperate enough to try anything, to keep the two of them working on the balloon. You didn't quite know why you were doing this. It wasn't some kind of charity. You'd find a use or a buyer for the contraption, only you hadn't found one yet, but you were still gambling like a maniac to scumble together money you scarcely ever had to fix up a great balloon so two crazy eejits could try to fly in her. Likely it was you were the crazy one. Finally the day came when they told you "Republica" was ready for a trial. Archie Cameron and Tam Linton grinning as if they were a pair of schoolboys and this some big adventure they'd dreamed up. Well, they'd dreamed about this trial thing for long enough. Find an open space away from the

town and fire her up and see what she might do. That was the way
Tam Linton spoke of it at any rate. Archie Cameron said less, as
though maybe the charm for him was the work, that somehow it
meant more to him than the thing itself. Mattie Tytler scarce said a
word to you. You weren't trusted, that was plain. A pity, for you liked
her, but it couldn't be helped. "Republica" was ready, after all the
time it had taken, and in a fit enough state to be taken out to a field
somewhere and set loose into the sky. You watched them load the
balloon and its basket on board the cart and set rattling off up
Blackfriars Wynd and toward Queensferry. You waved them off,
saying you'd someone you had to meet, then followed at what you
reckoned was a safe distance. You'd tell one side you were keeping
an eye on a known associate of James Tytler's. You'd tell another
thing elsewhere, not that the telling would get you any money. You
wondered exactly where Tam and Archie were taking the cart and its
load of silk and ropes and whatever else they needed. The two of
them had clearly reckoned the wind from the Forth would be too
strong, for they headed inland, till they came to a field out beyond
Hawes and begun to unpack the balloon. There'd still been a wind,
sharp enough to make you glad of the cloak on your back and to
wonder if they'd manage to get the balloon in the air at all. They'd
found a few sticks and set a fire going so that the bag filled with the
hot air, though the doing of all that had taken them long enough.
The bag had blown this way and that, and it had taken both Tam and
Archie a good while until it had filled enough to be able to lift
"Republica" off the ground. You watched the two of them clamber
into the basket, as if the thing were made of china or had snakes
inside it, they seemed that unsure they wanted to be in it.
"Republica" had lifted slowly at first, and you wondered if it were
going to get into the air at all. It had, all the same, and a fine sight it

made for the two minutes or so it was in the air. Then a gust of air caught the balloon and it veered and danced like a man at a rope's end, and you'd wondered if that was to be the end of it. Then Tam was hauling on a rope, and the great silk and canvas shape began slowly to drift back toward the ground. You'd noticed a coach then, its horses pawing the ground and digging hooves into the mud of the road. You'd stared at it for a moment, and at the frightened little man, sitting safe inside it. You wondered if you'd been seen by anyone, but decided not to worry. Your eyes turned back to the figures on the ground, packing the balloon away, laughing a bit, happy in spite of their wee mishap. Happier than you were, that was certain.

Auchterless Terrace, Perth

The three of them had been in the car a good half hour when they heard the scream. Rob, startled from his doze, flicked open the car door and was on the pavement in seconds. Tulloch and Eddie clambered out of the car, following Rob up the short path to the front door of the small house. Light came from an upstairs window. The rest of the place was in darkness.

'We can't go barging in' Eddie whispered.

Rob was about to ask why not, when Eddie's voice hissed again. 'What are we going to look like?'

That was a daft question as far as Rob was concerned, coming from someone who looked as if they'd lost their way to a fancy dress party, but he didn't want to start a rammy at someone else's front door, specially if they were about to rescue them from being murdered by a Special Branch nutter.

'I mean,' Eddie continued in conspiratorial tones 'we might not be thanked if they're ...'

'Having a massive heart attack?' Tulloch asked innocently.

The sound of footsteps on the stair was followed by light spilling through the fanlight above the front door. Eddie drew a deep breath and pressed the buzzer.

A sharp scream, similar to the one that had propelled Rob out of the car was followed by several seconds of almost silence. Someone was inside. The only question was whether they were going to open the door. Finally it inched open, and three pairs of eyes glimpsed a tired confection of pink tulle, barely covering the woman who blinked at them in shocked surprise through layers of smeared make-up.

'We heard a noise ...' Eddie began.

None of them was quite prepared for the bawl that emerged from the woman as her feelings finally overcame her.

'He's deid!'

A further heavy sob heaved its way off her décolletage.

'Stupit eejit went an died on me right ... '

Emotion overcame her once again, and the three men were able to observe at first hand the dreadful effect of mascara on a woman in distress. Eddie and Tulloch managed to persuade her off her own doorstep and back into the house. Rob followed at a distance, having first closed the door behind him before all the neighbours got cricks in their necks.

Tulloch's mind raced, but still couldn't grasp the intricacy of potential chaos into which his mission to Dunpark House had so rapidly descended. First there had only been him and Eddie Corcoran. Then Rob had joined them. Eddie's car had broken down so they had agreed to borrow the dubious John McGrath's until it was repaired, in exchange for driving him home. Only he'd had a fit of the carnals and they'd been parked outside the love nest until the woman blubbing her way up the stairs ahead of them had screamed. Tulloch's only remaining surprise was that the remains of his sanity weren't giving way, so far at any rate.

Eddie was oblivious of Tulloch's mental condition, but aware their lives were about to become considerably more complex as a result of McGrath's unexpected demise. He was driving McGrath's car. He was one of the last people to see him alive. Any member of Perthshire Constabulary was fully entitled to view one Edward Osnabruck Corcoran with considerable suspicion. He wondered how much worse it could get.

Edinburgh, the underground city

The Omnivore remembered the city slip past the coach window. He'd known that he would be in Perth before the day was out. The man who had been his visitor a few days before had come to see him again before he'd caught the coach, and had given him the names of two people who might, as he'd put it, "make themselves known to him". The names were forgotten by the time he got into the coach. His visitor also asked if he spoke Gaelic, and told him it was a pity when the answer was no. The Omnivore asked if the business he was mixed up in was dangerous. His visitor had smiled and told him that of course it was. Before he'd a chance to reply, the man was shouldering his own portmanteau, ushering him down the stairs, all the while telling him he mustn't miss the coach, till he found himself in the middle of the Grassmarket, the coach door open for him and the man shaking him by the hand, wishing him a safe journey. There was no denying that the commission, to design and build an ice house for the Laird of Dunpark, was timely. He had been told that an old Masonic Temple stood a little away from the main house. The Laird wanted it turned into an ice house, to store salmon from Loch Tay. Archibald, the heir, was learning law in Edinburgh and costing money. Salmon were still common, but a commodity nonetheless. If he could make something of this commission, he told himself, others might come his way. A recommendation by the Laird of Dunpark was nothing much itself, but maybe enough to persuade the likes of the Duke of Atholl to think of employing him. Hope is needed when there's little else. The coach was still some way from South Queensferry when the thing suddenly appeared, as if from nowhere. It had emerged from behind a high hedge, enclosing some field or other. It looked like nothing he had ever seen. It seemed to be a gigantic onion floating above the ground. There was something underneath it too, a little box or basket, but big enough for the two men who stared toward the ground, then gesticulated at someone who couldn't be seen, on the other side of the hedge perhaps. Next thing, the two men were hauling on a rope, which led toward the ground, and then gesticulating again, at each other this time. Whatever the thing was, it rose again in the air, swayed a moment, and then began descending rapidly toward the earth. Where it landed, among tall trees and surrounded by high hedges, could not be seen. The horses pawed, neighed, and refused to go on for several minutes. It was only then that he realised it had to be a balloon, a thing not seen since James Tytler's experiments with one a few years previously. What a balloon was doing a few miles out of Edinburgh could only be guessed. The Omnivore had puzzled over it for the rest of his journey. Perhaps it was simply a couple of enthusiasts, trying to imitate Tytler's feat. The Omnivore wondered what they might be doing, apart from frightening a few cows. Not to mention the horses that drew his coach ever closer to Perth. He wondered whether he ought to be frightened himself, there being so much else to be frightened of in these very strange times. The Omnivore tried putting it out of his mind. He'd enough to think about, after all. He tried to distract himself by seeing if he could recall the names he'd been given. "The East Indian" was one; he'd been told the man was called that because of having sailed on an East India merchant ship. The other called himself a Laird of some sort. He felt his stomach shrink when he realised these two names were all he had. Even if he ever came across them, there was no guarantee they would help him. Supposing he did meet them, he was unlikely to be much better off than he was now: unarmed, ill informed and on his own.

Auchterless Terrace

The ample buttocks of the late John McGrath mooned at them from the expanse of a generously proportioned double bed. 'Cheek of the man' thought Eddie, quickly suppressing any thoughts of humour before the woman standing next to him suspected he had any. He didn't know her name, so thrusting out his hand and speaking in a tone more suited to an undertaker, he introduced himself.

'Eddie Corcoran'

'Jinty Morrice' the woman responded, shaking Eddie's hand in an absent-minded way, before turning to the figure on the bed. 'Stupit!' She paused, turning with a still-fetching blush. 'No you, son! Him!'

She gestured toward McGrath.

'He'll need tae go back tae Annie.'

After a pause, she went on.

'Annie's his wife. Was his wife, I should say. I'm the wee bit on the side. Which was the way we both preferred it, before you start to wonder. But Annie was still his wife, an she deserves to get him back.'

Eddie was about to point out it would be a strange world if we all got what we deserved, then thought better of it. His two companions were still digesting the information and what it might imply when Jinty broke in on their thoughts.

'Come on,' she said quietly 'let's get poor John's breeks back on him, then we can have a wee cup of tea and think what's the best thing to do.'

Eddie gathered McGrath's trousers from where they lay on the floor. Tulloch and Rob moved toward the bed as Jinty disappeared down the stairs.

Even wearing a dressing gown designed with comfort rather than vanity in mind, Jinty Morrice remained a fine looking woman. Watching her pour tea steadily into three dainty cups, Eddie tried imagining her as one of his aunties over in Northern Ireland, but it didn't work. He was quite certain no Ulsterwoman of the Corcoran surname he'd encountered in his youth would have possessed a blush pink teddy, nor dreamed of handing round Hobnobs dressed in one. Tea poured, Jinty brightened, as if observing social niceties made the situation a little less bizarre.

'He will need to go back.'

The three men felt each in their own way threatened by Jinty's statement. There comes a point when no sensible man argues with a woman, especially if it's clear her mind is made up. Jinty's mind obviously was, and as possessors of the only available transport, their duty was clear enough to her.

'He's Annie's husband. He never talked about divorcin her, an I doubt he'd ever have had the gumption to dae it.'

She paused, brushed her hair back and started again.

'So Annie gets him, an that's only right. Problem's goin tae be the neighbours. Eyes on stalks, the ones that dinnae have binoculars, that is, an near every one o with the kind o minds I wouldn't want a look at.'

Tulloch and Eddie could guess what was on Jinty Morrice's agenda. Rob was already round that corner and heading for the hills, trying hard to avoid the woman's desperate, pleading look. He wasn't succeeding any more than his two companions. The ensuing silence felt longer than it was, as they each wondered how they might be able to avoid the upcoming topic of conversation.

'How d' you plan to get him back?'

Tulloch's question surprised even Eddie, who gave him a look that suggested a swift, sharp kick could be heading Tulloch's way at the earliest opportunity.

'I was kind of hopin you boys might be able to help me.'

The disingenuousness of Jinty's statement bowled Eddie over into wondering how the thing might be managed. Jinty ploughed straight on, as if dealing with possible objections was already shaping the plan she was putting forward.

'It's near half eight now. Annie's an early bedder, or so John always said. Chances are, by the time you got there, she'd be well asleep.'

Jinty watched as the implication sank in.

'We'd have tae break in.' The tone in Rob's voice wouldn't have been out of place in a bad melodrama.

'No break in. It's no as if you were going to steal anythin ...' Jinty's voice trailed off. She had by now tucked her legs up on the sofa, and was eyeing her guests with serious curiosity. Her plan depended on them and she was going to need all her wit and powers of persuasion to get them to see it through.

'John's house is at Kinfauns.' Jinty went on 'Wee row o houses by the Tay, just off the main road ...'

'I'm no breakin in.' Rob's voice carried the certainty of one who knows he's about to find himself in bigger trouble than he's already in, and is powerless to stop it happening.

Eddie considered the implications of Tulloch's remark and began to muse on possibilities. Tulloch on breaking and entering, Rob on look-out, him on get-away and all of them up for more crimes than would fit on a charge sheet if they were caught. 'How far is it to Kinfauns, anyway?'

'No that far. You could be there in half an hour.' Jinty beamed round at the three of them.

Jinty tried telling herself it was no time for tears. There'd be more than enough time for them later. She hated losing him, but it was a glad thought that John would be going home, going where he ought to be, at any rate. She'd miss him. Miss him sore. He wasn't much, but he'd been good company, except when one of the horses he'd backed had come in last. Even then, he'd be cheerful again in no time. There was a cheery wee laddie look to him, especially when he'd backed a winner. He'd aye told her she was the best he'd ever won, and she liked to think he'd maybe meant that. She smiled at Eddie as he offered a handkerchief.

'We'd been friends a long time' she sniffed.

Using the past tense brought her up against reality she's not expected to face quite this way, or so soon. She became aware of the three men waiting for her to recover.

'Well,' she said, looking at them with more firmness than she felt 'I suppose we'd better get John ready for his journey.'

They assured Jinty they'd be fine. There were three of them, after all, and only the one John McGrath. Upstairs, they stared awkwardly at what they'd all be, hopefully later rather then sooner. 'Come along, Sir, I believe you have a home to go to.' Eddie whispered, making Tulloch choke quietly, as much at Rob's shocked expression as Eddie's remark. Rob took the weight on one shoulder as Eddie gently lifted the corpse from the bed. Slipping his free arm under one of McGrath's, Eddie watched Tulloch quickly clear their line of retreat from the room. At the stair head, Tulloch watched anxiously as Rob and Eddie lowered McGrath, while Jinty waited at the foot of the stairs. Eddie let McGrath's legs down slowly, till he was more or less upright. For a moment, he might have been any Saturday-night drunk brought home by his pals. Jinty looked him up and down and nodded approval.

'I've seen him worse' she murmured, then quickly gave him a soft, gentle kiss before turning away. Her face was straight by the time she turned it to the three men taking up most of her hallway.

'Better get moving' she said 'before the neighbours start wondering what kind of entertaining I do these days.'

Walking the body down Jinty's garden path was no bother at all. Getting it onto the back seat of the car proved another matter.

'The bugger willnae bend!' Rob wailed.

'Can't be rigor mortis' Eddie responded.

McGrath was proving more awkward in death than he'd been in life. He was also as ample dead as alive. Even when they'd persuaded him into a sitting posture, his bulk sprawled across the back seat of the car.

'I'm no sittin next tae a stiff!' Rob announced as soon as they'd got McGrath into the only position he was likely to stay in. Tulloch opened the opposite rear door with a heavy sigh and slung his weight against McGrath. Eddie sighed almost as deeply as he settled next to Rob's bulk. He hadn't been looking forward to this journey; now it was getting off to an even worse start than he'd imagined. Kinfauns in half an hour, or if Eddie could manage it, even less. Switching on the engine, he prayed that there weren't going to be any late-night balloonists on the road to Dundee.

the ice house, Dunpark

McIlwraith could feel the strength ebbing out of him as he wrestled the length of metal that was cutting his palms to ribbons back and forth along the length of the padlock's shackle. He could feel it begin to give way, but it stubbornly held against the ring of metal that was tightly screwed to the side of the chest. Then came a sound halfway between a pop and a rip, as the staple finally separated from the chest's side, to go bouncing into the darkness, along with the padlock. He'd done it! If he'd not been so exhausted, McIlwraith would have done some kind of victory dance. As it was, he turned and picked up the plate that had been thrust through the tiny slit of a window a while back. The food was nearly cold, but McIlwraith was that hungry he'd have wolfed down near enough anything.

As he chewed, it dawned on McIlwraith that he probably didn't need to worry about the police battering down the door or kicking it in; he'd torn out the phone line, and there likely wasn't another house round here for a good two, three mile. The old guy that had put him in here wasn't going anywhere as long as the lassie he'd helped him carry down to the house was in the state she'd been in, and it could be long enough till she was out of it. McIlwraith digested the implications along with the cold food. He could take his time; only he didn't have much of that. Cameron was supposed to have lined up folk that could get him away, but if he had, they'd likely given up on him by now, and he'd never trusted Cameron anyway. McIlwraith turned back to the chest. He took a deep breath. What if there was something as bad as or even worse, in this one? Stop being an eejit, he told himself. The lid came up easier than he'd expected. He put his hand in, and to his surprise his fingers fumbled onto what felt like wee bags. As he drew one toward him, he could feel its weight. Fumbling at the drawstring, he got it loose and thrust a hand in. Small hard lumps pricked against his inquiring fingers. He drew one from the rest. He couldn't quite believe what he'd got hold of. He'd seen uncut stones before, and the one he held in his hand looked almost exactly the same. A diamond. So that was what Cameron had been up to, and what he had been so keen McIlwraith get from Dunpark. He turned back to the chest and began to count the number of bags.

'The problem with turning the old mason's lodge into the Laird of Dunpark's ice house was how the melting ice was to be drained. A hole was dug in the floor as deep as the level of the Loch. Then a tunnel was dug off it, which would be a channel leading to the Loch. When it reached there, water flooded in so fast it came up to the level of the floor, so it had to be drained and dug again. The Laird sent to Perth for a stonemason to line the drain, and grumbled about more expense. The folk about the Loch grumbled, too, for when the men the Laird had employed weren't working, Maclaggan made sure they spent their time and what money they had in his howff. With the harvest approaching, there were plenty who worried that those who could earn their money more easily by working for the Laird wouldn't want to bend their backs getting the harvest in. Also, folk worried that the new Militia Act would take the same men away to serve the King in some far off place. It might be well enough for laird's sons to play soldier in a fine uniform, they would say, but their own lads would be the ones that could be sent heaven knew where, leaving their families with few hands for the loom or the plough. As summer wore on, a rumour came from Perth that ministers and schoolmasters would be told to write down the names of men that could be put in the militia. Some said that it was all simply foolish talk, and I wondered whether the Duke would put his name to such a thing, but I knew that if it should come to that kind of pass, the Duke would have to do so, for appearance sake, if for no other reason. I had a strange dream then, Nathaniel. I was playing my fiddle for the Duke of Atholl and Angus Cameron and some other folk, and I knew I had to play as slow as possible, for if I didn't, it would be bad for all of them. Only my fiddle wouldn't let me play slow. Instead, I was playing faster and faster and I couldn't make myself stop. When I woke I could feel the sweat and the chill of fear.'

Kinfauns, Perthshire

'Told you we'd have tae break in.'

Tulloch and Eddie stared at Rob. A further rummage through McGrath's pockets had failed to produce anything that looked like a set of keys to his own property. Having clambered cautiously out of the car, they'd edged toward a house that looked as if it might rear up and scream at them if it noticed they were there. Two storeys high, with not a light showing on the ground floor or through any of the dormers above, it looked forbidding enough. A hurried rummage beneath the doormat had produced no spare key, so Eddie gingerly led the way around the side of the house toward the back door, Tulloch following reluctantly. The back door had been locked, of course. They slunk back to where Rob was waiting, ready to state the obvious in his annoyingly blunt way.

Aye, Rob thought, looking at the pair, I'm no the sharpest knife in the box and I dinnae say much, but there's nothin else for it, one o the two of youse are goin tae have tae break in yon place, 'cause I'm no settin foot anywhere I'm no invited. No wi Inspector Macquarie out there somewhere, waitin for me tae dae somethin stupit.

'It's not as if we're going to steal anything …'

Tulloch repeated the argument first voiced back at Jinty Morrice's house, only for Eddie to respond 'Probably nothing worth nicking in any case, unless you fancy a stuffed salmon.'

Tulloch resisted the temptation to tell Eddie precisely where he could stuff any salmon he came across. It took a couple of minutes to get McGrath upright. He was even less easy to manipulate than he'd been when they'd brought him down the stairs at Auchterless Terrace.

So this is why they call them "stiffs", Tulloch thought, as McGrath's weight rested against his own. Eddie appraised the home of the deceased with the eye of a battle-hardened commander approaching a fortress, then disappeared round the side of the house leaving Rob and Tulloch in charge of the body. They looked morosely at one another.

'You known that nutter long?' Rob's question caught Tulloch off guard, sending his mind reeling into a part of his memory bank he hated drawing from.

'Long enough. Too long, I sometimes think' he mused. 'Then again, I doubt I know him at all.'

The mystery that was Eddie Corcoran came softly from the shadows of the house.

'Amazing how far a Swiss Army knife can get you if you know how to use one' Eddie observed quietly, adding 'I've got the back kitchen window open but there's not enough room for me to squeeze through the way it is. Looks like it's your turn for breaking and entering, Tulloch.'

The look Eddie got from Tulloch held homicidal fantasies, which Eddie ignored as he passed him the knife.

'It'll be easy enough' Eddie reassured him. 'I slid this under the frame and it came away easy as anything. All you have to do is slide it up and in you go. Bob's your uncle.'

Tulloch felt like pointing out he had not now nor ever had had an Uncle Bob; instead, he shrugged and padded in the direction of the kitchen window.

It was more difficult than Eddie had suggested to prise up the heavy sash window far enough for Tulloch to clamber through. Turning to Eddie, who had followed him at a cautious distance, he whispered 'Hold it steady!' as he carefully slid between window and casement. Suddenly he was through, standing in a small room filled with strange dark shapes.

'This'll be the kitchen, then' Tulloch said to himself, his eyes growing slowly accustomed to the gloom.

'Find the door and let us in.'

Tulloch's eyes flicked right. He could see what looked like a door and made toward it. He felt for the handle, ran his fingers down the edge of the door till he felt a keyhole. No key in it. He tried the handle. Nothing.

'There isn't a key.' he whispered.

'What?'

'No key in the lock. Have another search of his pockets.'

'We already have done, remember?'

Tulloch heard Eddie sigh, then his receding voice, muttering something about 'Having another go, in case'.

The wait for Eddie's return felt as interminable as an overnight stay in hospital, and barely more comfortable.

'Found any keys?'

'We found something else.'

'What d' you mean?'

'Come and take a look.'

Tulloch didn't like the tone in Eddie's voice. Something told him that whatever had been discovered was bad news.

'Give us a hand out of here, then.'

Tulloch scrambled through the opening while Eddie held the window, then followed Eddie till they came on a very worried looking Rob holding a leather wallet.

'Didnae feel right takin a look.' Rob mumbled with embarrassment.

'As well you did, though.' Eddie reassured him.

'Noo we're up tae oor necks in it.' Rob shook his head.

'Up to our necks in what?' Tulloch asked, knowing fine he'd not appreciate the answer. Rob waved an identity card with McGrath's face smiling grimly up at them.

'Tellt ye the bugger was flamin MI six an three quarters!'

Eddie had to admit it looked pretty convincing. John McGrath was, or had recently been, working for H.M. Gov.

'Keep your voice down.' Eddie whispered in remonstration. 'Or the whole village will hear us.'

'We're done for!' Rob exclaimed, ready to run for the nearest hill. His mind was clear about one thing, though. If Macquarie was on this particular case, it was for his own reasons, and they were very likely not legal ones. If those two wanted his opinion, they should dump McGrath and run like hell.

'We seem to have put ourselves inadvertently in charge of the mortal remains of a former Special Branch Officer.' Eddie was speaking as softly as he could 'I'm not sure I know what we ought to do.'

Eddie disregarded the look of panic on Rob's face, and carried on.

'I've made an agreement to go to Dunpark House to interview some people called Cameron. I'm going to help you get this bloke, whoever he is, was, back in his house, then I'm taking this car to Loch Tay. Neither of you have to go anywhere near if you don't want to. If you want to carry on with me, that's fine. If you don't, say so now and no hard feelings.'

Eddie swallowed hard. He could be landing himself in more trouble than he'd been in his life to date. The card Rob had shown him did look convincing, but if McGrath had been Special Branch, or something like it, why had he been on their case? They'd done nothing to merit attention, and he doubted Rob was much of a danger to anybody but himself. McGrath had looked past retirement age, and if he really had been selling fishing books for the past few years, what, or who, had prompted him to begin stalking overweight comics and moody lighting technicians for a hobby? Eddie searched for a little more inner strength. At the end of a rather dreadful day, there wasn't much left, but enough to let him hold on to his decision. Dunpark House and damn the consequences, he decided.

'So, who's for carrying on?'

Tulloch squirmed. He was going to be driven to the door of Dunpark House if he stuck around. If he didn't, he'd a long walk ahead. He almost wished he'd said "no" to Luce when she'd first asked him to go there. Now something seemed to be going on that had all the marks of landing him in even bigger trouble than they were in right now.

It was clear to Rob that if he wasn't travelling with yon nutcase in the dressing gown he wasn't travelling at all.

The pair gave Eddie the ghost of a nod.

'Right,' said Eddie 'that's settled. Now let's see how fast we can get the dear departed into this place without waking anybody and then how fast we can get the hell out of here.'

Christ, he's a fair weight, Rob thought. Getting McGrath round to the back of the house wasn't that bad, but getting him through the window was another thing. Eddie directed operations, with Tulloch, inside in the kitchen, McGrath's feet gripped in both his hands. Rob's own hands were telling him to put the bugger down.

'Up your end a bit, Rob' came Eddie's instructions. Ignoring the temptation to pass a smart remark, Rob obeyed, his muscles protesting against cruel and unusual punishment.

'One more shove.'

The deceased slid as cleanly through the window as he might do into the incinerator of a crematorium. There was a stifled scream of protest from Tulloch. Eddie shushed as Tulloch emerged from beneath the body of McGrath.

'Keep quiet, Tulloch. Stop standing on him while I give you a hand ...'

Tulloch grumbled as he tugged the deceased out of the line of Eddie's size fourteens.

'Keep a look-out, Rob.'

Eddie's plea fell on empty air as his eyes caught sight of Rob's retreating back. A quick motion of Eddie's head indicated the door he presumed led into the hall. Putting his arms under McGrath's shoulders, Tulloch tried moving toward the door. He hadn't been that big, but in death felt several stones heavier than he likely had been in life. Even Eddie looked as if he was struggling.

'Put him on the table' Tulloch whispered breathlessly. 'Have to open the door.'

They shuffled McGrath alongside the table top, then with even more effort onto it, his length bizarrely almost matching it. Tulloch grabbed a cloth and gently turned the handle of the door. No creaks or squeaks, thank God. Eddie was tapping him on the shoulder.

'Casters. The table's got casters!' he whispered, with the excitement of a schoolboy. Tulloch stared at him; Eddie whispered loudly in his ear.

'We can move him on the table!'

'What if it makes a noise?'

Eddie grabbed the cloth from Tulloch's hand and waved it in his face.

'We use this!'

Tulloch shook his head, but Eddie had taken the cloth and was busy measuring it against the table's width. His eyes met Tulloch's with a grin and an affirmative nod.

'Fits like a glove.'

Eddie was already on his hands and knees, sliding the cloth beneath the casters. Standing up, he motioned Tulloch to one end of the table and took hold of the other end. It didn't move. Eddie thrust with his whole weight. The table creaked in complaint but stayed where it was. Eddie looked as though he might kick something.

'Stretcher?' Tulloch offered.

For a moment, Eddie wondered what Tulloch was on about. Then it dawned. He nodded breathlessly at Tulloch as he planted his feet and lifted. Heavy, all right, but so long as they took it slow and steady, they'd have McGrath by his own fireside in no time.

Then Tulloch banged the table against the doorframe. They stood still, breathing as shallowly as they could, waiting for the sounds of a wakened sleeper, footsteps, a call in the night. Nothing. How long they stood, neither of them could have told, though it felt like half an eternity until Eddie broke the silence as softly as he could.

'Come on.'

It took some time to manoeuvre the table, with McGrath still aboard, into the hall and then to slowly turn gently right. All the while, Tulloch imagined a flick of a light switch revealing half the constabulary of Perthshire arrayed on the staircase. The front room door was closed, but Tulloch managed to twist his hand round and over the doorknob, nudging the door softly open ahead of his weight. Backing carefully, squinting into the gloom in search of potential ambushes shaped like coffee tables or footstools, Tulloch let the table down.

Eddie didn't anticipate this, and McGrath's head slid in the direction of Tulloch's lower abdomen. A barely suppressed yelp from Tulloch caused Eddie to drop his end of the table more rapidly than he'd intended. Eddie and Tulloch watched each other hold their breaths. Still nothing. The wind shifted direction, rattling a stray tree branch against the windowpane. They both started, looking in the direction of the door.

'Let's get him settled' Eddie whispered, as if speaking about a child. Eddie slid McGrath onto the sofa and drew him into an almost upright position. He drew back, looked at the body, then rearranged its legs in a more "natural" position, took another look and nodded satisfaction.

'Reckon that'll have to do.' he sighed, flicking a look toward Tulloch.

They all but ran with the table back to the kitchen and quickly got back through the window, walking more slowly to the car. McGrath had looked almost innocent, thought Eddie.

Neither of them had noticed a small piece of paper flutter across the kitchen floor when Tulloch first clambered through the window. If they had, and had picked it up and read it, they'd have realised they had one less cause for concern.

Dear John,

I'm sorry you're not around so that I can say this to your face, but you're out gallivanting as usual. I've decided to leave you. I can't stand worrying about how I'm to pay for things any longer, and wondering if I'll have a roof over my head in the morning. I'm going to stay with Auntie Ethel until I sort out divorcing you. Stay here if you want, but I expect that Jinty Morrice will be pleased to see you, and more fool her.

Your soon to be ex-wife, Ann.'

Loch Tay

The trial with the balloon had been a disappointment. The thing had got off the ground, right enough, but the winds had been too strong. It had looked so proud and mighty when it had the wind with it, but as soon as the direction had shifted, trouble started. Tam Linton and Archie Cameron had done what they could, and now they were talking about making adjustments – a bigger burner, as Tam called it, to make more hot air. You wondered at their enthusiasm, for you'd little enough left. Truth to tell, you were in a mess and hadn't a notion how to get out of it. Those who paid you wanted information you didn't have. Those who believed you were still loyal to them wanted information you couldn't give. You wanted to tell both packs of fools to go to the devil, only whichever of them found you first would likely send you to that same devil if they knew what you were up to. Did you know yourself? You'd a balloon, or rather you might have a balloon, but what was the use of that? You were still trying to work out what you could do with the thing when you had two visitors. You were lucky they didn't call at the same time. First the man from the United Irishmen, who told you that the Militia Act would be likely to be resisted. Not by everyone, and perhaps not everywhere, but probably by some. It would be well if those doing the resisting were given every assistance. They could be the germ of a revolt. Then he started to repeat the usual nonsense, parroting the phrases you'd once blethered yourself, till Government caught you by the heels and threatened to string you up if you didn't do what they told you to. After he left, it wasn't long before the Government's man pitched up. Same tune, different words. The Militia Act would likely be resisted. Not by everyone, and perhaps not everywhere, but probably by some. It would be well if they were watched. They could be a danger to the state. You didn't believe one iota of what either of them told you, but each of them clearly believed every scrap they'd been told. Whichever particular set of rogues had started the rumour you didn't know and cared less, except that the rumour put you on the spot in a way you didn't care to be. You'd damn near been caught, as well. Ten fewer minutes between the two of then turning up at your door and you'd have had a hell of a lot of explaining to do, supposing you'd been allowed to do any explaining before they stabbed, shot or garroted you. Time to move on, as far and as fast as you could. The question was, how? You were being watched, but you knew that, expected it, even. So no point taking the coach to

Glasgow or God knew where, nor trying to sneak aboard a boat at Leith or Newhaven. What other way out was there? Only the one that had been staring you in the face for months. You'd been so caught up on your own plans you'd never thought of it before. "Republica" would set you free. Another trial. The lads were keen to make one, so let them. You'd go along and somehow, you'd get them to fly you as far from Edinburgh as they could. Let either set of madmen try and follow you. Wherever the wind took you couldn't be any worse than where you were now. So that was your plan, as far as it could be called a plan. None too clever, but then you'd not been too clever yourself, simply lucky to have got away with serving two masters as long as you had, since neither one was that clever either. Off you go and talk to Tam and Archie about another trial. They've been saying to you for long enough that they want to make one. If they ask any awkward questions, you'll find the right sort of lie to tell them. You always have up to now. Fingers crossed, for the bigger the lie, the more likely it is to be believed.

Luncarty, Perthshire

'I reckon' Eddie said slowly 'we should find a quiet pub somewhere, have a drink and decide whether we push on now, or take our chances and see if we can't find somewhere to stop over night. I don't know about you two, but I'm pretty knackered. Either of you lads know a decent pub in these parts?'

Eddie felt less relaxed than his words might have suggested. He had, along with his two travelling companions, recently broken into a house and left a dead body behind. The police had not been informed, on the grounds he was now driving a vehicle that had been effectively stolen from a dead Special Branch Officer, even supposing he was an officially retired one. The case against Eddie Corcoran, he thought, was starting to look pretty compelling.

'We ought to do something.' Tulloch observed, half to himself.

Rob all but leapt off his seat.

'Suppose we went tae the cops, what d' you reckon they're goin tae say? Tell them we reckon John McGrath might have been Special Branch, an by the way, it's no Eddie's car, it was his, an no we dinnae have the insurance or nothin. You're no givin them the option o daein anythin bar arrest the lot o us!'

Rob settled back in his seat. He'd not said as much in a long time, but someone had to tell the pair of them what the real score was.

'Let's see if we can find a pub' sighed Eddie. He changed gear and set the car in a direction that he hoped the police did not frequently patrol. Not that the promise of alcohol seemed to raise the spirits of Rob or Tulloch. After a few miles of fields bordered by dry stane dykes, they were cruising toward a collection of houses. Eddie began slowing the car to a crawl. The halogen lamps mounted on the ends of the building shone unremittingly on a sign that read "The Duke of Lennox. Beers, Wines and Spirits. Slainte Math and Haste Ye Back"

'Why not give this place a go?' Eddie suggested, clamping on the handbrake. As they approached, Tulloch heard loud female voices with accents he couldn't quite place. Opening the door, they were greeted by a stunned silence, till someone screeched 'Get a load of Rasputin!'

Eddie smiled ingratiatingly at a dozen women circling the bar, turned to his two companions and sighed 'Right lads, what'll it be?'

As he drew out his wallet, his gaze was drawn back to the women round the bar. One of them looked remarkably like someone he used to know. Dismissing the unlikely possibility of encountering her again in the middle of Perthshire, Eddie concentrated on attracting the barman's attention. He knew that neither of his companions could buy a box of matches supposing they had a whip round, and his Regimental Sergeant Major father had instilled in young Edward a delicacy where other people's impecuniousness was concerned. Rob and Tulloch responded suitably by ordering half pints. None of the three of them were sure they wanted to stay long in the company of twelve hormone-high young women, now singing "She'll Be Wearing Silk Pyjamas When She Comes" at the top of their respective ranges. A trio of musicians perched in a corner was trying hard to adapt their usual repertoire of Scottish dance-band standards to the women's eclectic requests and failing miserably. Eddie thrust drinks into nervously waiting hands.

'John McGrath, God rest him' he proposed.

Tulloch glanced over to the women. What a hen party was doing so very far from the bright lights, he'd no idea. Curiosity had always been his weakness. He ventured over to one of them.

'If it's not a rude question, who or what brought you here?'

'A bloody great bus driver did, then ran away, pal.'

Tulloch felt a wee bubble of completely out-of-order laughter struggling its way to the top of his throat. Then he clocked the look on the woman's face.

'Bastard bus went an bastard broke down on us, so it did. Driver promised us a tour of Perthshire afore we got tae Freuchie – that's oor next stop. Then the bus breaks doon an he says he's goin tae have tae take it tae a garage in Perth, then has the cheek tae leave us stranded in a dump like this.'

'Where are you from?' Tulloch asked, though he'd no doubt what he was hearing was broad Glasgow.

'Birmingham' came the response. Defying his disbelief, she rattled on 'Maist of us that is, apart frae Dawn ower there – she's frae London.'

'That doesn't sound like a Birmingham accent to me' Tulloch replied.

'Ah come frae Shettleston, but I've been in Brum for years.'

'Hen party?'

'Cricket team.'

The sight of male eyebrows being raised was clearly one the woman had seen before.

'Five Ways Ladies, that's us. Nae stupit jokes, if you dinnae mind. I've heard maist o them. Twice.'

'So what are you doing in the middle of Perthshire?'

'Well you may ask. We're up here on a tour. Friendlies, like. My daft idea, by the way. We played in Glesca yesterday, an we're supposed tae be playing Freuchie Ladies on Friday, always assumin we get oor bus back.'

The band seemed to be playing better the closer Rob and Tulloch got to the bottom of their glasses. Rob felt a tap on his shoulder and turned to find himself in very close proximity to a pair of large breasts.

'You dancing, sweetheart?'

Rob glanced at the two left feet he'd been born with, wishing they hadn't come with an inability to say "no" to any woman who gave him a smile. His shoulder slumped as he rose from the table. Tulloch turned to his own thoughts for long enough to almost forget where he was, only to be forcefully reminded when he was all but birled off his seat by the same large woman waltzing a pink and perspiring Rob the length of the bar-room. A pair of scared "rescue me" eyes struggled to catch Tulloch's as Rob went down for the second time as the fiddler struck up "The Mason's Apron".

Eddie waited while the woman he wanted to talk to reeled off a list of drinks. Tequila Sunrises and Manhattans didn't cause the barman to blink, but mention of Sex on the Beach did. You could understand why there wasn't much of that in Perthshire. Dawn. It was her. Eddie couldn't believe it. Not in his wildest dreams and certainly not in wildest Perthshire had he ever expected to see Dawn again. The memory of stupidly losing his wallet ran in his mind. The one that had had Dawn's number, carefully tucked into the little button-down pocket on one side. With it had gone any chance of seeing her again. Or so he'd thought. He clocked Dawn looking in his general direction. Fear of embarrassment wrestled instinct. For a full thirty seconds it was an even contest, till instinct slammed a full headlock on any restraint and Eddie found himself walking up to the bar and smiling – he hoped ingratiatingly – at Dawn. He breathed deeply, took a shaky further step forward and succeeded in wedging himself between Dawn and one of the pillars supporting the bar gantry.

'Dawn Blackwood I presume? I very possibly do presume, since it was quite some time ago, but ... '

Tulloch clutched his half as Rob and the woman waltzed back in his direction. He decided there ought to be something in the European Convention of Human Rights on no dancing in bars less than six foot wide. To divert his mind, he studied a potted but cheerfully illustrated history of the pub screwed to one of the walls.

The original publican, John Maclaggan, had claimed to be illegitimately descended from the Earls of Lennox. Mixed up in some riots in 1797, or so the plaque claimed.

"*A Public House has stood on this site since the 1780's, when John Maclaggan, also known as the "Duke of Lennox" because of a supposed connection to the Lennox family, first began to brew and sell ale here. As well as being a publican, John Maclaggan was believed to be a member of the secret society called the United Scotsmen. Active in the late 1790's, the United Scotsmen aimed at the creation of a new social order based on the principles of the French Revolution. Unlike its sister organisation the United Irishmen, the United Scotsmen did not take part in armed rebellion. However, they may have helped instigate riots in this part of Perthshire in 1797. John Maclaggan is supposed to have been a leader of the rioters and was active during them. Afterward, he may have left the area, and no further mention of him exists.*"

Eddie and Dawn had found a table in a corner that no one seemed to want. Dawn hadn't so much left theatre as moved sideways, into "Corporate Communications" – teaching the socially cack handed the "skills" needed to deal with the obdurate, the obnoxious and the plain bloody minded, which all too often also included most of the customers to whom such unfortunates had to "relate". She'd followed Eddie's career since their first meeting at some distance, but didn't seem either particularly impressed or jealous of his success – if a seemingly endless round of clubs and student unions, with slowly increasing amounts of radio work could be called success. After a pause in the conversation, Eddie asked the question he realised could be fatal.

'Are you going out with anyone these days?'

He wanted to bite his tongue off, but Dawn simply smiled at him.

'Can't say that I am.'

'I don't believe that' Eddie blustered, hoping it was true.

'I won't say I've been waiting for you to call, but now and again I wondered why you didn't.'

Eddie took a deep breath and told the truth. Leaving his wallet on a bar counter possibly sounded a bit far-fetched, and Eddie wasn't sure how far he could take their conversation, but he didn't know how much time he had left to impress the woman of several of his dreams. The imminent arrival of a bus loomed in his consciousness, not to mention the potential arrival of some Perthshire constabulary, asking questions he couldn't, or would rather not, answer. You do love to complicate your life, young Edward, he could hear his father saying. Leave me alone, Dad, for all you know I might be chatting up your future daughter-in-law.

Unaware of her potential future status, Dawn appraised Eddie; there was indeed a touch of Rasputin about him, and those caftans he wore added to it. She could understand why Eddie wore them; he simply wasn't comfortable being the size he was, though that was the size God, his genes and a healthy childhood had made him. Well, Dawn, if you buy the package, you buy the package. Did he really still fancy her, or was it male hormones working his mouth? Bit early to tell, bit early to dismiss him out of hand either. If you don't stay for the big picture Dawn, you'll never know how disappointed you could get.

Eddie looked back at her. She was still absolutely gorgeous. "Honesty is always the best policy Edward" his dad would have said to him. Sometimes it is, Dad. Sometimes it can get you in big trouble. Eddie took another breath.

'I wasn't joking when I told you that there's this bloke who still fancies you rotten ...'

Dawn looked at him, then away, around the room, seeing Rob, red-faced and panting against the bar, Tulloch staring wistfully into the middle distance. Then she was back, looking straight at him.

'Who could that be, Eddie?'

Dawn struggled to keep the flicker of a smile off her face as she watched Eddie turn a fetching shade of beetroot. Then she was on his side of the table, finding his lips for a lingering kiss which sped him back over two years.

Tulloch was lost in thought; he'd only agreed to Luce's pleading because it meant he wouldn't have to think what he was going to do with the rest of his life for another few days. The money wouldn't last forever and he wasn't made to sit idly watching one fat bloke waltz round a bar while another sat chatting some woman up in a corner. His eyes flicked toward the television screen, silently flitting through the day's news above the bar. He recognised the face, frozen in a photograph of presumably several years ago. John McGrath was staring accusingly at him, several feet and an eternity above contradiction. As Tulloch rose from his seat, he witnessed the most unexpected event of the evening.

A large man in a caftan and a woman in a black top stumbled past him.

'Getting a bit warm in here' observed Eddie.

As the door closed and the two figures disappeared into shadow, Tulloch's attention turned back to the television screen. No-one else in the pub appeared to have noticed McGrath's television appearance, nor that of the dour Chief Constable that followed. The crowd of Five Ways Ladies round the bar looked as if they wouldn't notice if World War III were declared, but Tulloch didn't fancy his chances of explaining the events of the past few hours to a police officer or a procurator fiscal.

One of the women demanded loudly

'Where's Dawn got to?'

Rob, thankful to have been finally put down in a corner,

wondered what all the fuss was about. He caught the note of panic in the big gallus one that had near jigged him off his feet. She was getting up a search party. Tulloch signaled to Rob with an unspoken indication it was time to leave. Following the women into the night, they slipped away in the opposite direction, walking as noiselessly and quickly as they could toward where Eddie had parked his car.

'That was our John McGrath on the telly' Tulloch told Rob.

'Eh?'

'Late of Special Branch, according to you.'

'An the papers he had on him. On the telly?'

'Time we found Eddie, wherever the hell he's got to.'

'Did I no see him leave wi some bird?'

Tulloch nodded, already sure that same said female was the one for whom the Five Ways Ladies had decided to organise a search party. For a wee village in the middle of Perthshire, there seemed to be an awful lot happening on a quiet night.

Edinburgh, the underground city

'So you're the one they cry The Omnivore!' his employer, the Laird of Dunpark, had said at their first meeting. 'You don't look as if you've eaten a damn thing in weeks!' A joke that was almost true. He'd eaten the way he had because he couldn't survive any other way. With luck, that might change. When the horse he'd hired in Perth had finally reached the shores of Loch Tay and he came within sight of Dunpark, he could see what he thought must be the building that had been described to him. It was small, quite low and not as close to the loch side as he'd hoped it was going to be. Ice houses needed a drain, somewhere for melting ice to be channeled away. A river or loch was near perfect, but whoever had seen to constructing this building had cannily sited it away from the Loch. Whether for fear of erosion or high tides was no matter, it would make the change to an ice house that bit more difficult. He foresaw that much digging would be required. Enough soil would have to be moved to make a channel from the building's foundations to the Loch. He'd made his way toward the big house, standing not much further from the Loch than the one he'd been looking at, and was shown into a large room on the ground floor. The man who had been sitting behind a wide desk rose and introduced himself as the brother of the previous Laird of Dunpark. He went on to explain he was trustee for his nephew, studying law in Edinburgh. Nonetheless, the man went on, his was the real power at present. It was then the Laird, as he called himself, had made the joke about his nickname. What struck The Omnivore was that the coldness of the Laird's manner hid a deeper coldness. It frightened him, though quite why he couldn't have said. After a few brief pleasantries, he was told he could start work immediately. The interview with his employer being over, he made his way toward the ice house, drew a sketch pad and pencil from the satchel he was carrying and began to make a preliminary drawing. Then a voice came, as if from nowhere.

'Guid day tae ye.'

The man walking slowly toward him stood about five feet tall, dressed in grey clothes that might once have been clean, with a battered top hat sitting above the tartan scarf that bandaged his head. How or why the injury had been inflicted was something the Omnivore wondered at, but was wise enough not to ask about.

'I'm the Duke o' Lennox. Pleased tae meet ye, Mister ..?'

His real name, The Omnivore learnt from other people, was John Maclaggan. He began by asking what a man he'd never met was doing, making sketches of 'the auld Ludge', as he called it, and when he was told, the man announced that he 'kent fine' a dozen or so who would be glad enough of a few days work, hard though it might be. They were family men, so Maclaggan assured him, grateful for anything that put a little more food on their tables. After one or two comments on the weather and its fickleness, he decided to explain why he called himself the "Duke of Lennox".

'I've more rights by law tae the title than them that claim it. Seein as I'm one o the gentry, I'm for the government an Viscount Melville, though it'd dae me nae good if I were tae say so in some places. If ye're the man anither man told me to look out for, mind the Duke o Lennox when you want an opinion o some o the folk roon aboot here.'

He disappeared almost as quickly as he had appeared, leaving The Omnivore to puzzle what he'd meant by his last few words and whether he could be trusted on the strength of them. The Omnivore decided that his best way would be to trust no one, and he was sure he ought not to trust a man who claimed to be a duke.

Luncarty

Eddie and Dawn were running through the previous two years of their lives at a gentle canter. Eddie began to feel a nervous butterfly flit up and down his stomach; they'd hit the point when flirting becomes a roller-coaster of uncertainty; when you're no longer sure who the hell you really are and no idea who you're with. Eddie was loving every terrifying moment of it, and so it seemed was Dawn. Curling into one another in the front seats of the car, their lips brushed as they talked about her move to Birmingham, his first BBC gigs, made jokes about theatres they knew, techies they'd worked with, each small self-deprecating joke and deliberately near-miss kiss a tiny step in a dance they were both enjoying far too much to think very seriously about where it might lead. Dawn stiffened slightly when she heard her name called from somewhere in the darkness. Eddie had moved the car from where he'd first parked it down a side lane leading off the road. Eddie glanced at Dawn twisting nervously in the direction of voices calling her name, released the hand brake and let the car freewheel slowly further down the lane.

Rob and Tulloch moved as inconspicuously as they could in the direction of where Eddie had parked the vehicle. Rob's stomach lurched as he realised it wasn't where he reckoned it ought to have been. Tulloch knew this was where they'd parked; only there was no sign of either the car or Eddie.

'Bet you he's done a runner' Rob surmised, his expression a plea in Tulloch's direction, desperate to be told he was being daft, that the car was sitting safely out of sight round the next bend. Tulloch was about to turn the corner when there was a sudden jerk on his shoulder. He spun back to see Rob's contorted features, a hand gesturing wildly into the semi-darkness.

'Tellt ye the bastard widnae let us alane!' Rob was tugging at Tulloch's coat sleeve. Ahead was a car, and a man standing beside it.

'It's fuckin Macquarie!' Rob pulled Tulloch back round the corner. 'Listen,' said Rob, his head now close to Tulloch's 'we've no much time. I wis yon bastard's stoolie for years, informer, ken? Never tellt him much, but I learnt this aboot Macquarie, he's bent as a nine bob.'

'Not a hanging offence. Not these days, anyway.'

'No like that! He's aye on the lookout for the main chance, and if he's up tae somethin, we're in trouble. I kin feel it.'

Tulloch digested Rob's words, trying to decide what might be true and what was likely pure imagination.

'I'm gonnae shift my arse afore he starts sniffin aboot. If you ken what's good for you, you'll do the same. I'm headin in this direction, so dinnae follow me.'

Tulloch didn't altogether believe Rob's assessment of Macquarie, but although McGrath's death might have been the natural outcome of extreme activity on an already overburdened heart, Tulloch didn't fancy trying that explanation on some member of Her Majesty's constabulary.

By now, Rob was already a shape in the distance, moving faster than Tulloch would have given him credit for. He began walking quickly in the opposite direction. Hearing a car engine start, then begin turning over, slowly at first then more rapidly, Tulloch's walk became a swift jog, then a sprint he was quickly forced to slow to a hard canter. Glancing toward the other side of the road, Tulloch could see a dyke. Scrabbling, he heaved himself over, the sharp edged stones cutting into his fingers. Dropping into pitch-blackness, knees hitting the ground harder than he'd hoped, he could already feel the sting of the cut to his hands. Breathless, scared, but not enough to run immediately, his eyes blinked into darkness, desperately focusing for a way out of the space he'd leapt into. He could barely make out anything. Tulloch legged it till he tripped and stumbled. Recovering, he hesitated, listening for any sound like footsteps but nothing broke the silence. Canes lay around him in huddled clumps. A rasp field. Earlier in the year he could have sated hunger on handfuls of fresh raspberries, but hunger was no longer uppermost in his mind.

Tulloch lay still as he could, dampness seeping into his clothes, his constricted breathing the only sound he could hear, till a car engine started, revved up, then grew fainter as it moved off. Having waited a little, he rose slowly and walked over to the wall. Tulloch gazed at it, impressed by his own recklessness. It was higher than it had appeared on the other side. He peered into darkness, looking for a handhold that might add impetus to what he knew would be an almost impossible struggle to the top of the wall. He made out a stone jutting from the rest, which his fingers could touch if he stood on tiptoe. Jumping, he fought gravity to a draw, his feet swinging till he pushed against the wall, struggling upward. He felt he was about to lose his tenuous grip, then pushing harder against the wall, he jerked his weight onto the tiny ledge. Almost at once gravity dragged him earthward, and he thrust his hand toward the coping stones on top of the wall. Clutching at one, Tulloch swung free of his perch, his legs kicking air. One more pull, and he'd be there. One more pull, if he had strength for it.

The world beyond the wall came in sight, and the shapes of hills slowly emerged from the darkness as his eyes began to refocus. Then, as if out of nowhere, a pair of car headlights swung in his direction. The car came toward him at such speed that Tulloch realised what rabbits must feel like. It stopped sharply, then the driver's door opened slowly.

He was wee, right enough, if he was Macquarie. A swagger to the walk, of which the small figure hardly seemed worthy. He stopped a few feet from the wall and gazed up at Tulloch.

'You look a right Humpty from where I'm standin, son.'

The voice had enough edge in it to make Tulloch think twice about his next move. He had the advantage of height, but not surprise.

Macquarie looked up at the figure perched precariously on top of the wall. Thirty, perhaps a bit more. Fit enough; the wiry ones generally were. There was no danger he was going up there after him. If he couldn't persuade the bastard to come down to his level, he'd have to wait, which might be a bit embarrassing.

'Inspector Macquarie's the name. I have reason to believe someone stole a car from outside a house at Kinfauns. I got a call that a car similar to the one that was stolen had been seen parked near the Duke of Lennox. Don't suppose you'd ken anythin about that, son?'

Macquarie paused to let his words sink in. Tulloch had listened carefully to every one of them. If the man really had been at Kinfauns, then he very likely knew McGrath and also knew he was dead. Tracking down McGrath's vehicle, however, was good luck or good judgement on a scale beyond Tulloch's comprehension and credulity, especially in what seemed a remarkably short space of time. He shook his head in disbelief, but Macquarie remained feet away from him, asking questions Tulloch decided it was best, at least for the moment, not to answer.

'I don't think I can help you, Inspector.'

'Can I give you a hand off that wall, son?'

The conciliatory tone in Macquarie's voice almost caught Tulloch off guard.

'I'm fine where I am for the minute. Getting my breath back.'

Tulloch gazed down at the figure standing beside the car. He didn't look that big, but he was willing to bet he'd be big enough if they ever met on the same level. He considered the options. If Macquarie was on his own, chances were he didn't want police involvement. Even if Rob was right about Macquarie, what Tulloch had in mind was a very big gamble, but perhaps not as big as he might have thought a few minutes before.

'It's no that far to jump' Macquarie observed.

'Right enough, it's not.'

Let the wee shite freeze his arse off, Macquarie thought. He was in no hurry. Leaning against the side of the car, he looked up at the sky, as if Tulloch was no sort of problem at all.

The wall was getting cold. Correction, he was getting cold, but it was his own fault he'd ended on top of a farm dyke in the middle of wildest Perthshire. The daft notion that had crept into his brain refused to go away. If he was wrong, he could be in even deeper trouble than it looked as if he was. Whatever Tulloch did, he was still in trouble. He coughed loudly, and then paused for effect.

'I have something might interest you.'

'Doubt it, son. Doubt that very much.'

Tulloch fished in his pockets and cupped something in his hands.

'Why don't you come over and take a look?'

Macquarie shrugged and ambled away from the car

'All right, what is it?'

'It's a wee kind of thing. You'll have to come closer, or I'll drop it.'

Macquarie edged closer. He was a couple of feet from the wall by now, Tulloch reckoned.

Macquarie was on the ground before he realised what had happened. The man had got hold of him by the shoulders and was rifling his pockets.

'Car keys.'

Too stunned to speak in any case, Macquarie wasn't going to say anything likely to help the wee shite. It'd take more than this to loosen Maurice Macquarie's tongue. Then he was yelling in pain, but not so loud he didn't hear the whisper.

'Where are they?'

'In the car!' Macquarie screamed. 'They're still in the ignition!'

Tulloch ran toward the driver's side. Yanking the door open, he wrenched out the key and began to run. Then his leg gave way.

Stumbling forward, trying to avoid contact with the tarmac, Tulloch hobbled as fast as he could away from the car. He calculated that if the man had got to his feet by now, with a good lungful of air he'd be faster than he was with a twisted ankle. Turning, he glimpsed a figure leaning on the bonnet of the car. A few seconds and he'd be up and running. He began circling his arm, building up momentum. A patch in the road surface caught him unawares and his ankle buckled. As he tumbled toward the ground, he let go the keys, hearing them rattle against the road surface somewhere ahead of him. That would have to do. On a night as dark as this, it would take the other man more time to search for them than it would take him to get as far away as possible, maybe even as far as somewhere he could hide and rest up.

Tulloch legged it as fast as his hobble allowed. He glimpsed a hollow in the hillside, whin bushes either side. He was almost half way toward it when his arm was suddenly gripped and he lurched forward.

'Wheesht!'

Tulloch looked the way he'd come. No sign of anyone, and no sound either.

Rob had a quizzical look on his face, as though Tulloch was going to have the answer to his question.

'What's the script, then?'

Tulloch hadn't thought beyond getting away. The last few minutes had been filled with only that. In the dark and the quiet, he admitted to himself they really had lost Eddie. Or Eddie had lost them. Whichever way round, he and Rob were on their own and out there somewhere was Inspector Maurice Macquarie, who didn't seem to have their best interests at heart. Tulloch didn't have a clue what the script was, apart from simple survival, which was maybe enough to worry about. For the moment, Dunpark House looked as if it would have to wait. All he wanted was to be somewhere safe and warm, and if he couldn't have both, he'd settle for safe. He turned to Rob, who looked about as done in as he felt.

'There's a bit hill over there' Tulloch spoke quietly, in case Macquarie was nearer than he thought. 'with a few trees'.

'Ay' was Rob's phlegmatic response.

'I was thinking it was as good a place as I was like to get to spend the night.'

'I've slept in worse places,' conceded Rob. 'No without a sleepin bag, though.'

'It's barely September! No-one dies of exposure in September.'

'First time for everythin' Rob complained, as he followed Tulloch toward the slope.

the ice house, Dunpark

McIlwraith felt chill again. Not the way he had when the two figures had appeared from out the first chest, but real, freeze your bones, chill. It was night by now. He'd discovered what he had been supposed to pick up, and the knowledge of that made him a dead man walking. He'd been that desperate to get out of Northern Ireland and off a charge of murder, he'd gone and swallowed Cameron's bait, hook, line and bloody sinker. The bastard never meant him to get out of this alive. McIlwraith decided he was getting out alive, whatever it took, if only for the pleasure of seeing Cameron's jaw drop when he, McIlwraith, did what he wasn't supposed to and walked away after all. The thought of that was almost enough to keep him warm. Almost. The question, though, was whether he'd manage to stay alive long enough to see the slick smile slide off Cameron's baby cheeks. McIlwraith could barely make out the door and its frame through the gloom. He moved toward it, and began to feel his way up and down the side of the frame where the hinges had to be. What his fingers discovered didn't cheer him up one little bit. There were three hinges holding the door, each of them screwed firmly into the frame, which had been given a thorough coating of wood preservative at some time. He was going to have to work hard if he was going to get himself out of here before Macquarie or Cameron himself pitched up, asking awkward questions and likely not bothering about an answer. He tightened his grip on the spike in his hand. He'd better get back to work.

'Not long after I had that dream, the schoolmasters and ministers began to get word to make lists of those who could be taken in to the new militia. As soon as I heard that, I knew what my dream meant, not that there was anything I could do to stop what was happening any more than I could have stopped playing in my dream. Work went on with the ice house for the Laird of Dunpark. Though, as I told you, it went slowly enough. John Maclaggan and his crony James Menzies got the lads to do the digging and carrying, while they sat around like lords, telling the others what needed to be done but not lifting a finger themselves. By now folk started seeing the ministers and schoolmasters with books in their hands, ready to write down the names of those who were to be enrolled in the militia. No-one knew what was to happen when men were enlisted. What folk did know was that men had already been sent away or overseas, and nothing done to prevent it. So there was no reason to believe what the gentry said about them only having to serve in their own localities – and what did these folk mean by "locality"? It might still be miles from their own homes, and who was to get the harvest in if they were absent, and how would that be done? Their questions weren't answered, so folk worried the more. I noticed that Angus Cameron was

often on the road, though when I asked him why, he never gave a straightforward answer. There were a fair few on the roads apart from him, and one or two of them told any that would listen about the Navy mutinies earlier in the year, or how the French had landed somewhere – anything that would get them a glass of something and a bit of notice. The harvest time was growing closer all this while, yet work, apart from on the Laird of Dunpark's ice house, was hard to find that summer. Some said that it was the war with France and fewer folk with money in their pockets, but when there's folk with little in their pockets and less to lose, there's aye the chance of trouble. It was plain enough that the taking of names for the militia might be the spark to light the bonfire, but of course there were those who could not, or would not see what was in front of their face. Though the Duke of Atholl pays me to play the fiddle for him, I'm no more than a weaver body that has a skill he can hire. He has less reason to value my opinion than those of the great folk round about him. Yet if you live among humble folk, as I do, Nathaniel, you can learn a lot from them. You also learn to be grateful for what you've been given and to grumble less. Some might say I've been a coward, but when your livelihood depends on others, you learn when to keep quiet. For all that, though I know I've been fortunate, I've also know many less fortunate that had less to lose than I have. What the great ones forget is that if you've little enough to lose, you can be the more willing to risk what little you have if you think even that may be taken from you. When people become that desperate, they become more dangerous.'

Luncarty

'I have to get back, Eddie.'

Dawn smiled, but Eddie could see the determination lurking behind her eyes. Of course she had, and he had to find the two he'd left in the pub and sort out what the three of them were going to do. He didn't want to, any more than he wanted to take Dawn back to the Five Ways Ladies and the prospect of never seeing her again. He wondered how much of his mind Dawn was able to read when she made her suggestion.

'We're going to stay overnight in a hotel in Perth. The bus company has booked us in, seeing the bus broke down. You look done in. Why don't we see if they can't put you up as well?'

The thought of a decent night's sleep in a comfortable bed, especially if it might also contain Dawn, made him pause. Then Tulloch and Rob came back to mind and spoiled it all. He couldn't abandon them.

'I'd love to, but I've two travelling companions to think about.'

'How d' you mean?'

Eddie managed to edit John McGrath out of his explanation of how he came to be in the company of Ninian Tulloch and Rob Ainslie.

Dawn listened, smiled and swept objections before her.

'They can come too! Bet you we can swing it for them!'

Eddie looked into Dawn's eyes again and believed she could, if anyone could.

'We can try,' he conceded.

'Let's get back to the Duke of Lennox and see what your pals have to say.'

The minute they opened the door, there was a loud cheer followed by more questions than Eddie had answers for. Fortunately, most of them were aimed at Dawn. Eddie tried standing to one side, smiling and looking pleasant. It didn't work, of course. The Five Ways Ladies were not so much irate as incandescent. Dawn had disappeared minutes before the replacement coach had arrived. The Ladies had been out searching for Dawn, and arrived back barely in time to stop the coach driving off without them. They were now keeping the driver under close guard, and had been on the point of phoning the police when Dawn and Eddie walked through the door. Used to charming audiences, Eddie found the Five Ways Ladies a very hard one. Coming up with an explanation of why he'd attempted to abscond with their teammate wasn't easy. 'It's not Eddie's fault the 'bus turned up while we were outside' Dawn broke in 'and it hasn't driven off without us. So what's the problem?'

There was a moment's silence, then came the question Eddie dreaded someone was going to ask.

'Haven't you been on telly?'

'He looks familiar, doesn't he?'

'I've been thinking that since he first walked in here.'

'You're the Funky Chicken, aren't you?'

Eddie's shoulders sagged. It was a nightmare that kept recurring, ever since he'd agreed to do the adverts. His agent had threatened to drop him if he didn't do them, and fair dos, they'd been a nice little income steam, but the price he'd paid had been heavy. He hadn't dared enter a club or dance hall for months after the adverts had gone out, in case the DJ decided to play *that* number. His mother was under strict instructions to deny her son was now or ever had been Robinson's "Funky Chicken", capering round a pile of outsize tins marked "Funky Chicken in White Wine Sauce", "Funky Chicken Italian", or "Funky Chicken Tikka Masala". Even now, the thought of chicken in anything brought Eddie out in a cold sweat. He looked at the enquirer as if she'd suggested he molested sheep as a hobby.

'I'm Eddie Corcoran' he replied with as much dignity as he could manage. 'whatever I may have done in a previous existence has no bearing on this, madam.'

'Told you he was the Funky Chicken' came a voice from the back of the crowd.

'He's probably suffered enough, then' said a woman who vaguely reminded Eddie of a slightly younger version of his mother.

'Just don't think you can get away with kidnapping Dawn again, that's all' said another of the Ladies. Small chance, Eddie decided regretfully. He looked round for Rob and Tulloch, but saw no sign.

'The two blokes I came in with, where are they?' He asked the barman, who shrugged his shoulders and carried on polishing glasses. They couldn't have gone far. Eddie's eyes raked the smallness of the bar with the keenness of a food standards inspector on payment by results. Nothing. No-one. He swung the door open, went out and scanned the road in both directions.

Pacing first in one direction then the other, he called 'Tulloch! Rob!' until he was nearly hoarse, to no response. He went back inside and tapped Dawn, busily talking to one of the team, on the shoulder.

'No sign of them. I'll have to take the car, try to find them.'

'What'll you do if you don't?'

Eddie hadn't thought that far ahead.

'If I really can't find them, phone the police, I suppose.'

'I'll sort something out for you at the hotel. It's the Breadalbane House Hotel. Right on the main street, I'm told, so I'm sure you won't miss it.'

The Five Ways Ladies were already making their way to the bus. Dawn picked up her bag from beneath a table. Eddie caught her as she opened the door.

'Miss you, though.'

Eddie's lips connected with a cheek where he thought a mouth ought to have been. He really was out of practice, he decided.

'I'll have a whisky waiting for you. Don't make it stay up too late.'

He waved forlornly as the bus disappeared round a bend in the road. Once he'd got into the car and switched on the ignition, Eddie realised he hadn't a clue which way to go. He knew the main road ran on to Aberfeldy and Loch Tay, or back to Perth, a neat whisky, a warm bed and Dawn, but there were any number of side roads leading God knew where. He edged the car gently into gear, watchful for any road sign that looked as it might lead somewhere.

Eddie glanced at the clock. It read almost eleven fifteen and still no sign. He'd stopped the car at least half a dozen times, got out to yell 'Tulloch!' and 'Rob!' at startled birds and dozing cattle. Nothing. If they were out there, either they couldn't hear, didn't dare respond, or ... A huge yawn told him how tired he was. If he drove slowly, he could still be in Perth before midnight. He'd go to the police station, tell them ... well, as much as he felt able to.

It would probably be best to leave out John McGrath and his car, which he'd abandon before going to the police. If they didn't arrest him on the spot, he could hire one tomorrow and get back on the road to Dunpark House. Assuming they let him.

It was after midnight before the door of the police station banged shut behind the bulk that was Eddie Corcoran. He'd told the desk sergeant as much as he dared, but he could tell the man didn't believe him. He could almost feel the quiet dismissal in the desk sergeant's slow repetition of Eddie's statement, his asking Eddie if he wanted to change anything, anything he wanted to add. He'd done the best he could. At least Tulloch and Rob were now listed as potential missing persons, for whatever good that might do them.

He walked slowly until he saw "Breadalbane House Hotel" illuminated by a half dozen halogen lamps. Amazingly, the front door was still open and as he wandered across the deeply carpeted foyer, he saw Dawn, seated at a table at the far end.

'That whisky's been waiting over an hour for you.'

'I didn't find them. Went to the police in the end.'

'And?'

'I don't think they believed a word.'

'Drink your whisky, Eddie. It won't make things any better, but you must be frozen.'

Eddie drank, lent back in his chair, and suddenly realised how tired he was.

'Hello. What's the time?'

Eddie woke to find himself looking into Dawn's eyes. Very nice eyes to wake up to, he decided.

'Six o clock.'

'In the morning?' Eddie asked, incredulous.

'In the evening, you daft idiot.'

'How long have I been asleep, then?'

'Since you got here.'

Eddie thrashed upright. If that was true, he'd been asleep for nearly eighteen hours.

'Is it really six o' clock? In the *evening*?'

'Yes, Eddie, it really is.'

It had happened before, once when he'd compered a twenty-four hour horror film event in his student days, then after "Corcoran's Weekend Wander", a series of shows in comedy clubs in Glasgow, Liverpool and Manchester on Friday and Saturday, Birmingham and Coventry on Sunday. He'd felt almost as exhausted after that lot as he did now. His own peculiar version of petit mort. Not dead, merely sleeping, usually for a hell of a long time.

He'd lost a whole day. He ought to have been to Dunpark House by now, done the interviews, and been halfway back to Edinburgh.

Instead, he was almost as far away as when he'd met Dawn. Slowly his brain caught up with the present. He didn't know where Tulloch and Rob were, and he didn't know if this Inspector Macquarie character was still out there somewhere, and … He ought to get out of bed and … He wasn't sure what the next move should be, but his whole body told him he wasn't able to make any sort of move. He collapsed back onto the pillows.

'Why didn't you wake me?'

He'd meant to yell the words, but they came out as a flat whisper. He felt weaker than a very sickly kitten.

'I did try, but you'd open your eyes, smile and go straight back to sleep.'

'Dawn, any chance of a cup of tea?' he croaked.

No point setting out now. Stay another night and get on the road in the morning. Sleep, please. More sleep. Lashings of it, with no dreams of wild children, balloons or waving women, unless they looked like Dawn.

Loch Tay

After your two visitors left, you wondered and worried whether "Republica" would ever be ready for a flight again. The one above South Queensferry had set Tam and Archie thinking of all sorts of notions of how she might stay in the air longer, be more stable and any other sort of improvement their minds could come up with. You didn't give a damn about any of them, so long as "Republica" could get you away from the ones who might be after you at any minute, and that as fast as possible. Things were starting to get too hot for you to cope with. You'd heard stories of the sailors that had mutinied at Spithead and the Nore. The mutinies hadn't come to much and it seemed Government now had the upper hand once more, but there was still a chance something might flare up again. There had been some sort of mishandled landing of French soldiers at Fishguard, wherever the hell that was. The Welsh coast, someone had said. Talk of the Militia Act in Scotland could turn into more than talk at any moment. You'd wondered what to do about the balloon when you first heard that Thomas Muir was too ill to travel. For all the wild notions that you'd once had about what you might do with "Republica", all you wanted now was to use her to get away. You were a fool and chancer and there were plenty would give you a worse character than that, but you'd always known how to get out of whatever scrape you were in. If you'd only Tam and Archie to deal with, you could talk them into taking "Republica" far enough away from Edinburgh and the mess you're in. Not a chance Mattie would let you do that. Nor let Tam and Archie mix themselves up in it. You decide to talk to Tam and Archie about another trial, only nowhere near South Queensferry. "Republica" had already caused enough of a stir there. Along the coast at Prestonpans, or somewhere thereabouts, perhaps. It's no surprise Mattie is against the notion, but she has a point that there are more soldiers about now. The disturbances have made Government nervous and though there's no crime in flying a balloon, it would likely attract suspicion. You push the harder for making the test somewhere away from Edinburgh and prying eyes. Eventually it's agreed Tranent would be the place. A hamlet with a few coal pits seems unlikely to attract the military. The following Tuesday, a man who has a horse and cart is talked into giving the loan of it to carry "Republica". Tam takes the driver's seat and the three of you perch on the rails of the cart and you're off. It takes a couple of hours from the centre of Edinburgh to the outskirts of the village, only when you get there, on the narrow main street, a confused mass of people and horses have blocked the way forward. Soldiers on horseback struggle to control their beasts as people throw stones and whatever else comes to their hands. In front of what looks like the only hostelry in the place a man tries to read from a paper, his voice drowned by the confusion and shouts of the crowd. You'd read about riots in newspapers, but never thought such a thing might happen without warning in some small village. Riots are things that happened in towns, not in places in the country. A stone flies by your head, Mattie screams, and at once you're scared one of the soldiers hears her and you're all done for in a minute. But the noise is too great for that, and by now others are screaming as well. Tam persuades the horse to turn, gets the cart into the middle of the narrow road, facing the way it came, then takes it slow until you're all well out of sight. Everyone is silent all the way back to Edinburgh. They don't want to risk another trial, but if there isn't one, you've no chance to escape using 'Republica". Somehow, you've got to persuade Tam and Archie to make another attempt.

Perth

Eddie clocked himself in the wardrobe mirror. The sight of nearly eighteen stone of humanity, even one's own, can be a shock to the system. He'd vaguely hoped the best part of two days without proper food would have helped him slim down. He didn't look as if he'd shed a pound, and decided against canceling his gym subscription. The hands on his watch were edging toward 8.00 a.m. Eddie dressed quickly, discovering a ravenous appetite in the process. He was that hungry he could eat a pig's hind end. In fact, he decided, that was exactly what he was going to eat, probably with a couple of eggs and some sausages. He hoped the hotel did a buffet breakfast, then wondered how Tulloch and Rob were, and where they were, come to that – but decided he'd think better with food in his stomach. Then he remembered the car. It was still, he hoped, where he'd parked it when he'd arrived in Perth, some thirty hours ago. He hurried downstairs. A thin elderly woman in a garishly patterned housecoat was vacuuming the carpet while holding a conversation with a younger version of herself behind the reception desk.

'Everything all right for you?' the younger one enquired in a tone that sounded as if it had been acquired on a crash course in "hospitality management".

Eddie nodded quickly, smiled politely and rushed through the doors, hoping he wasn't going to meet a group of policemen waiting to interview him about the recent death of a certain John McGrath, and asking awkward questions as to how he came to be in possession of the deceased's vehicle.

The car was still where he'd parked it. Part of him wanted to get on the way as soon as seemed decent, but the police station would have to be visited again, unless the police decided to visit him. Since they hadn't on the previous day, Eddie reckoned they were unlikely to, but it was just possible some word had come in. He wandered back to the hotel, working out what to say to the police that wouldn't land him or anyone else in trouble, yet still keep Rob and Tulloch on their minds.

Halfway through toast and marmalade, Dawn appeared and settled herself beside Eddie, a smile on her face, obviously waiting for him to speak. Eddie continued chewing, so Dawn opened the conversation.

'The match with Freuchie isn't till Friday. I thought I could come with you to Dunpark House.'

Almost choking, Eddie tried to think of a simple way of telling Dawn why she couldn't, but failed to come up with one. Instead, he tried a smile that might even have made a used car salesperson suspicious.

'I'm not going to tell you there's a perfectly simple explanation for any of this, 'cause there's not.'

Dawn gave him the sort of encouraging smile you give five year olds at a nativity play.

'Nor am I going to tell you to trust me and everything will be all right, 'cause I'm not sure that it will be.'

Dawn slipped her hand across the table and into Eddie's.

'I don't care what you tell me, Eddie, as long as it's the truth.'

Edinburgh, the underground city

It was a poor summer. The dawn threatened rain, then the light grew slowly brighter, till it looked as if there might be sunshine, only for clouds to gather from seeming nowhere and lour, and then for a cool, damp haar to herald slowly smirring rain, lasting so long it was well past the dinner hour before any more sun appeared. By six o' clock, dusk was creeping across the parks and precious little work had been done. "Progress" was too optimistic a word for the snail's pace at which work on the old ice house proceeded. The Omnivore had been watching for more weeks than he cared to count as the old building crept toward something like the ice house he had first planned. The floor had taken a good two weeks to dig out. Then a central shaft had been dug to the depth of the Loch. That had taken two more weeks. Once the shaft seemed deep enough, they had begun a narrow tunnel from its bottom, running toward the Loch itself. It flooded three times in as many days. It had to be let dry out, then dug again, the still-clay soil now more heavy to move, so slowing the work to even less than the snail's pace it had gone at before. A stonemason was hired, at the expense and grumbling of the Laird. He took one look at what was expected and fled back to Perth, from where only larger amounts of money, paid in advance, could induce him to risk his person and reputation on the task of lining the walls with granite. The Duke of Lennox took great care that those he had caused to be engaged on the work were not paid off, but found trivial occupations between breakfast and the opening of his hostelry, which paid enough for them to spend the most of the little they had earned in that establishment. One day, with the weather grown better than it had been for some time, The Omnivore made his way to the Duke of Lennox's howff. He needed the men working, but he'd discovered nearly all of them spoke only Gaelic, bar a handful of English words they proudly mispronounced whenever he was in their hearing, becoming unable to understand a single word as soon as he asked them to do anything. Determined to make John Maclaggan appreciate the need for the work to progress more speedily, he found the workforce spellbound by a tall figure wearing what had once been a soldier's coat. He was told the man was Angus Cameron, and he had been on campaign in Holland, been captured but had won home and was now working as a wood merchant. The Omnivore wondered if he might be speaking against the new Militia Act, since he spoke so quickly and passionately, and if that were so, whether he was trying to persuade the others to the same opinion. Yet Angus Cameron gave the impression of a solid, respectable sort of man, the kind who work steadily, attend church, often more than once on a Sabbath, and are well regarded by their neighbours, all things likely to make this one the more dangerous an agitator. It was clear Maclaggan held him in some awe. If Cameron were indeed involved in some sort of plot to make mischief against the raising of a militia, he would be well to be watched. However, he gave the impression of one who kept his own counsel most carefully. Watch, he had been told. Watch and listen, and if what you hear seems worth telling others, be sure we are the ones you tell. Already he'd begun to hate what he'd been told to do. The men staring at Angus Cameron as if he were some kind of wonder posed no more threat to Government than he did. If these were the men the United Scotsmen hoped to raise in rebellion, they were to have a hard job. The men looked at Angus Cameron, listened to him in silence, but stirred not an inch. Whatever Cameron might hope for, it seemed unlikely that any of them would raise so much as a finger at his word. Yet the lists that were being drawn up of those who might serve in the militia were hated things, and there could be no telling the way the people might react once they appeared. The Omnivore wrote all this in his letters to Edinburgh, though he doubted any one there paid the least heed.

Luncarty

Tulloch woke to a cold shiver running the length of his body. Brushing his hand across his coat, he felt the cold of the dew, and how damp his clothes were. Haar was drifting through the branches above his head. The rest of the tree and the hollow beneath became clearer as dawn broke steadily through the haze. No cars on the road, nor any sound of movement. He hadn't a notion where Eddie had got to; he was likely miles away by now, with luck sharing a nice warm bed with the woman he'd seen in the pub.

He tried standing up, and immediately stumbled back to earth. His ankle hurt like hell; he squirmed round, looking for anything that would at least let him get into an upright position. A broken branch lay tantalisingly out of reach, halfway up the side of the hollow.

He glanced back to where Rob lay sleeping in a position as undignified as it looked uncomfortable; his head curled onto his chin, his legs drawn under him, making him look as if he were praying on his side. Tulloch's nerve ends chorused in pain as he inched toward the branch. His hand curved around it, drawing it down to his side. He dug one end into the ground and began slowly pulling himself upright. It still hurt, but at least he was on his feet. He looked round slowly, wondering in which direction they should go.

Find the river; that was the first thing. Once they'd found the river, he'd know the way. Tulloch shook as he moved one shambling foot in front of the other. Jolts of pain from his ankle combined with uncontrollable shivers to slow his movement to shuddering spasms until he had to stop, readying himself for the next step.

He staggered as far as the roadside, proud of his effort and faintly hoping it might be rewarded by a passing car that would take two hitchhikers and wasn't driven by someone called Macquarie. Nothing came, and he stumbled back to wake the sleeping Rob. A wee nudge of the big man's shoulder was like waking a monster. Rob groaned, twitched, flipped onto his back and stared fiercely up at Tulloch.

'What the hang did you go and do that for?' Rob accused him.

'You looked uncomfortable the way you were sleeping' Tulloch told him 'Not to mention a bit ridiculous.'

'I dinnae criticise the way you sleep' Rob grumbled as he got to his feet. 'What time is it, anyway?'

'After eight, if my watch is still working.'

The sun made fitful attempts to break through the haar, which was reluctant to loosen its grip of the low hills. They couldn't be far from the river, Tulloch reckoned. The sooner they could work out where they were, the sooner they'd be able to work out what to do.

Eddie was God knew where, doing ... well, Tulloch could guess what, but in any case nowhere near this forsaken spot. They could trek the roads for days and never meet up with him. Tulloch could throw in the towel, try and thumb a lift back to Edinburgh and simply say, sorry, I knackered my ankle. He'd made a promise to a pair of sparkling eyes, though, and had no intention of receiving a reproach from them. Pain ran through him as the cold of the early Perthshire morning seeped its way into his bones; all he wanted was his bad leg good and food that wasn't likely to poison him or require the dissection of a small furry creature.

He moved away from Rob, toward a sound he couldn't quite make out and couldn't quite believe. It sounded like the lap of a river, not far away. He began to make out the shape of it between the trees, and decided the river could only be the one he'd hoped they'd stumble on, the Tay.

His feet began to pick up speed, almost in spite of themselves, and he tripped and stumbled his way down the track till he felt his body lurch forward and darkness swept over him.

the ice house, Dunpark

McIlwraith's hand travelled over the edge of the hinge, as he tried to gauge how much of the paint that covered it he'd managed to work away with the point of the spike. Not that much. At this rate it would take him long enough to work this hinge away from its fastening, and there were two more after that. The preservative paint was clarted all over, and the damp had affected it, but not in any way that made the work easier. He must have been picking at it for hours now, with precious little to show for his efforts. McIlwraith hunkered against the wall, struggling not to give in to sleep or despair. There was nothing else for it but to keep going, working the spike round the edge of the hinge till finally he'd worn away the stuff and could get at the hinge itself. Like some reluctant schoolboy at the end of break, he forced himself to push the nail against the hinge and start work again.

John Maclaggan and James Menzies seemed to grow even thicker between themselves as the building of the Laird of Dunpark's ice-house went slowly on, those early days of August. Angus Cameron kept them company sometimes, after the day's work was done. They'd gather at Maclaggan's and put the world to rights in their way of it. They said that there would be resistance to the Militia Act all across Scotland. How they came to believe that, and whether it was true, I'd no idea. Get a handful together and the can passing, and you'll hear rumour. That was all their talk was thought to be at the time. There were other stories going about, though, of soldiers being sent into Scotland, not regular troops, but Volunteer units from places in the south. That made me wonder, Nathaniel, for Volunteers are mostly gentlemen who have no notion of how the poor live; ordinary soldiers are more like ourselves, not that it would matter if they were acting under orders. Those were the kind of thoughts I had when I heard there might be soldiers coming to enforce the Militia Act. Those around Loch Tay became more and more ready to do anything that would prevent the Act ruining their lives, as they saw it. Easier, maybe, to calm frightened beasts than frightened people, their heads full of stories, all of them with bad endings. There's a sort of trick I've learned from the gentry, over the years. That is, to seem as if you're paying attention to every word you're told, but to never listen to anything at all. You find a sort of still place inside yourself and never go away from it, so that people can tell you their most dreadful troubles and greatest fears and none of the hurt touches you in the least. It's a grand way of not letting yourself think too much. It was a big help to me, those days in ninety-seven. It let me listen to the nonsense that was being spoken – and there was a powerful lot of nonsense about the place, let me tell you – without having to say a single word of what I might be thinking myself. Some of the crofter lads would talk about what they would do to the gentry if they tried making them join the militia, and some of the lairds would talk about buying muskets or sending to Perth for a cannon. Strange, the way folk brag when they're terrified. All the same, you have to pay them heed, listen to what they say, nod and shake your head at the right places. Always remember, neighbours can intimidate you as long as you're in their reach, but Government has a longer arm, with more power in it. For all that, the rumours flew about and folk grew more anxious, till the whole Strath of Tay was like a kettle boiling, ready for the lid to fly off. I watched Angus Cameron, coming and going, talking to John Maclaggan or James Menzies and I wondered what might become of us all, if their talk led to actions. The ministers and schoolmasters kept themselves busy taking notes of their congregations and classes. A stranger coming amongst us might not have noticed that everyone here lived as if on the surface of a volcano that might erupt at any minute, but all of us knew that to be the case.'

The Old Gaol, Perth

Dougie Simpson eased his bulk onto the stool opposite Rob.

'There you go, Son. Nothin like a wee Scotch pie wi yer cuppae tea, this time of a mornin.'

Rob wasn't going to argue. As soon as he'd seen Tulloch fall, a couple of hours ago, it had been clear he wasn't going anywhere in a hurry. Clear, too, that the sooner he could find somewhere for the two of them to rest up that wasn't a freezing cold patch of wilderness, the better it was going to be. That Dougie Simpson might still be at the Old Gaol had been a memory feat close to genius. Mind you, getting Tulloch from wherever they'd been hadn't been any sort of doddle. Rob was still scared Macquarie would appear round every bend, and had near enough panicked when a car slowed down and the driver asked if Tulloch was ill. Rob had managed to convince him that Tulloch had had a rough night and Rob was simply walking him back to sobriety. Some walk, all the same. He was relieved to find Dougie was still at the Old Gaol. Dougie had told him about landing this job the last time Rob had seen him. It had been taking a flyer, chapping the door of the place, hoping Dougie hadn't got the sack in the meantime. The thought of finally outwitting Macquarie had been great, though. Macquarie was never going to look for the pair of them in a prison. Dougie had opened up and been decent enough not to look down his nose at a couple of scruffs trying to talk their way into a nice dry cell. Rob had done the talking, of course. Tulloch hadn't looked as if he had the strength to go one round with Rob's granny, even supposing she'd had both her arms tied behind her back. Dougie and he'd near enough carried Tulloch into one of the cells, Dougie assuring Rob it was dry and the blankets were clean. They'd left Tulloch to come to in his own time, and now Rob had a smile on his face again; a pie on a plate in front of him and a cup of tea in his hand. If he could have wished Macquarie off his case as easily, he really would have had something to smile about, but as his granny might have said "If that's what you want, Rob, you'll just have to want". He stared down at the plate in front of him, picked up the pie and was about to take a bite when Dougie spoke.

'Would ye like tae tell me what the hang this is aa aboot, Rob?'

Rob cleared his throat, took a long swig of tea, and wondered where to start. Sitting facing Dougie, warm and about to get some food inside him, the past thirty-six hours seemed like some daft laddie's ploy. But Macquarie was real enough, he'd thought the ghosts in the tunnel were too, and all the business last night had been no kind of dream as far as he was concerned.

'D ye mind me talkin about a guy cried Macquarie?'

Dougie shook his head.

'Well, the mad bastard's aifter the pair o us ...'

When Rob had finished, Dougie stretched in his chair, giving Rob a look, which was a mixture of sympathy, disbelief and incomprehension.

'Yon Macquarie must be hard up for entertainment if he's chasin you an yon fellae the length o the country.'

Rob shook his head.

'He's no daein it for fun, but I'm damn sure he's daein it for profit.'

'How d' ye mean?'

'Think aboot it, Dougie. The man could have us collared in nae time if he wanted. Whatever he's up tae, it's no on the up an up. An if it's no legal, it has tae have somethin tae dae wi makin him a few bob. Stands tae reason.'

Dougie nodded, digesting the implications.

'Rob, I dinnae mind you an your pal bidin here till he's got his strength back, but soon as he has, it'd be the best thing if you an he got on yer way. There's a kin o Board run this place, an I never ken when one o them'll turn up.'

'What is it ye do here, onywey?' Rob enquired. 'I mind you tellin me you'd got the job, but I never really kent whit it wis.'

'The idea was to make it a kind o tourist thing, wi tours o the buildin, but it never worked oot like that. Noo it's workshops an offices, business start-ups an the like. They're aa right, maist o them. Nae a lot tae it bar keep the place clean, an the lights workin. There's this Board meetin every couple o months, an I mak sure they've tea an sandwiches an gie a wee spiel aboot hoo it's gaein frae my side. Bit o doddle, maist o the time, tae be honest.'

Rob's eyes took in his surroundings. He'd never been in a prison voluntarily before. He had to concede it wasn't a bad place. It was solid enough, the cleaned-up stonework glinting in the late morning sunshine beaming through one of the few large windows in the place. A wee thing chill, owing to a lack of plaster and wallpaper, but clean. Dougie likely earned his wage, even supposing he was being casual about it. It'd be okay working in a place like this, Rob reckoned, somehow managing to forget about a certain period of time spent at Her Majesty's Pleasure.

'It's no bad' he allowed. 'Any chance o a job here?'

Dougie shook his head. 'If there wis two o us workin, they'd easy spot hoo much o a doddle this is, an then where wid I be? Come on, I'll gie ye a wee tour o the place while we wait for yer mate tae wake up.'

They walked the length of a corridor, Dougie pointing out names above doors as if he were a tour guide.

'Meikleour Management – couldnae manage their wey oot a paper bag, that lot, an they're behind hand wi their rent ... Smith an Souter, bespoke gairden ornaments – ye'd think folk wid hae mair sense than clutter themsels up wi the like o yon, but na ... Ach, ye get aa sorts here, an maist o them near as gyte as I have tae be tae put up wi them. Here's a thing, though.'

They were standing outside a door with the words "Archive Room" painted neatly above the door.

'This is a bit o a hangover from the days this place wis goin tae be the tourist trap o Central Scotland' Dougie announced, turning the handle and throwing the door wide. Rob stared at the shelves ranging almost the length and height of the room and at the dozens of volumes, solidly bound and consecutively numbered that stood on them.

'Ay,' Dougie nodded 'there's a fair bit leather went in the making o them.' His hand waved in the general direction of the room's principle occupants.

'Ye might be surprised at the number o poor folk get a mention in these record books here. Then again, mebbe no. They're aa the old prison records. Must go back to nineteen oatcake an then some. There's folk come frae the universities, sometimes, wantin tae take a look, dae a bit research, like. I take a look at some o them mysel, times, when it's slack an I've nothin better tae dae. An I'll tell ye this, some o the stuff the folk diggin through aa this come up wi – it's pish. Pure pish. There wis this fellae writin up stuff aboot a couple o guys mixed up in riots roondaboots here, an I got tae see whit they'd dane.'

'Ay?' Rob was starting to feel he was on the receiving end of a rant; it was a bit like listening to Macquarie, but politeness got the better of him, and he was smiling and nodding almost before he knew he was.

'Thing is, you cannae get inside onybody's heid. For sure you cannae when they're deid. Only some folk seem tae think ye can. It's like your ain charge sheet read back tae ye, ken whit I mean? Ay, it's mebbe aa the facts in the right order an that, but it's missin ... I cannae explain what, but ye ken it's no the whole story. Ye have tae laugh aboot it. The stuff that gets missed an naebody the wiser. Laugh or ye'd mebbe go cracks thinkin aboot it.'

Dougie began to stare ahead, his arms gesturing helplessly in a way that made Rob nervous. Finally Dougie sighed and shook his head.

'Ach, that's enough o my blethers. You look like you could use somethin mair tae eat. There's a wee kinda coffee stall place by the main gate – did ye no see it on yer wey in? We'll get a cup o soup there, then mebbe you can gie me a hand wi the East Wing. It's needin a right clean. They used tae keep the criminally insane ower there. Nothin much changes ...'

Tulloch woke with a start. He'd no idea how long he'd been asleep or where he was. He still shivered, in spite of the blanket he pulled quickly round him. He looked up, his eyes drawn by the light from a window high in the wall. Turning his head, he could make out a strange pattern on the opposite wall. He stared at row upon row of notches, tallied off in sevens. There seemed to be hundreds of them. Tulloch began to count, but quickly lost patience as the notches almost ran into one another, advancing across the wall like an army marching across the stone blocks. Someone had carved something else. He peered at the shapes, trying to turn them into words. Slowly, they became letters and he could make them out:

"James Menzies. Held here. God help me"

The scratched rows made sense to him now. How many days, weeks, months? Whoever James Menzies had been, he'd kept track of time, maybe counting down the days till his release, more likely simply counting the days out, not knowing if he'd see the outside ever again, fearing he might die in this place. Tulloch shivered again, this time for a different reason. Then he heard voices coming toward the door. It opened to reveal Rob and a man he seemed to remember from when he'd entered ... wherever he was. Tulloch tried rising from the bed only for the floor to spin in front of his eyes till he found his weight had deposited him once more on the mattress.

The other man was shaking his head.

'You're going to need another night's rest afore ye're fit.'

Whoever he was, he was right, Tulloch admitted to himself.

'Well, ye cannae stay in this place overnight. I switch on the alarms afore I leave, an I'm no humphin my arse back here at God kens when because one o youse pair tripped one o them.'

Dougie shook his head.

'Only thing I kin dae is take ye back tae my place. Wee cottage the other side o Dunkeld. There's a spare bed an a settee that's no bad so long's you dinnae want tae stretch.'

Rob and Tulloch digested the invitation, deciding in almost the same length of time it was the best they were going to get, and nodded almost in unison.

At least it isn't raining, Tulloch thought to himself as he padded away from the accommodation of the previous night. The outskirts of Dunkeld were soon behind him, but it was going to take him a good while to get near Loch Tay, never mind Dunpark House.

Rob watched Tulloch almost disappear before he began walking in the same direction. Tulloch hadn't asked him to travel with him, which was no surprise to Rob, though it felt like a small rejection. Rob wasn't the one with some strange mission to fulfill, but he knew fine Tulloch had one, same as he knew he wasn't likely to last five minutes without someone watching out for him, so Rob had decided he was the one who ought to do the watching. At a distance, of course. Wouldn't do for Tulloch to think Rob might be worried about him.

Tulloch had stepped off the road to rest for a moment when he heard the sound. It seemed as if it might be human, but he couldn't be sure. Wondering if a trapped animal would make a noise like that, Tulloch moved in the direction the sound had come from. What met his eyes after a minute or two of walking wasn't anything he'd expected to see in the middle of wildest Perthshire. Lying on the ground, a man in a grubby overcoat was clutching his arms and legs against his chest in an almost foetal position, moaning now and again as he rocked back and forth. It was several seconds before Tulloch recognised him as the man who'd pursued Rob and him after they'd left the Balornie Arms.

'Inspector Macquarie?'

Macquarie stared up at the man whose question was more of a statement than an enquiry. He struggled to place the tall, skinny fellow looking directly into his eyes, till he remembered the man on the wall outside Balornie and the time he'd spent looking for his car keys.

He'd given up the struggle, the other night in Balornie, and instead spent the rest of it freezing his arse off in the car. Come the dawn, it had still taken him a good few hours to find them, so long that he'd been so knackered the only thing for it was another kip. Today had been no better, and if only he'd not spotted that lassie wearing near damn all, he wouldn't now be lying on the ground, realising that whatever revenge he might have been planning on the wee shite standing over him was going to be a dish he'd be eating very cold.

'What brings you to this part of Perthshire, Inspector?'

Macquarie didn't like the skinny bastard's tone any more than he liked the turn the conversation was taking. All the same, he couldn't help his eyes flicking toward the abandoned car or the camera still lying where the other woman had put it before running off after the one that had been sitting on the rock in next to nothing.

That was what had caught his eye, of course. He'd got out of his car to answer a call of nature when he'd heard voices, and that's what had led him to where he was now, lying on the ground with what felt like near enough half his bones broken. He'd been looking at the lassie for less than a minute, but it was long enough for the other one to spot him and take the legs of the camera and beat him round the head with them. Then, when the one he'd been watching had run off, the other lassie had left him with his bruises till the bastard in front of him appeared out of nowhere. Macquarie knew another question was going to follow the first one, but he wasn't going to let his tongue go loose on him this time.

Tulloch looked to where a car sat with its doors open. He recognised it almost immediately, though he hadn't seen it in three years. On closer inspection he could see some clothes lying on the back seat, along with a bra. Tulloch didn't know if a police examination would reveal his fingerprints on the clasp, but the size looked about right. His mind was flashing to part of his conversation with Luce, when she'd told him that Heather wanted her to pose for a photograph that would reproduce something one of the early photographers had done. Julia something Cameron. Yet another one. Maybe he was jumping to a conclusion, but he felt certain Luce was around here somewhere and probably freezing to death by now. He looked at the bra again, then turned to Macquarie, still lying on his back, but quiet now, walked over to him and stuck his face close enough to Macquarie's to feel his nervous breath on his face.

'Where did she go?'

Macquarie stared at him as if he was mad. Then Tulloch had his hands on the lapels of his coat, and was shaking him hard as he repeated his question.

'Where did who go?' Macquarie responded, knowing fine who

was being asked about, the same as he knew he'd need to give him an answer or get another beating worse than the one he'd already had. Only he'd always been more stubborn than was good for him, and service training had drummed into him that you give away as little as possible

Tulloch didn't have the benefit of any training that might help in this situation, so he used brute force instead. Macquarie suddenly found himself on his back, his arms pinioned in a savage full nelson. Tulloch sat astride him despite his squirming, his voice demanding

'From the top! Tell me what happened and which way she went.'

'I only stopped tae have a pee! Then I saw this lassie sittin on yon rock ower there, wi nae mair than a vest on an ... I had a look, at wis aa! I didnae dae anythin else, honest I didnae!'

'Then?'

'This other lassie, she had a muckle great camera an she sees me, yells tae the lassie sittin on yon bank o scree ower there, then comes at me wi the tripod thingummy an starts hittin me wi it.'

'Sounds as if you deserved it. What happened next?'

'The lassie I'd been lookin at runs off, an the other lassie runs after her, an that's aa I ken till you grabbed haud o me.'

'You must have seen which way they ran.'

Macquarie could do no more than jerk his head.

'That way! Toward yon trees!'

Thinking again of the bra lying on the back seat and of Macquarie's fingers anywhere near it was enough to make Tulloch want to give the man's arms a further twist, but that would have taken time he didn't think he had. In a second, he was up and running in the direction of the stand of timber.

Macquarie pushed himself over on to his side and allowed

himself to sob. He'd have lain there for long enough, only he heard something like footsteps that might be headed his way. He struggled to his feet and looked around. No sign of anyone so far, but no sense in taking chances, any more than taking another beating. He recollected he still had a car around there somewhere, if he could remember where he'd parked it. At least this time he wouldn't have to spend the night looking for the keys.

Loch Tay

Stories of what happened at Tranent come dripping slowly into Edinburgh over the next few days. Unbelievable that six at least had been killed that day. Unarmed, or so it was claimed, but in any case killed outright by the soldiers. The story goes that the rioters that have been caught will be put on trial. There's a chance they've picked up someone who could mention your name, or worse than that. Tam and Archie do little more than stare and mope, exactly when you need "Republica" up in the air again, and as soon as possible. You wheedle and even plead with them, but the shock of the affair at Tranent stops them doing a damn thing. Eventually you persuade them that they ought at least to fire up "Republica" if only to see she's all right. By Friday, you've managed to get them to agree to that. If they only manage to get her burner going, you'll take your chance. The next day comes and by the late afternoon, "Republica" – or at least the bits of her – are lying close by the houses of Lower Calton. Tam and Archie take their time, but eventually the burner is fired up. Tam is about to damp the fire back down, only you grab him before he can do that and swing him sideways. You see Archie glaring at you. Pulling the pistol from under your coat, you wave it at them. They're taking you away from here, you tell them. Archie tries a lunge, but you shout at him not to be a fool. You tell them you're taking the balloon. You hope the damn thing will get you as far away from here as possible. Tam and Archie stare at you as if you're mad. Maybe you are, but perhaps that's what you have to be to think a balloon like "Republica" is the best means of getting away from all this nonsense. It's only then you realise you're in the hands of Tam and Archie, far more than they are in yours. It scares you a bit when you think of that. The thing is, they don't trust you any more than you can trust them, and you're none too certain they're capable of taking you anywhere you might want to go in any case. You gesture with the pistol for Tam to fire up again. He does, though it's plain he's none too keen to do it. Then Archie asks where you want to be taken, and you've no answer to that, so give a great laugh, as if you really were mad, and point the pistol at Tam again. He lets the fire flare and you feel "Republica" rising off the ground. You hold yourself for a moment, keeping your eyes on the pair of them till you can't resist any longer and you take a peep over the side to watch as the city below grows smaller and smaller and you're heading toward the Forth and whatever sort of future you may still have. You're in command, or so you tell yourself, but Tam and Archie command the balloon, so far as it can be commanded, seeing as the wind can drive it in any direction it chooses. The fire is dying now, and the balloon is losing height. You're still over the Forth and none of you want to come down over water, with the only chance of rescue some fisherman with more superstition than sense. Tam gets the flame going once more, nursing it till the balloon starts making height again, and then steps back. You still have the pistol pointing at them, though you all know that there's damn little point to your performance. You might kill one of them, but the other would be on you in a second and in the confined space of the basket, you wouldn't be sure of winning the fight. So here you are, the three of you, sworn enemies that once were friends, tied together for as long as this journey lasts. You've no idea how long it will, and in one way, you don't want it to end. As soon as it does, you'll be back to earth with more than a bump, seeing that wherever you land, one bunch or the other will be after you. You can't stay in the sky forever, though you've no idea where you want to go anyway. You have to travel on, and no matter how hard it is, you have to hope.

Perth

Dawn and Eddie crossed the street. "Premier Vehicle Hire, Where You Are Always First" read the sign above a building that had been new when Queen Elizabeth II was first on the throne. Now it looked as if it was quietly going to seed, and Premier Vehicle Hire along with it. Dawn had already told Eddie in no uncertain terms that he was completely out of his mind, and Eddie reckoned she was probably right. He considered the case for the prosecution; transporting and depositing a dead body, failing to mention same to the local constabulary, appropriating the deceased's vehicle, then proceeding to try and hire another car, naively hoping thereby to avoid all said previous offences coming up on police radar. Guilty, m' lady, all too guilty. Still, needs must, if he was to get to Dunpark House.

The woman behind the counter looked up from *Hello* as Eddie and Dawn entered.

'We'd like to hire a car ... '

Eddie had barely got the words out before a glossy brochure was thrust across the counter at him.

'That shows all the models in our fleet, sir, along with hire charges, by day, week or month.'

Eddie flicked through the brochure till he came on what looked suitably anonymous, speedy yet economical enough for his both his purpose and his wallet.

'How about this?' he asked Dawn, who was studiously looking out of the showroom window.

'I'm afraid we don't have that particular model available, sir.'

Eddie sighed loudly. Asking why, if it was in the brochure, there wasn't one available clearly wasn't going to get him anywhere.

'What about that one?'

The woman smiled and shook her head.

'Why don't you simply tell me what you do have?' Eddie suggested.

'All we have available at the moment is that one.' A jerk of the woman's head took his eyes in the direction of a Volkswagen Polo, the unfortunate victim of some particularly nasty accident earlier in its career, which a bad repair and even worse re-spray completely failed to disguise.

'It's perfect. We'll take it' Eddie announced.

The woman's jaw dropped almost as far as Dawn's.

'How much?'

The woman's reply all but dropped Eddie's jaw. He dragged a credit card from his wallet, thinking that the cost of his trip so far had all but wiped any surplus from his fee for the documentary he hadn't yet started to make.

Still, if he'd not taken up the chance to make it, he'd never have met Dawn again; on the other hand, if he'd never had that encounter in the Assembly Rooms, he could have had his feet up in his Vauxhall flat by now, his hands round a warm cup of coffee, wondering whatever happened to a certain lady who might have been in his life.

Eddie and Dawn approached their new vehicle with a caution normally reserved for booby traps and Jehovah's Witnesses. Dawn wished Eddie would stop playing with the keys. She was beginning to feel nervous about the whole Dunpark House idea and Eddie wasn't helping. Then Eddie stopped dead in his tracks and began to stare at the sky.

Above him, in the middle of the street, a balloon floated. Although there was practically no wind, the balloon came toward him, low enough for him to see the basket below it clearly and the young woman standing in it. Her eyes seemed to reproach him. Eddie felt his stomach pitch as if he were about to be seasick. Though the air was chill, he could feel heat rise to his cheeks and sweat break out across his chest. Then the balloon rose and began to disappear northward till it was a bare pinprick against the sky.

Of course he didn't believe in apparitions or whatever you called them, certainly not in broad daylight in the middle of large towns, but he had seen it. The balloon was no more a figment of his imagination than it had been the last time he'd seen it, and explaining it away as a hallucination was more nonsensical than admitting he'd seen what looked like an eighteenth-century flying machine cruise the length of Perth High Street.

'What's the matter, Eddie?' Dawn's voice seemed to come from somewhere far from where he was.

'I've seen something' Eddie replied softly.

A peek into Eddie's eyes told Dawn he wasn't joking. She tried lightening his mood.

'Not after you, is it?'

'I rather think it might be.'

'Eddie, what are you talking about?'

'A damn great balloon.'

'Not talking about yourself again, are you?'

The look Dawn got from Eddie stopped the words almost as she was saying them. Whatever Eddie had seen, it wasn't good news.

'I've been seeing this thing on and off since I started the journey. Exactly what I said. A damn great balloon. Well, sometimes it look bigger, sometimes it's smaller ...'

His voice trailed off. Dawn hadn't got a clue what he was on about, and there was no reason she should.

'You're serious about this, aren't you?'

Dawn was appraising Eddie with the attention a psychiatrist might give a particularly disturbed patient. Eddie nodded.

'When did it start? I mean, when did you start seeing it?'

'We were about half-a-mile from the Forth Road Bridge.'

'And it was a balloon?' Dawn repeated.

'Yes. Not a kid's balloon, nor the sort of thing you get at fairgrounds. There was a basket, with a woman in it.'

'What did she look like, this woman?'

Eddie thought for a moment. He didn't know how to describe what, or whom he'd seen.

'She was waving.'

'Waving at you?'

'I supposed she was. Then again, I am a bit self-obsessed.' He was the one trying to lighten the conversation now.

'You really believe you saw this, don't you?'

Eddie nodded and Dawn shook her head.

'Eddie, I do want to believe you, I really do, but ...'

'It's all right, love. I'd be a bit worried if you did, to be honest.'

They stood bewildered by their mutual incomprehension.

'Thing is,' Eddie began again, feeling his heart somehow stumble into his mouth. 'Thing is, I think she wants me to follow her. The woman in the balloon, I mean. I can't explain it, I know that, except maybe to a psychiatrist, but that's what it feels like. As if she's trying to tell me something. If she is, trying to tell me something, I mean, then I reckon it's to do with Dunpark House.'

'What in heaven's name makes you think there's a connection?'

'I'm not certain there is a connection. I simply can't believe there isn't one. I've seen it in four different places along the route I'm taking. Maybe it is all nonsense and the best thing you can do is get me locked up and throw away the key.'

'Chance would be a fine thing!'

Dawn's eyes wrinkled suspicion, but her mouth was getting the better of the contest between anger and amusement.

'So what do you propose doing about it?' she asked.

'Not much I can do. It pops up when I least expect it to. So it's not as if I can take any sort of avoiding action, nor do I know where to be on the off chance it's going to appear again. I've no idea what to do, to be honest, except get myself to Dunpark House and do what I said I'd do.'

'What about Tulloch and this Rob whatever-his-name-is? I thought you said we had to find what had happened to them?'

Eddie sighed. He never liked his conscience pricked. It meant having to pay attention to it.

'I did. We do. I've this feeling it's all tied together in a way. Tulloch's his own reasons for this journey. Not that he's told me what they are. I wouldn't be surprised if we get to Dunpark House and find he's there already.'

'We get to Dunpark House?'

Dawn's tone didn't phase Eddie completely. Like most men, he'd assumed Dawn would do the decent thing and be completely supportive of his idea of what they ought to do next. Oh dear, Edward, he could hear his father's voice piping up, you're going to have to be more careful in future.

'Small matter of a cricket match, Eddie' Dawn continued. 'In which I've said I'll play.'

'I've told you this won't take long. It's only doing a couple of interviews.'

'It was "only a couple of interviews" till your two friends disappeared, you told me you'd "borrowed" a car off a dead bloke and we had to lose it and hire ourselves another one in case some mad inspector from Special Branch was on our tail. Now you're having hallucinations. Eddie, you're trying my patience, you really are.'

Eddie bowed his head at Dawn's verdict. Nothing else for it but make an outrageous promise and hope he could keep it.

'The match is on Friday, isn't it?'

Disconcerted, Dawn nodded.

'Right. You'll be in Freuchie, wherever that is, on Friday morning. That's a promise.'

'You sure about that, Eddie?'

'I wouldn't say it if I wasn't sure' Eddie told her.

Dawn looked steadily at him.

'Lets see your hands, Eddie. I prefer you to keep them where I can see them.'

Eddie raised his hands above his head, the fingers of both still firmly crossed.

Dawn couldn't help the smile she didn't entirely feel.

'Well, Eddie, all I can say is I hope you're right. For both our sakes.'

Edinburgh, the underground city

News scarcely reached so far as Loch Tay, certainly not the kind that had made Edinburgh a hothouse of rumour since the start of the year. The sailor's mutinies at Spithead and the Nore, when whole ships' companies defied their officers and the red flag flew at mastheads alarmed many. The mutinies had been put down and a few of the ringleaders hanged, but Government stayed nervous, fearful on the least provocation. The French had actually landed, in Wales of all places, near a town called Fishguard, but only in small numbers, and had been defeated more by good fortune than good generalship. All this The Omnivore knew before he left Edinburgh. But he had to rely on others to tell him what might be going on around Loch Tay. Maclaggan and Menzies were always ready to turn the most unlikely of rumours into incontrovertible fact, particularly if they thought there might be a dram in the telling. The Omnivore had no Gaelic, which meant Maclaggan and Menzies were his only means of discovering what the folk who lived by the Loch thought of the news from Edinburgh. He could only sift every snatch of Maclaggan and Menzies' talk for whatever grains of truth there might be, however few these were. The new militia, he knew, was being spoken of, chewed over like a piece of gristle no one wanted to swallow, but could not spit out. Demonstrations against the Militia Act had begun even in country places. There was one tale, possibly true, of one such in Wigtown. Already there were folk moving around the country who seemed to have no reason to do so, greeted warmly by others who appeared to know their business. Government claimed it knew what the United Scotsmen planned before it had been agreed among the United Scotsmen themselves. The Omnivore thought little enough of such confidence. Frightened people do not act with sense or caution. The folk around Loch Tay watched and waited, as if they sensed two prizefighters pacing around each other, waiting for an opportunity to strike the first blow, yet nervous of dropping their guard or exposing a flank. Viscount Dundas was already arranging for volunteer soldiers from England to move to those districts where it was believed the Militia Act might be resisted. In safe and heedless Edinburgh, Dundas' clerks carried on their work unaware of the rumours flying in far-off towns and villages where fear of authority barely smothered a quiet, growing rage. On the first Sunday of September a greater number than was usual attended the kirks around Loch Tay, and when the morning service was ended at Dull, many stayed on to listen to Angus Cameron explain, in his own way, what the Militia Act would mean to them. Whether it was Cameron or some other persuaded them to march to Blair Castle to petition the Duke of Atholl to have the Act set aside, The Omnivore never discovered; all he knew was that a vast crowd filled the road between Dull and Blair, women as well as men, Maclaggan and Menzies among them. The number that took part ran into hundreds, and it likely seemed to those who watched them walking up the long approach to Blair Castle that the whole of the Strath was on the march. They ringed the wide space in front of the castle, standing as if uncertain what they should do next. One individual stepped forward, a paper in his hand. It was a letter, asking his Grace to abolish the Act for their own sakes, and by implication his. It was some time before a reply was sent to the waiting crowd. When it came, it asked that his Grace the Duke be given more time to consider the letter. As the duke must have hoped, his response meant that those gathered outside were left with nothing to do but melt away in ones, twos or larger numbers, till there were none left standing at his door. They did not, however, return to their homes. Instead, they gathered again on the braes around the Loch, lit bonfires and waited.

II

UP AN AWA WI
THE LAVERICK

Fearnan, by Loch Tay

Heather Inglis surveyed the damage. The camera's tripod was the thing that vexed her most. It could be repaired, of course, but that would take time and money, neither of which she had a great deal of at the moment. The car stood as she'd left it when she'd first realised that Luce had run off. Heather had initially been sure that Luce couldn't have got far in the time it had taken her to give the nasty wee creep who'd been spying on them a piece of her mind and a sharp slap, before she lost her temper completely and took a swing at the man with the tripod of her camera. A really stupid thing to have done, Heather told herself, as she struggled along with the battered tripod, her eyes searching the ground for any components her blow had loosened. There was still no sign of Luce, and Heather had no idea where in the wide country spreading out across the hillsides her companion might now be. She decided the only thing to be done was to collect up what pieces belonging to the tripod she could find and wait. Heather was sure Luce wouldn't make for Dunpark, despite the fact that where she'd parked the car couldn't be more than a mile or two from the edge of the estate. Her plan was collapsing, and she didn't have another one. It had seemed simple when, one warm summer afternoon, she'd sat down at a table outside a café, and before she'd picked up the menu, glimpsed an old man smiling at her from the next table. At first, she'd not recognised Professor Roderick MacLennan. When they began to talk over what they could do about Luce Cameron, Heather had imagined that if she could persuade Luce on this trip into Perthshire, she could somehow get her to Dunpark and achieve reconciliation. Now it seemed a fool's errand, with her the fool. A noise made her turn to watch as a large man in a dusty tracksuit emerged from the woods.

"Scuse me, but you've no seen a fellae in a muckle leather coat?' Rob asked.

Heather was too surprised to do more than shake her head.

'Thought it was a bit o a long shot, but ye dinnae ask ... '

His voice trailed off as he surveyed the chaos scattered round about them.

'What happened?'

'Long story' was all the reply Heather could manage.

'I'm no in a hurry.'

'Once upon a time' Heather almost smiled 'There were three lassies and they decided they were going to be the best band they could possibly be ... '

It took Heather and Rob the better part of the next half hour to talk through as much of their past histories as they were prepared to reveal to a total stranger. When they'd both finished, Heather gave Rob a determined look

'I'm going to Dunpark House, tell Luce's father what's happened and see if he's willing to organise a search party or at least phone the police. Coming with me?'

Rob thought for what seemed like a full minute, and then shrugged.

'I lost sight o yon Tulloch a while back, but he must've come this way. Mebbe he's caught up wi yer pal bi noo. I only hope yon Macquarie's no caught up wi either o them. So ay, let's gie Dunpark Hoose a go. I dinnae have a better idea'

Heather gave him a brief nod and they moved toward the car.

the ice house, Dunpark

It had taken McIlwraith long enough to work the central hinge free. It had to have taken the best part of a day at least, for he'd been fed again, though there was less on the plate this time. They must be running out of supplies. He still had the top and bottom hinges to work on, and it felt as if they were going to take at least as much time as the middle one. McIlwraith didn't know if he had that much time; He must be at least two days overdue by now, and there was every chance Cameron would have sent Macquarie or some other idiot after him. If he hadn't, then sooner or later the guy that was keeping him here would find a way to get help. For all McIlwraith knew, he could be phoning the police right now. He gripped the spike as if it were his dearest possession, which in a way it was, and felt for the bottom hinge.

'The following Sunday, Angus Cameron attended the service at the Kirk at Dull, as was his custom. After the service was over, the folk that were there began to ask him about the Militia Act. Pressed to explain it to them, he clambered up on the wall that went around the Kirk and, so some said afterward, told them that they ought to resist it. Whatever he or any others may

have said, before long there was a great crowd walking toward Blair Castle, and as they walked, the women began to take off their stockings and find stones to put in them. I suppose they feared that some of His Grace's people might offer them violence, though none did on that occasion. By the time they arrived at Blair Castle, the crowd must have numbered in the hundreds. There might even have been a thousand there. A petition was already drawn up for His Grace to sign, in which he promised that the Militia Act would never be put into force in Strathtay, though how he would have been able to promise such a thing I can't imagine. In any event, what His Grace did was promise to read the petition and give his opinion on it once he had. This was simply playing for time, of course, and I've no doubt that a fair few in the crowd, Angus Cameron included, must have seen the ploy for what it was. Although the folk who had gathered outside Blair Castle walked down its long driveway without an answer, they did not disperse. Instead, as the day wore on, bonfires began to appear on the hillsides around the Loch. It was then that I first saw this thing in the sky above Loch Tay. It looked very small at first, and I wondered if it was some strange kind of creature that I'd not seen before; but as it grew bigger, I could tell it was no sort of creature at all, though it was like nothing I had ever had sight of in my life. A huge globe of a thing was coming through the air, almost as it seemed toward me, with something smaller tied underneath it somehow. As it came lower and lower I could tell that there were people in what looked like a great laundry basket. The closer it got, the more sure I was that I recognised at least one of the three figures in the contraption. He looked very like your cousin, Tam Linton, and it was then I realised what the thing was; a balloon. I'd never seen such a thing before, but I'd heard that Tam had been helping James Tytler, who'd flown such things in Edinburgh a few years back. Before I could be sure it was Tam, a sudden gust took the balloon and sped it down the loch shore. I followed, though it was a few minutes before I caught sight of it again. By that time it was down on the ground, and the three men that had been in it were arguing, or rather Tam and one of them were angrily waving the other man

*away. It was then I realised the man standing beside Tam was Archibald
Cameron, heir to Dunpark. How the pair of them had got here I'd not a notion,
but they'd picked a bad time to visit, with Strathtay in the state it was. Tam
and Archie were packing the balloon in its basket when I came up. I told them
the best thing would be to find them somewhere to hide till things got a bit quieter,
and that I thought I knew a place where they could do that.'*

Royal Infirmary, Edinburgh

The skeleton of a herring gull drifted slowly past the window,
followed after a gap by a face that reminded him of an uncle he'd
known as a boy; the shape in the sky seemed to have his uncle's
plump cheeks and to be smoking a cob pipe. As the clouds continued
to drift and to change shape as they did so, Professor Roderick
MacLennan began to recollect what had happened. The floor had
slipped away from him and he'd fallen heavily. He'd no idea how
long he'd lain, till the postman rattled the letter box and shouted
loudly. Then the key in the door and Mrs. Toulmin from downstairs
telling him she'd called an ambulance. He shifted position, trying to
hold the cellular blanket against his body. How long had he been in
here? An hour? More? He knew he was luckier than many. He could
have been lying on the floor for days, undiscovered. Instead, he was
here in the hospital, waiting ... for quite what, he didn't know. Then
he saw her, coming quickly down the length of the corridor toward
him. Lucette. He'd known her from before her earliest tottering
steps, and even heavily disguised in something that looked as if
Florence Nightingale had been the last to wear it, he knew Lucette
Cameron. She was almost level with the trolley now, and he
stretched out his hand, drawing her closer to him.

'Lucette?' He didn't need the confirmation, except to reassure himself he was still alive.

'Uncle Roddy!' The shock in her voice and look were telling him things he didn't want to accept, but he smiled as strong a welcome as he could manage.

'What's happened? What's the matter?'

'Had a bit of a fall. Lucky for me the postie had a parcel for me and knew if I didn't answer the door something must be up. They had me in here in no time, I'll give them that. Trouble is, I've no idea how long I've been here, waiting to be X-rayed.'

She took hold of his hand again, told him she'd find someone to ask and was gone. A long trail of cumulonimbus spread to reveal a little old man at the controls of what might have been an areoplane, both man and machine gently breaking up as the cloud began to stretch and lengthen. MacLennan decided that as soon as Lucette came back, he would tell her.

Luce tried to still the voice in her head, the one that was telling her that the man she still called Uncle Roddy, though he was no kin to her, was dying. He'd looked so weak and small lying on the hospital trolley, barely recognisable as the man she'd known almost as long as her father. She tried to be sensible, telling herself he was over seventy and had lived alone for almost as long as she had been on the planet. The woman he'd married late in life had died before Luce had known her as more than a name who gave her birthday and Christmas presents. At the far end of the corridor, a figure moved from one doorway to another. By the time she reached the same spot, there was no one there. She turned and walked back to where he lay.

'Lucette!' The voice was urgent, and MacLennan struggled into a semi-upright position, pushing urgently upward with his hands straining against the sides of the trolley.

'Something I must tell you. It's to do with a manuscript I found in Dunpark once. Always meant to talk to you about it. It's by Neil Gow.'

'Don't talk now. You'll tire yourself out.'

'Must talk. Have to tell you about it.'

Luce was putting her arms around his shoulders. He pushed himself up till he was almost level with her face.

'I discovered the manuscript in the library. By Neil Gow, no doubt about it.'

'Uncle Roddy ... '

'Music by Scotland's greatest fiddle composer that's never been played! Think of that!'

A figure was striding along the corridor, the self-importance as evident as the sound of the footwear. The nurse wasn't alone, for a small white-coated doctor and a stout auxiliary struggled to keep up with her. Before Luce knew what was happening, Uncle Roddy was being wheeled away from her, down a side corridor.

'Lucette!' he called faintly 'Remember. Neil Gow is at Dunpark. Don't let him be lost ... '

Whatever else Professor Roderick MacLennan had to say was muffled by the hospital's labyrinths.

Standing alone in the corridor, Luce could scarcely remember when Roderick MacLennan had not been part of her life; Luce's mother had died not long after she'd turned five, leaving her to become the sole focus of her father and his childless friend. Later there'd been university, and Uncle Roddy the only person she'd known in Edinburgh at first. They'd The Forest in common, the bar he drank and she played in. The prospect of loss hit her like a sharp slap.

A figure was walking in her direction from the far end of the corridor. Sensing herself the target, she tried to will the nurse to walk on, to be on any other errand than what she sensed this one was.

'Ah ... Miss Cameron? I'm very sorry to have to tell you ...'

Luce scarcely heard the rest. She couldn't bring herself to look at the nurse, but stared through the high windows illuminating the corridor with fading sun, travelling to another place and time, where Roderick MacLennan waited, his eyes lighted with the enigma of a smile around his lips.

She stood lost for a moment, a child once more, expecting him to appear from nowhere with a "boo!" and reassurance that all was well, he hadn't left her. Then her mind began to race. There were all his friends and drinking cronies to phone round, then ... She didn't want to think about then. She felt like having a stiff drink, and The Forest was close. She hadn't set foot in the place since the band broke up, but decided to risk the stares and questions of where she'd been for so long. There might even be someone there willing to set foot in Dunpark House.

As she turned out of the hospital gate, she saw Ninian Tulloch standing by the bus stop, like the answer to an ill-made prayer. Her first instinct was to avoid him, but that was going to be difficult on a narrow pavement. Then, for no better reason than that he was one of the few people she could say she really knew, her mind raced ahead of reality. She'd hoped she could simply say "hello", tell him calmly what had happened and ask what he thought she ought to do about Uncle Roddy's last request.

Instead, 'Uncle Roddy's dead!' had blurted from her lips before she knew she'd said the words and the sad comfort of Tulloch's look brought the tears stinging her eyes. The notion she'd had crumbled to bits and a sort of madness swept it away. Luce couldn't tell even herself what made her lead Tulloch down the incline and into the huddle of buildings around the hospital.

She knew where she was going from the first step, but it was only once she'd swung open the double doors leading down the corridor that she knew why. Tulloch gazed at her as if he thought she might be out of her mind, which in a way she was. That would have been her excuse, if she'd felt she needed one, opening Dan and Billy's secret stash, pulling out the two pairs of boxing gloves and slipping Tulloch's uncomprehending hands into one of them.

You didn't need to be particularly bright or obsessed with psychoanalytic theory to have a notion of why she'd wanted to lash out at someone, anyone, or even why Tulloch had been so tempting a focus of her wrath. What, Luce wondered, as she surveyed her bruised eye the next day, had given Tulloch the strength or patience to put up with so much from her, and what had made him agree to visit a place he'd never been on what might well turn out to be a wild goose chase? The thoughts felt as if they were crowding her brain, too much to deal with at such a ridiculously early hour. She hadn't slept well and felt as if she'd not slept at all. The memories she wished she didn't have kept returning, sometimes connecting or colliding in odd ways, sometimes passing one another by, going in directions she scarcely understood. She wanted to let go of most of them, or for them to leave her in peace, but even a further attempt at sleep failed to quieten them.

It was the phone ringing that woke her. Luce had startled at the sound. Who on Earth could be telephoning her at this time? One of Roderick MacLennan's cronies who'd picked up the news of his death? Tulloch? Then Heather's voice came on the line, with another reminder of something Luce would have preferred to forget.

'Luce?'

'Yes, what is it?'

'I thought I'd better remind you about Wednesday.'

Luce had gone from blank to panic in seconds. She'd promised Heather their foray weeks ago. The last twenty-four hours had been a switchback of emotions which Heather's interruption hadn't help to calm.

Luce had breathed deeply before she spoke.

'You'll not have heard.'

'Heard what?'

'Uncle Roddy's dead.'

'What!'

'He died last evening.'

Heather could scarcely believe Luce's words. She'd spoken to MacLennan only days ago. She'd always puzzled a little about the easiness Luce had with her godfather, in spite of the almost fifty years between them. Any time he had wandered into The Forest and Luce had been there, they were in a huddle in minutes, chatting with a closeness that seemed to Heather both mystery and miracle. You're going to miss him like hell, she thought, wondering also how she'd manage without her fellow conspirator.

'Oh God, Luce, you're going to miss him.'

The silence on the line felt it might last forever, till Luce broke it.

'Yes, I will. I already do.'

Mere chance had placed Heather and Professor Roderick MacLennan at adjacent tables in a cafe one sunny summer's afternoon less than two months before. After politeness and inconsequence, conversation had turned to Luce. Since "John Knox's G Strings" had split, Luce had kept herself very much to herself. Never encountered at any concert, nor in any of the dozen or so pubs across the city where you could get a tune at least one night of the week and usually more. Never, of course, to be met with in The Forest, and so far as Heather's gentle probing could discover, without a boyfriend. Heather had been pleased MacLennan was as concerned about Luce's aimless drifting as she was, and intrigued by his unorthodox plan. Getting Luce out of Edinburgh, let alone as far as Perthshire, seemed to Heather impossible, till she discovered the photograph. Attributed to Julia Margaret Cameron, a pioneer photographer whose work dated from the 1860s, it showed a young woman in a theatrical version of "Celtic" dress, perched on a rock beside a burn.

What was miraculous and disturbing was the face, which might have been Luce's. Even the photographic model's dark skin tone seemed a match for the dark copper of Luce's own. Finding the photograph among a small collection "attributed", but not certainly, to Margaret Cameron was the catalyst of her plan but it was the Professor himself who came up with the strangest ingredient. Heather doubted Luce would believe a word of it, and whether there was one more or fewer Neil Gow manuscripts in the world didn't matter that much, surely?

Roderick MacLennan seemed to think it did, though, and he was so pleased with his scheme that Heather didn't have the heart to point out the details which might unravel it completely. Heather's silence was taken as approval. He'd tell Luce he'd been doing some research on Gow and realised a manuscript he'd seen at Dunpark had to be a tune of his. When Luce told him that Heather wanted her to be the model for one of her reconstructed photographs, MacLennan would pretend surprise, and suggest they meet up in Perthshire. The pressure exerted by the two of them and the proximity of Dunpark would somehow force Luce into the final step.

It had sounded convincing when she and MacLennan had been plotting it. Now, with the Professor dead, Heather could pick more holes than there were in a string bag. She'd pressed Luce so hard to be her model that even now, with so much else changed, Heather could only carry on with her side of the plan, in the faint hope something might come of it without her having to do anything. She'd ploughed on, trying not to sound as callous as she was sure she must.

'When's the funeral?'

Heather's enquiry switched Luce's mind to realities she wasn't ready to face. MacLennan had lived alone. Luce hadn't been sure which she dreaded most – a long-forgotten relative turning jackdaw among Uncle Roddy's possessions or going through them herself. He'd married late in life and his wife's death had left him stunned. He'd slowly reverted to an existence divided between his New Town flat, his office at the university and The Forest. With no surviving kin she'd ever known of, she'd felt a need to phone someone, his lawyer probably. Whoever he was.

'I may end up being the one making the arrangements, so I suppose I'm likely to be the first to know.'

Luce's imagination could travel no further than Monday morning, with the phone calls she'd have to make, then stopped. Professor Roderick MacLennan had lived alone for the last ten years of his life. The few friends he'd had who were still alive would be unlikely candidates to make funeral arrangements. She wasn't sure if he'd left instructions or even a will. Running away was an impulse she couldn't give in to, but a few hours out of Edinburgh might be exactly what she needed after she'd done whatever she was expected to.

Heather realised the perfect excuse to call the whole thing off was on the tip of her tongue. Luce didn't let it get further.

'It was Wednesday you were planning we do this, wasn't it?'

Heather stumbled back from the brink of assuring Luce she'd have too much to think of to worry about posing for photographs in Perthshire.

'Er ... Yes, that's right ...'

'When were you thinking of setting off?'

Luce was oddly keen to be away from Edinburgh. Then it dawned on Heather Edinburgh was probably the last place Luce would want to be while she waited to bury her beloved Uncle Roddy.

'We ought to leave about nine.'

'Let's see if we can do that, then.'

'Won't there be things you'll have to see to?'

'There will be things I have to see to, though it would probably do me good to get out of town, even for a few hours. Call me again on Tuesday night.'

Heather sighed as she put the phone down. Twenty-four-hour 'flu would be too transparent an excuse for Luce to see through. She began racking her brains for reasons not to go to Perthshire.

The morning, Luce decided, would come with what it came with. To be away from that, even for less than a day; not to have to listen while voices she hardly knew spoke unconsidered condolences down the telephone, brief acquaintances inflated themselves into lifelong friends or journalists cajoled for quotes they'd never use, to be free of them all for a few hours, she decided, would be heaven. She might even have time to think of Uncle Roddy. Any lawyers she knew – and, she was sure, any undertakers she was about to become acquainted with, would remain relentlessly professional in the face of mortality and do the thinking for her.

Too early for bed, Luce had dragged the battered cardboard box from its resting place on the top shelf in the hall cupboard. She really ought to throw away the box and its nonsense, but the thought of ridding herself of almost three years of her past still appalled her. The photograph of the three of them taken, it seemed so long ago, sharpened into focus.

She was disconcerted by her younger, smiling self, confidently looking back at her from some three years ago. This was someone who knew the world was before her, and relished taking on whatever it might present her with. She'd loved the life she had then: its unpredictability, its capacity to surprise and astound her.

Then she'd become surprised and astounded in ways she hadn't imagined and hadn't enjoyed. She'd run away from all of that and continued to feel guilty at what she'd done.

"*Triple talents unstring John Knox*"; they'd all hated the strap line, almost as much as the inanely patronising article spread across the centre pages of the Scotsman "*Weekend*" magazine.

"*Down at The Forest something is stirring. Six months ago three young women formed a band called 'John Knox's G Strings', and are now ready to launch their first album. Strings and Bows will mark their passage from playing in Edinburgh's Forest bar to a professional folk scene thriving with new talent. In the crowded bar where they first met, Heather Inglis, Luce Cameron and Kit Barber spoke of their plans for the future...*"

Encountering Tulloch had brought back memories she'd been trying to bury for almost three years. Luce skimmed the article, entranced and appalled in almost equal measure.

'Anyone who's ever played in one of these sessions,' Kit Barber explained, 'knows that now and again you come across someone you can really play with'

'You find you're on the same wavelength. You click with them and the other way round.' We move on to more recent events. 'The US tour went far

better than any of us expected,' says Heather Inglis. 'Though I'm not sure what we expected in the first place.'

'I expected you to know which side of the road we were supposed to be on!' jokes Luce Cameron, going on to explain that as the only driver, getting from gig to gig fell to Heather: on one occasion they'd been stopped by a Highway Patrol car, for cruising along the "wrong" side of the road!"

Luce returned the page to the box, then another article caught her attention.

"INTERROGATION; LUCE CAMERON:
Which living person do you most admire and why?"

Oh, that had been an easy one

"My godfather, Professor Roderick MacLennan. He taught me, and loads of other people that asking questions is sometimes a frightening thing to do, but something all of us should do, all the time.

What is your greatest extravagance?

Well made clothes. Though as far as I'm concerned, they're not extravagant, they're essential."

Easy enough to say, with a record deal in hand and a tour booked.

"What is your favourite journey?

The road from the Forth Road Bridge to my old home, Dunpark House on Loch Tay."

Once upon a time it was. Now it'd be the hardest one to make.

"What is your favourite word?

Detail."

Still true.

"When would you prefer to live?

When women weren't bullied and stereotyped. That must have been a long time ago.

Where would you like to live?

On a Greek island where the sun shines every day of the year."

Somewhere I can live at peace with myself.

"How do you enter heaven?

Wearing my best ball gown and playing my fiddle.

What film plays endlessly in Hell's cinema?

The Great Escape, of course

Who or what is the greatest love of your life?

My fiddle. It's Perthshire-made, eighteenth-century. It's supposed to have belonged to Neil Gow. A twenty first present from my godfather."

It still is my greatest love.

"What do you consider the most over-rated virtue?

Courage. An awful lot of the time it's simply doing the right or the decent thing. The rest of the time, it's attention seeking."

How our words can come back and haunt us.

"Have you ever said 'I love you' and not meant it?

I've always meant what I've said, though I've meant things in different ways."

What a smug little cow. How did they ever put up with me?

"What is the most important lesson you've ever learnt?

That it gets no better than the moment you're in. If you don't savour the present, you're in danger of leading a disappointed life, expecting something better round the corner."

Reading the silly, flip article made her wince. Disappointed at the way it had turned out? She considered for a moment. Three years since the band had split. Since she'd come downstairs, told Heather no more than that she was leaving, and never looked back. Not true. She'd looked back every time she'd walked past any pub with a session going on.

As the "G Strings" had taken more time and place in their lives, Luce had sensed relationships changing; she and Kit were still the best of friends, but as far as she'd been concerned, it was she and

Heather who were the force behind the band's public face. There was an ease between them, an understanding neither of them needed to notice, it seemed so natural.

'That was Tullibardine Lodge' Luce had smiled at Heather. 'Can we do a wedding on 22 June?'

'That's a Friday. We've the Ochil Arms on Saturday night. How long do they want at Tullibardine?'

'Three hours, I should think.'

'Seven till ten, and they can whistle for any longer.'

They'd been great days. Heather had done a lot to make them great days. Meeting her in Edinburgh again had been difficult at first. Heather was the one who had made a career for herself after the "G Strings". Luce hadn't. She wasn't going to admit to jealousy, though that was what she felt. Not resentment, but an acknowledgment Heather was able to let the past be the past, move on without feeling she was leaving something precious behind.

There had been no question or reproach from Heather since that day she'd stumbled down the stairs at Dunpark House, mumbled words she could scarcely remember now, saying there was no more band.

The two of then had agreed to close that chapter and never go back. Luce was more than grateful Heather never mentioned those days. She didn't miss them, Luce kept telling herself. Didn't miss the smoke-filled pubs or tacky venues with plumbing as dodgy as the electrics, the predatory stares of males whose ideas of what women with dark skins were like and liked as unconsidered as their allegiance to the Celts or the Huns. But God, she missed the music.

She'd lost confidence in her ability to play, because now she played so rarely. Coming in tired from a day's tour guiding, she'd barely energy to turn supper out of pasta and tinned tomatoes. Every so often, she would lift her fiddle from its case and slip into "Coilsfield House", the tune they'd always opened with.

A happy little number, which only made her feel more sad, but the one she always came back to; it was better than nothing, and she'd begun to have more than enough of nothing the past few months. She bent and unpacked the fiddle once again, caressing it as she no longer could one who would never hear her play again.

Heather had never been able to say what it was about the battered photograph that made her think it was the work of Julia Margaret Cameron. In spite of the caution of experts, she believed that somehow it had to be. Cameron and her work were well known long before Heather became interested in – her friends said "obsessed by" – the woman that potted histories almost always referred to as "a pioneer photographer" before illustrating this bald statement with reproduced calotypes of pre-Raphaelite maidens, all flowing hair and ankle-length dresses.

Heather had gone to classes, learned as much technique as she had time to these days, and finally tracked down a decent plate camera and accoutrements at a price she couldn't afford but somehow managed. She consciously tried reproducing the Julia Margaret Cameron style, but her results always felt contrived.

She knew she was getting better, but there still lurked, in all the photographs she took, a naïveté, an almost gawky self-consciousness. Getting better at what Heather had stopped regarding as a hobby was the real obsession as far as she was concerned, while the fading print became part of the plan she'd concocted with Professor MacLennan. She'd spoken about the photograph when they'd met, and almost at once MacLennan had seen Heather's wish to recreate it as an opportunity. Heather had talked to Luce about how she might reproduce the image; a young girl dressed in a thin cloak, a theatre-prop broken sword and helmet clutched in her hands. "They make a desert place and call it peace" ran the crabbed written caption.

Heather had asked Luce if she would be the model, giving a handful of lame reasons; Heather needed a model who'd bring more than sulks and demand a mighty fee; Luce looked like the girl in the original photo; at which Luce snorted, pointing out that even if the girl in the picture looked almost as dark as Luce herself, the age of the photo was the only reason. Heather countered by saying that having a Cameron pose for a copy of a Cameron photograph was appropriate. Eventually Luce had smiled and given in.

The dim sum and vegetable rice Luce had bought at the take-away on Marchmont Terrace lay barely picked at beside her bed. A near full moon struggled through the clouds passing her window. It must be nearly one, she thought, pulling the duvet with her as she struggled up from the futon. The dreams she'd had were close enough to nightmare to startle her awake. She'd heard the sounds again, as if of deep panicky breaths, of something close to struggle. Kit's face came toward her, dimly lit, her eyes wide but absent, looking through and beyond her as her mouth opened ... Shivering as she came out of the bathroom, a conversation with Heather came back. Where did Luce think it might have been taken? What looked like birch trees crowded the background, casting shadows, the sitter framed in a pool of light. It had been Luce's suggestion, as wine and warm sunlight relaxed her.

'I can think of a place.'

'Where?'

'Not far from Aberfeldy. There's a bit of scree going up ... maybe thirty feet or so. Birch trees, of course ...'

A shiver of nausea had run through her, like some sort of premonition. She was being told what she knew already; that she didn't want to go through with this.

She'd phone Heather. Tell her the trip wasn't going to happen after all, at least not with her. She hadn't been thinking clearly; the funeral was still to be arranged, there were people to phone, write to; she wasn't in any state to be of use to Heather. The only reason she'd agreed was to get out of all that. Luce paused; phoning Heather would renege on her promise. In any case, they'd be miles from Dunpark House. The chance, after all, of meeting anyone she'd not wish to was remote. You're not a little girl, Luce, so stop acting like one. Forget about what might happen till there's a reason to think it might.

Loch Tay

By now "Republica" is veering westward, across Fife. It must be a wind off the sea that's doing it. You let Tam feed some more sticks to the fire, and it blazes up, sending sparks flying in all directions. One of them gets you in your eye and you lower your head to try and get the stinging cinder out. Tam and Archie make a move then, almost wrestling you to the floor of the basket before you manage to fight your way back up. The basket is swinging more wildly than a crazy man on a rope's end, but somehow you keep your feet. The basket swings again as you pull yourself upright, to find you're staring into their eyes. You realise they're near as afraid as you are. As long as you don't let them know how scared you really are, maybe you can keep them from finding that out. You wave the pistol in a way that says keep the fire lit and your hands off me and maybe none of us will get hurt. It seems to work, for Tam works the burner a bit more, which takes the balloon up for a while. The wind has calmed for the moment, and you find "Republica" is drifting west with the wind. Moving northward as well, which isn't the direction you want to go. Too much to hope that "Republica" could make landfall in Ireland, which isn't where you'd want to be in any case, but north isn't a direction you want to go in either. You realise then that you're trapped here in this small space as much as you'd ever be anywhere on the ground. "Escape" is only an illusion, after all. If you really want to escape, you have to know both what from and where to. You think you know the answer to the first part of that, but you've really no idea about the second. Never did have, that's been your trouble. Whatever your thoughts on the matter, "Republica" is still moving with the wind, and by now there's barely enough sticks left to feed what's left of the fire. Before long you'll have to let Tam and Archie take her down somewhere. It's going to be difficult, you know that. You won't be able to watch them as easy on land as you can in this cramped basket. Tam gives a yell; he's seen something through the trees and he throws the few sticks left on the fire. He's playing the air now, letting "Republica" dance her way down toward the ground, allowing her to rise and then fall again as she moves closer and closer to where he wants her to land. There's a great loch, almost a sea, and then the land comes close and the balloon is down. The basket dunts against the earth and Tam and Archie scramble clear, but you don't. You clamber over the side after them, and drop the pistol in the process. It's two against one and you don't fancy the odds much. They let you catch your breath and then let you have it. One blow and you're on the ground and they're telling you it's over; they'll go their own way and thank you to leave them alone. As you wander in the one direction that's got a house on the horizon, you can see the first streaks of dawn breaking through the clouds. You look back at Tam and Archie, taking the brazier out of the basket, getting ready to pull the bag to the ground, and you can't help but marvel. Neither Lunardi nor Tytler himself ever got a balloon to travel this far. How many miles from Edinburgh? You've not a notion, but it must be a good many. There'd be plenty willing to pay for the secrets of how to do that, to pay for the privilege of learning what 'Republica' had to teach them. Maybe you've only now discovered why you kept on with what seemed a mad scheme. Perhaps you somehow knew all along that your destiny was tied up with that contraption, only you didn't understand why. You look again at Tam and Archie, now trying to hide the thing behind some bushes. They think they've seen the last of you. You're not so sure that they have.

Albion Road, Edinburgh

She could be the most annoying woman in creation, Luce Cameron. Heather Inglis had known that before there'd ever been "John Knox's G Strings". Maybe it had something to do with Luce having been born with half a canteen of silver cutlery in her mouth. So it seemed to Heather, till Luce had taken the band to Dunpark House, and Heather had realised that in her own parent's home you didn't have to give the water twenty four hours notice you were going to have a bath, and at least in their council house in Bannockburn you could manage to keep warm. Heather didn't have as much awe for Luce after those realisations, but for all that Luce was the one who had made them into a band. Kit was rare; she could draw sounds from a fiddle no-one else Heather knew ever had. She could glide into a fresh tune with a confidence she and Luce could follow wherever Kit chose to take them; Luce managed the band, but Kit was the glue that held it; without Luce they would never have got started; without Kit, Heather had known they were finished. Everything has its time and place and Heather had known the "G Strings" would finish one day.

She'd been lucky; moved on, found another band in need of a player, gone solo for a bit and not enjoyed it, bar the travel and playing the music. Something was missing, though. Something Heather needed, even if she hadn't a name for it. The sense another person could make of her playing, that was what she really wanted. Luce Cameron, for all the bother she could be, was the only one, apart from Kit, Heather had ever felt comfortable playing with. It was a crime she didn't play these days. A crime against music, and against herself. Heather knew the reason fine.

Luce had been the one to come down those stairs and say to her there wasn't a band any more, she was sorry but that was it. Heather had guessed the reason without Luce ever saying a word. What was likely to happen had been obvious almost from the moment they'd set foot in Dunpark House. Obvious, it seemed, to everyone except Luce. When Kit hadn't reappeared in Edinburgh and was never heard of or seen playing anywhere, you didn't need to be a genius or do any sort of detective to work out the likely reason.

What the hang did Luce think she was doing, pretending to be a tour guide? She was hiding away in a corner and wasting her talent. It had to stop. Heather remembered the moment she'd glanced through the window at the fading August sunshine and thought she was going to really have to stop trying to re-organise Luce Cameron. Luce ought to be left to make her own mind up about what she was going to do with the rest of her life, Heather had almost decided, till a "No!" screamed back at her, because a talent such as Luce's wasn't one you met every day. Leaving her to stew out the remains of something that didn't have anything to do with her was not, Heather reckoned, what friends were for. Eventually Luce would have to go back and face up to what she'd turned away from. The question Heather didn't have an answer to was when that day would come.

Then the day came when she found herself sitting a café table away from Professor MacLennan and the conversation led to their separate thoughts crystallising into a plan. Crazy, but a plan, nonetheless. One she owed her dead co-conspirator the respect of trying. The shock of MacLennan's death slowed her thoughts. She needed a clear head with some space in it to consider how she could make it work. Wednesday. A strong pot of tea was what she needed, Heather decided.

Edinburgh, the underground city

Seven days since near a thousand had walked from the Kirk at Dull to His Grace's castle at Blair Atholl. From that day, the valley had not known peace. Fires blazed every night on the hills around the Loch. In almost every village, the people had defied their ministers and torn down the hated lists. The Omnivore watched as a few feet away, the Laird rested both hands on his cane, giving attention to the voice booming from the pulpit. The security of the country, the voice said, depended upon respect for those who led it. Near enough every congregation in Perthshire heard the same sort of thing those summer Sundays. The Militia Act was not mentioned, but those who were told their obedience was not simply to the words of Jesus but to those set over them knew well what was meant. The duty of the able-bodied to defend their native soil had became a topic, along with the need to secure property against those who would follow the example of the godless French. The Omnivore listened, not seeing those in the pews behind him; the cottar folk, crofters and others that never saw a Frenchman from one year's end to the next, but feared starvation more than the lairds and gentry in front of their eyes. He'd heard talk of ministers who had become very eident in seeking out backsliders and Sabbath breakers who now had even less inducement to step over a Kirk threshold of a Sunday morning. Shepherds and any others who could find excuse to stay among the hills and trouble neither God nor their fellows were glad to do so. Lairds took greater interest than before about the numbers and ages of their tenants' children, and of those who worked on every farm and inhabited every cottage. The Omnivore began to realise he'd never taken heed of the world he lived in. Or that the world he lived in never took heed of anything except itself. The men that Maclaggan and Menzies brought to lift and carry stones for the ice-house said little. Their lives said more. These were folk who worked patches of land that would never be worth the hours and sweat spent on them, would never be profitable in ways that would make sense to the men in Edinburgh's drawing rooms. Yet not one of these men would have walked away from the poor scraps of land they could never own any more than any of the lairds he'd met would sell his estate, save in direst need. When harvest came, even the poorest piece of land would need every pair of hands that could be found to win a crop from these patches of earth. They lived from planting to gathering, any interruption at best a nuisance and at worst a disaster. The people knew all this perfectly well, and the making of lists had caused them to rise up, to try and stop their making. The knowledge that their name was in the hands of the minister or schoolmaster was a confirmation of their powerlessness at the hands of others. To pick out the letters of your name with unfamiliar wonder makes you chary of its use, anxious it may be stolen and fearful for it in the world of those with greater power. Better your name be erased than used to send you or yours far from your own land, beyond the seas to fight in wars, to die friendless and forgotten far from home. Such were the thoughts in the minds of those who tore down lists and threatened ministers and schoolmasters and who now sat around the bonfires blazing up and down the Strath. The Omnivore could see all that as clearly as he saw that he could do nothing to prevent it. This understanding had not come suddenly or at once; only as the days passed into weeks did he begin to see what the men working on the ice house already knew; that they were less than a speck to the lairds and to Government, whatever they might do. The Omnivore knew as well as they that he was no more than such a speck himself.

Marchmont Terrace, Edinburgh

Luce stared at the face in the mirror. The reflection staring back at her looked as if it was posing for a publicity shot for a women's refuge. It wouldn't look as bad in a minute or two. She couldn't deny present reality, however, any more than how she got it or what happened after. Tulloch was … she didn't know where Tulloch might be. Luce wondered if he really would make the trip to Dunpark House and search out the manuscript Uncle Roddy had been so sure was there. Busying herself with coffee making, she watched the sky shift slowly into dawn sunlight. The coffee mug warming her hands, she decided there was no point giving space to the unknown. Three years gone, and she hadn't even managed to change flats. She resented how difficult it was to move from where she'd stayed so long.

Heather had done that. Found a new band to play with, then gone solo. Luce tried hard not to admit her resentment. Heather Inglis was a successful performer. The music magazines and weekend supplements told her so. Luce, on the other hand, had picked up and dropped a number of options since the "G Strings" had ceased. None had lasted. Her yearning for those sounds the three of them had made together was an ache that stayed. You never know what you have till you throw it away. She'd no idea who had said that, but it was true for her. For a brief space, she'd been defined by what the three of them created together. Those days, that sound, were gone and she was bereft as a friendless child.

Heather and she would see each other from time to time, but she missed doing what she felt she'd been born to do. "John Knox's G Strings"; created one night in a pub drunk on it's own noise, surviving long enough to cut three CDs, do a few tours and attract some notice. She knew there were plenty bands who'd done less, yet guilt clung to her like an old coat she couldn't bear to throw away, no matter how tattered and sad it looked. She was the one who had ended it, from a sense of betrayal, hurt and a jealousy she didn't want to acknowledge. Heather had accepted reality and got on with her life. Annoyed at herself, Luce flicked her way through the directory and dialed.

'Good morning, Rankeillor, Arbuthnot and MacDonald. How may we help?'

'I believe your firm represented, er … acted for, I'm not sure what the term is, but I think Professor Roderick MacLennan was one of your clients?'

'May I ask the nature...'

'He's dead. I'm his goddaughter.'

There was a pause while the voice at the other end digested the information.

'May I ask you to hold, madam?'

She waited for several minutes before another voice came on the line.

'Good morning?'

'My name's Luce ... Lucette Cameron. It's about ... I'm sorry, I'm not used to this. Professor Roderick MacLellan is dead.'

There was silence at the other end of the line.

'Hello?' Luce's voice sounded louder to her than she'd meant it to be.

'Roddy MacLellan dead!' There was another pause. 'I'm sorry, we were friends, you know. Well perhaps you don't. You are Lucette Cameron?'

'Yes. I'm his god-daughter.'

'Of course you are. We have met, though you probably don't remember, and no reason why you should. My name's Magnus MacDonald. I'm afraid Professor MacLennan dealt with another partner. My brother, actually, but he's not in the office at the moment.'

'I'd like someone to help me ... ' Luce wasn't sure what she wanted help with. What she really wanted was someone who would take her hand, tell her it was all going to be all right and do all the things she didn't want to admit were going to have to be done without her having to even think about them anymore. A small cough echoed in her ear.

'The first thing to do is locate the will. We should have a copy here – in fact, I know we must since my brother would have drawn it up, and he'd have ensured Professor MacLellan made one. Then there are the funeral arrangements to be made ...'

'I wouldn't know where to begin ...'

'I'll give you a number to ring. They're a good firm, but try not to let them add on things like an extra car that you may not need. We'll make a proper inventory of any relevant papers, property, furnishings and so on. Then we'll tot up any outstanding debts – I doubt there are any serious ones, but the estate will be liable for any unpaid bills and such. It probably sounds a lot but it's pretty straightforward.'

'I see' responded Luce, who didn't really.

'I'm sorry to have to ask you this, Ms Cameron, but do you have a death certificate yet?'

'Er ... no.' Luce felt as if she'd forgotten to do her homework, as if this was something she ought to know but didn't.

'We'll need one, in order to begin probate on the will.'

'Will?'

'As I said, I'm sure we have a copy. Ah yes. Here we are. The computer is telling me my brother was the partner your godfather dealt with, which I knew, of course. He's the executor of Professor MacLennan's estate, along with yourself.'

'Me? I don't understand.'

'It's quite straightforward, and not something you really have to worry about. My brother Marcus will do pretty much everything that's needed. It's what we get paid for'

'I see' Luce replied, not certain what was meant, but grateful for the assurance.

'You could say, I *would* say, that Roddy MacLennan was my oldest friend. There was more than twenty years between us, though it never seemed to matter. He was very fond of you, and very, very proud. It's really not the time to say this, and not my place, but it's a pity we've not had a tune from you for such a long time, Ms. Cameron.'

Luce flinched at the unexpected mention of her past.

'One thing, though, before I give you that telephone number. Professor MacLennan dealt with my brother. I think Roddy felt I knew him too well. But if you've any questions you want to ask ... Well, Marcus switches on the meter the moment the telephone rings, if you catch my drift. If you think I may be able to help, don't hesitate to call.'

'Thank you.'

'Not at all, though Marcus would probably want me struck off for saying that. Look, this is probably the last thing you want to hear, but grief always takes the time it takes. You may find yourself in tears months from now, and wondering why you are. It's perfectly normal, believe me. As I said, whatever I can do to help, please believe me when I say that I will. Get back in touch, once you have the death certificate. Oh, I was going to give you that number ... '

The voice on the other end of the phone was taking her through what he kept referring to as his "instructions", interspersing these with delicate hints as to what items might cost, where corners might be cut if expense needed to be spared, always coupled with reassurances that the economical version was not noticeably inferior to the pricier item it replaced. The whole business made her feel uncomfortable.

Luce kept reassuring herself she wasn't the one who had died. She'd no intention of doing anything so final for a long time yet. One day she would, though, and the idea of someone else feeling remotely the way she was at the sound of the undertaker's drone wasn't Luce's idea of a good start to anyone's morning. It took the better part of an hour for her to go through this, and several minutes of nursing the remains of a cup of coffee before she could draw her courage together and pick up the telephone again.

'Good Morning, Saint Thomas and All the Apostles. May I help you?'

'I'd like to speak to someone about doing ... giving ... taking a funeral service.'

'May I ask for whom the service might be, and whether they were a member of our congregation?'

'I'm not sure about their being a member exactly' Luce tried and failed not to blurt 'it's for Professor Roddy MacLennan.'

A pause. Perhaps the voice was running through cerebral file cards, working out why the name should seem familiar, or was simply as stunned and shocked as Luce was.

'We always try to help, of course ...'

Friday afternoon was returned to several times in the conversation. Three o' clock in a church Roderick MacLennan had scarcely ever set foot in except to match or dispatch some crony of the same supposed persuasion. Luce had passed the place often enough, stuffed like an over-iced gingerbread between the university and the end of the Meadows. She speculated briefly whether it would be big enough for all those who were likely to claim Roddy MacLennan as sib, kin or friend and demand place at his funeral. That would be their funeral, Luce decided. She had enough to worry about, as the day wore toward noon. The insistent noise of the telephone interrupted as she bit into the apple that was her first concession to eating since breakfast.

'Hello, Ms. Cameron? Magnus MacDonald again. Something I ought to have mentioned. Nothing should be touched in the flat until we have probate on the will. I'm sure you aren't thinking of anything like that at the moment, but even taking a little memento's been known to gum up the works. I really ought to have said so when we last spoke, but there we are, I have now. Oh, and one other thing while I have you on the phone ...'

The gentle tone, quiet, reassuring yet relentlessly professional, confining Luce to answering questions, resumed. Something Shug at The Forest had once said struck her with all its shrewdness.

'The dead dinnae care. Mind that. They dinnae care a toss. But they aye matter.'

To matter to at least one person when we no longer matter to ourselves is maybe all any of us can hope for, Luce thought. Even Magnus MacDonald, anxious to do what he thinks right, confirms Professor Roderick MacLennan as more than leaking fluids and decomposing flesh. What he'd believed when alive was reason enough for others to take the things he'd said, written down and signed away as near enough stone tablets now he was dead. There was something rather noble about that, Luce thought. Trusting other people to do what you're no longer able to. Those other people believing it matters if not to you, at least to them, to do whatever they can for people who can no longer give a damn about any of it.

the ice house, Dunpark

He'd not removed much of the mortar around the central hinge while he worked on the other two hinges. Although his hands were a mass of blisters and sores, McIlwraith knew he had to keep at it; there was no telling when he might be interrupted by who knew what sort of unwelcome visitors. Nothing else for it then, and to his pleased surprise, the mortar around the bottom hinge came away a little easier this time. Maybe it had something to do with rising damp from the foundations that probably went as far down as the Loch's water level, though McIlwraith didn't care what the reason was, only that the work went a bit easier. He was more tired, though. In plain truth, he was puggled. He'd begun to lose track of how long he'd been in this damn place, nor had he any idea of how long it would be until he was able to get out. He felt what was left of the mortar carefully. Still a way to go. He pushed the metal into the crevice he'd already made and pushed hard. He was rewarded as tiny bits of mortar slipped away from the stonework. He pulled the spike back and thrust with it again even harder.

After that first Sunday in September, when Angus Cameron had made his speech outside the Kirk at Dull and the folk had marched to Blair Castle, and Tam Linton and Archie Cameron had come among us in a balloon, the bonfires blazed all night across the Strath of Tay. Sir William Ramsey's factor was threatened when he tried putting up a list of men that could be taken into a militia, some folk saying they'd burn his house around his ears if he tried again. The day following, a great crowd gathered in Blairgowrie village, demanding Colonel Allan Macpherson of that place sign an undertaking not to impose the Act on the people. Both Sir William and Farquharson of Persie were with him, the man Farquharson having had folk at his house the day before, demanding another of the hated lists be destroyed. None of them were able to persuade any of the folk gathered in the main street of Blairgowrie to go back to their homes until they gave an undertaking not to have any part in the business. It was the same in other places; lists torn down or burnt, ministers and schoolmasters terrorised, and everywhere the folk around the Loch demanding their lairds and other great folk prevent the Act coming into force. I knew fine that what the people wanted would never come to pass, but I also knew that in the mood they were, anything might happen, and it would be the fault of those who had refused to listen. Some, I knew, would say that the United Scotsmen were behind the demonstrations, but I saw little to prove that whoever they might be, they had any hold whatsoever over the folk that lived around the Loch. What happened, happened in the way a brawl or a ceilidh might start; it was what people felt ought to happen, and so it did. I'd played for all three gentlemen who were at Blairgowrie that day, so I knew them, though not that well. It made me uncomfortable to think how quickly the times had changed; before this, there didn't seem a great separation between the folk in the big houses and the ones that had less. Now, it was all becoming very different, and it seemed that it was all happening very fast. A dance is a fine thing, so long as everyone follows the steps and no-one breaks the circle. If they do, everything becomes confusion. What's lost is trust and respect, and those bonds, once broken, can never be repaired. The fires continued to burn on the hills above Blairgowrie, and I could see that folk moved from one fire to another, as they might from one house to another, greeting their neighbours and being sociable with one group and then another. It might have seemed harmless enough, if you didn't know what had gone before. The thought I had was of what these folk might do next, and I wondered to myself when the fires that were burning in folks hearts would ever be put out.'

A90

Heather Inglis had never told Luce how much she missed her. Not as a friend, though she liked Luce well enough, even if there had aye this thing between them. Maybe it was growing up in a council house less than a mile away from the muckle statue of Robert the Bruce on his horse, while Luce seemed to have had half of Perthshire for a playground that was the reason. Not that Luce was stuck up or anything; she couldn't help living in a great big house with Loch Tay for a pond in the garden. Luce simply knew about things she didn't, like how to open an oyster without making a mess all down your front, and Luce certainly knew how to dress. At times, things like that made Heather nervous. She wasn't nervous when Luce was playing. Heather had long ago admitted to herself that she couldn't set herself to organising the way Luce had, and whoever she played with these days, it was never the same as it had been with Luce Cameron and Kit Barber.

Heather was wrestling as fiercely with the possible consequences of her decision as she was with the wheel of the aging Triumph, manoeuvring the car off the motorway and into the slip road. Luce rubbed her eyes and yawned. She'd always been brighter the later the evening wore on; the morning light seemed sharp and harsh, hurting her eyes. She'd tried sleeping through their journey out of Edinburgh, but distractions kept waking her. Flat-bed lorries tipped scaffolding poles onto pavements beside New Town tenements; bigger lorries honked their way past on the way to the next supermarket drop; schoolchildren were deposited, shrieking, outside schools. The noises grew less as they reached the suburbs, ceasing altogether once the city was left behind. Luce curled into herself and drifted.

The day before was a dream; she'd done all she could think to do, made all the arrangements that could be made; the death had been registered, undertakers had been given "instructions", as many of Uncle Roddy's friends given the news as could be found at home or at the university. She'd steeled herself and phoned Shug at The Forest, in case there were any there would feel offended if they didn't get invited to the funeral. Now sleep was what she wanted, needed, most.

She woke to a blurred confusion of dark bluish-green water, the wind playing through it, its disturbance a sort of anger, the two elements seeming to test the strength and weakness of the other.

'The Tay' she said, immediately aware of how long it had been since she'd last seen the river and of all the contradictions both its name and the sight of it meant to her.

'Did you sleep well?'

Luce nodded. She'd had no dreams she remembered.

'You seemed that peaceful, I didn't want to disturb you.'

Luce smiled. No dreams she remembered, but sounds that she did. Notes and phrases and snatches of tune still flowed through her as they had done since they'd left the bustling streets behind. She smiled at Heather.

'Where would you like to have coffee?' she asked.

The two of them skimmed the cafe blackboard. Hot coffee and, they hoped, hot toast looked the safest option. A radio blared the previous decade's top ten at them from the safety of a shelf above the counter. Luce retaliated by mentally running through tunes she knew as well as the lines on her palm, tunes the three of them had practised and played till she had said enough. They still came back, of course, and she had come back to them, regretful of her neglect. "The Atholl Highlanders", "The Hen's March tae the Midden", "The Downfall of Paris", the tunes skipped and birled and went hay-fit, strae-fit through her head making straight for her heart. Yesterday's top ten gave way to a series of pips.

"The news at the top of the hour here on Radio Breadalbane. Police continue to search for a man believed to be in the Perthshire area, wanted in connection with an ongoing murder enquiry in Northern Ireland. A warning has been issued that the man is believed to be armed and may be dangerous ..."

Heather looked out of the window at the road that led along the river bank, stretching its glinting way toward Perth. Luce placed her cup carefully on its saucer and gently coughed. Heather nodded slightly as she turned round, and the two of them gathered themselves for the approaching struggle of settling the bill.

The sun had risen above the shade of the oaks framing the entrance to the car park. Luce flipped down the sun shield as gravel machine-gunned the chassis of Heather's car. Once they had turned back onto the main road, Luce began to turn her attention to the remembered landmarks at either side. Some remained almost as she'd imagined them. The fields straggled to a handful of optimistic acres as the land rose and the river took to bends and eddies.

The car took a corner and Luce reframed her memories. Things change and stay the same, she thought, seeing a pan-tiled cottage, but they also change, as she noticed it looked less beaten by the wind than it had before, freshened by paint and the conspicuous wealth of new town-working owners. They turned another familiar corner, and she glimpsed down a narrow track, expecting the dowdy barn which marked the Mains, instead seeing a clean, new-made road where a smartly dressed-woman was emptying shopping bags from a car. On the lea of the hill, new barns rose in aluminum-clad uniformity.

A signpost whirligigged familiar names. Trochrie, Inver. A turn here would take them in no time to Birnam Wood and to High Dunsinane. Luce remembered from school the wee shiver that skelped its way down her back when she imagined the Macbeth of Shakespeare's play lurking so close. Inver, where Neil Gow had been born, lived and died. Why had Uncle Roddy been so sure the manuscript would be somewhere in Dunpark, and not there?

Neil Gow, a man who knew where to take music. "Farewell to Whisky", "Neil Gow's Lament for his Second Wife". These were tunes that could take hold of you by the small intestine, gently squeeze the life out of you and bring it you back again. She'd never played any of them at a gig – listening to something like that was a demand too far on people wanting simply to enjoy themselves. Now and again, on her own, she'd taken her fiddle and followed, awestruck and oddly fearful, those great pieces of music to their end. They were the response of Scotland to the great sonatas; muckle, sinewy and sinuous patterns she marveled at and struggled to master. The jigs and reels were cheerful decoration, the pipe marches so much male posturing. The slow airs, though, could stand beside half the standard classical repertoire and blow them away with the grace of their simplicity. They were pure music and she loved them for that, and Neil Gow for giving them to people like her to play. Should they go west to Inver and see if they could find Uncle Roddy's missing manuscript? Luce shook her head. It wouldn't be there. Let Inver be Inver, a tourist shrine for the initiate, another halting place for those with a liking for their history in a glass case. They could dig and delve all they wanted, it wouldn't be Neil Gow they'd find. Luce eased herself back into her seat and let a set of tunes come on. The first in the set was, of course –

It Goes as Follies

"Rosin" it was called. A wee cake of stuff you ran up and down the strings of your bow to ease it across the strings of the fiddle. Luce had been nine when she'd first learnt to do that. The bow could matter more than the instrument, she'd been told. Was the instrument in some ways. A good bow could make a poor fiddle sound better than it truly was, and a poor bow bring down a good fiddle. It hadn't been easy to tuck the fiddle beneath her chin and keep it there. She'd wanted to play since the day she was able to crawl from one room of the big house to another, listening for the music floating in and out of the rooms. Sometimes simply a tune playing on a radio, sometimes her father picking out notes on his guitar. She thought she remembered her mother playing the piano, but as time went on, she became less sure. Eight, going on nine, when she first picked up a fiddle and held it, almost properly, her chin resting uncomfortably self-conscious against the wood. Then lessons, then more lessons, then something called "an exam", and after it was over, back to the lessons. It wasn't the only thing she was good at, but the music would come back to her and be welcome as an old friend when the others began to bore her. When she played, she was somewhere else, where people weren't cruel or stupid or trying to be funny only to be cruel in a stupid way. It had come to her slowly, that under the surface – under the skin she wanted to say– was the little matter of her colour. Luce made friends easily; affectionate in nature and wanting to see the best in people she liked, she'd pretend not to notice or hear what might hurt.

It was only when she'd started to play in competitions that Luce had sensed resentment expressed less in words that hurt, more in how people reacted to her, or more often didn't react. She got smiled at less, spoken to only when this was inescapable, avoided if it wasn't too obvious.

There's a lot can be done to children before their resilient optimism breaks completely; Luce never reached that point. She'd ways of finding and keeping friends who didn't care about the things that made others seem to avoid her. There were boys, of course, but most of them country-shy, awkwardly avoiding maturity; there was Nigel Oliphant too, taking her to concerts along with other pupils, thrusting CDs at her with a 'See what you make of that' and a shy smile, then disappearing into the night before she could bawl a 'Thank you' after him.

O Grades and Highers came and went, "Music" along with the rest, but none of that lessened her appetite. She'd wanted to do music at university, even if there wasn't a career in it her father could see; then her Uncle Roddy had pitched up at the house one day and spoken of the new course he was setting up "Scottish Culture; Material and Other Influences". He'd talked long enough to persuade her to at least think about it, and virtually made certain when he pointed out she could do some music courses as well. When she got to Edinburgh, The Forest was almost the closest bar to George Square and the university buildings, and the one where Uncle Roddy was most likely found.

The Happy Days of Youth

When she'd first started going to sessions in The Forest, she'd sat with her fiddle in her lap, listening and watching. Set two or three round a table and they'll start to talk, and as they talk you learn who they are; as they play you learn what they're good at, what they're less comfortable with, their style, their pace. Playing with Heather and Kit had been easy from the first. They really had 'just clicked'. She'd dreamt of being part of a band for long enough, and couldn't quite believe she'd found the makings of one so easily. Heather and Kit weren't as convinced as she. They were happy enough to talk about being a band, less enthusiastic when it came to the hard work of making words reality.

Her first attempts to set up gigs were embarrassing to look back on. She'd no idea how you set a fee, or how to make sure money that had been promised changed hands at the end of the night. How she'd managed it, and her university classes as well, Luce was never quite sure; thinking about it now made it seem one extended party, the sort you recall moments of, without being able to put any order to them. Madcap days, she thought now, a smile of nostalgia and regret playing across her lips. Playing small local venues at first, then arranging more and more events outside the city, with Heather as their driver, since she was the only one of the three with a full licence. Luce's father had come to see them at Perth, staying to chat and beam at her proudly.

The last two years at university weren't easy, all the same. She'd wished often enough she could throw in the towel; stick up two fingers, leave a note saying "gone to hell" and have done. Only neither her father nor Uncle Roddy would have let her, and the thought of the looks on their faces was enough to send her scuttling back to the library with a fit of the guilts. Her playing suffered and the band's tour dates thinned to a trickle as her final exams approached. She got through, as much to her own amazement as anyone else's; she remembered stuffing her degree certificate in its cardboard tube into a drawer as the horn of Heather's car blared impatiently. At last, she was going to make music again with the two people who really mattered to her then; heaven's gates had opened wide and she was back inside them.

Up And Awa Wi The Laverick

Boston. Chicago. Somewhere called Davenport, which sounded like a make of china, somewhere called Gary, which sounded like someone's name, and another city whose name none of them had been sure how to pronounce.

They'd an agent by then, with an agent's urge to send folk scarcely known on long-haul flights to places with strange-sounding names, there to languish in soulless hotels where the air-conditioning was dying along with the potted palms. Luce had stared into dressing table mirrors in these stopping places, wondering what had possessed them to agree to any of this, and how drunk they might have been when they did. Even the music wasn't the same. Perhaps it was the travelling, or playing in strange places, or simply the difference of it all. They'd never be the same again, Luce thought. Maybe everything simply has its time and season and theirs was drawing to a close. The tour had drained and disappointed them all. They'd been almost ten hours in the plane on the way home and scarcely a word had passed between them. It had been Kit, struggling her cases up the staircase of the Marchmont tenement, who'd turned at the stair head and called down to them.

'Stuff this for a row of Marmite soldiers! Let's go and play where we're wanted next time.'

The Raveled Hank of Yarn

Till then, Luce had wondered if there ever would be a next time, and she could have hugged Kit except for being two flights of stairs beneath her. So the agent had been called and told they'd take any gig so long as the hotel wasn't air-conditioned, the potted palms were real and they didn't have to wear dresses with tartan sashes.

They'd been called back the next day. Could they do Belfast the following Saturday. Where? The Student's Union. Benefit gig for the Student Helpline service. It felt both a come-down and a liberation, as if having failed to capture the heart of America they'd been freed to make other conquests. A strange elation contended with nervousness as they planned for the gig, which turned out to be not that far from the airport – they could fly over and be back to Edinburgh the same night. They talked idly about seeing if they could get more gigs in the North as they drove to the airport and Heather searched for a space to park. Seemingly they were appearing on the same hill as a stand-up comic called Eddie Corcoran.

Kit knew him, it turned out, but only through Tulloch, who had been his technician at one time and still loathed him. Kit had seen him perform somewhere. She'd said that he'd been quite funny, and he'd looked amusing enough when they found him standing in the auditorium, wrapped in a paisley pattern caftan of lurid greens and blues, musing on possible fates for student theatre technicians with amateurish attitudes toward performers of professional standing. They'd quietly ignored him, set up for a sound check and got on with it. Eddie brightened up the closer they got to show time, and the three of them brightened to him; they were almost flirtatious by the time Eddie excused himself back to his dressing room.

It hadn't been the best gig they'd played, and the organisers had seemed a bit disappointed at the turn-out, but it had still been manna from heaven, a drop of cool water for folk who had been parched, and they were grateful for that.

No taxis had been arranged for them and Eddie became their porter, protector and guide for the journey to the airport. He knew the city, certainly better than they did, and saved them from taking more than one wrong turning. Eddie had carried their fiddle cases down the hill from where the gig had been, to pitch up at a taxi rank perched at one end of the covered platforms of the central bus station.

Sandwiched between a couple of drunks and a pair of kids busily eating one another's brains out, they had continued to wait. Ten minutes later, they were on their own, anxious for a cab that would get them to the airport with time to check in before that last plane back to the mainland.

A cab had drawn up and a wiry man with a grin on his face jumped from the driver's seat, only to stagger as if hit from behind and collapse across the bonnet of his cab. Her mouth opened, but Luce never heard her own scream. The gunshot had been soft as a tennis ball on grass, and she heard no other sound, till a voice yelled.

'Don't stand there! Get after him!'

Eddie Corcoran had taken one slow, surprised glance at the three of them before turning toward the long street with its gable-end pictures of men in balaclavas and dark glasses, carrying guns which had seemed somehow too big for them. Luce watched Eddie running, faster than she'd have given him credit for, into blackness that nearly swallowed his shrinking figure. Hurrying footsteps quietening as they receded, then silence. The three women watched the police car coming toward them, light flashing. Its approach and the noise of the car's siren meant they had neither seen nor heard Eddie as he stumbled back.

It was only when she had heard the words "Lost him" that she had become aware of his re-appearance. The angry disappointment in Eddie's voice had been almost enough to make her jump in her skin, and a glance in his direction all the confirmation she had needed of how he was feeling.

An ambulance had arrived by then, and the man had been pulled gently from the bonnet, slid matter-of-factly onto a trolley and in through the waiting doors of the vehicle. Eddie and the band had found themselves travelling through the Belfast night, each in one of the several police cars that had arrived in the wake of the first. The questions she'd been asked had verged nervously between accusatory and banal. No, she'd not seen the taxi driver before. No, she didn't know the city. What was her relationship to Mister Edward Osnabruck Corcoran? She'd started to deny that she'd ever met anyone of that name before remembering they were talking about the comic with a garish taste in caftans, which led to even more questions. By the time they'd let her out into the chill fresh air, to wait alone for a police car to drive her to an airport from which her flight had left hours ago, Luce was ready to swear never to help a policeman across the road, never mind any of them with their so-called enquiries.

It wasn't their fault, she had told herself, wondering frantically if Kit and Heather were still cooped up in another badly decorated, over lit room, telling all they knew of every unsolved murder of the last ten years. When Heather and Kit finally did appear, the grey looks of panic in their faces brought Luce's arms round them firmly and quickly, as if they were two very frightened children, which was how they felt.

'What do we do now?'

Kit's question had hung in the air.

'We go home, and then .. ' Luce's voice trailed for a second. She hadn't got that far. They would do something.

'Then I'm taking you two to Dunpark with me and we're going to make another record.'

The words were out before she'd had time to think what she was saying. It had been the right thing to say, she'd been sure of that at the time. If she'd known what was going to happen ... She couldn't have known, of course. None of them could. Easier to predict the weather than the uncertain movements of human hearts.

In any case, their spirits had taken a battering that night. They needed a haven and Luce knew of one. Obvious, really.

Ask My Father

Not a particularly good joke, though it made Zen-sense in Luce's world. An American (of course) wanders into a pub when there's a session going on, goes up to the bar and orders a drink, leans back and starts enjoying the music. At the end of one of the tunes he turns to a young man leaning on the bar beside him and asks what the tune's called, and the man jerks his head toward one of the players. "Ask my father" he says, and the American replies "Is that right? Well, well, 'Ask My Father'". Too late to ask her father now.

After Belfast, Luce had decided they all needed time and space somewhere, free to think about nothing but the music itself and the pleasure to be had playing it. She'd take them home to Dunpark. There was enough room for all of them there, and to practise in, or they could always use one of the outbuildings if her dad wanted peace. Not that she expected him to. Even now she didn't think of him as old. He'd be fifty this year. Fifty and she'd not even sent a card. Guilt, she used to think, and still did, was a useless emotion unless or until you did something about it. Trouble was, she didn't know what to do. She hadn't then, and didn't now.

They'd headed north in Heather's car; a lot of laughter and silliness, as if they'd been let out of school, which in a way they had. Charlie Cameron was anxiously pleased to see them, fussing them to their rooms and wondering if he'd made enough supper for four. He loosened as the day wore on, saddling up Sugar Puff for Kit to ride, taking Tumshie for himself so he could show her something of the country. Luce felt as if they might be beginning to get back to where they'd been and where they belonged.

The first day had been great; Kit had never played better, Luce had thought, and her own playing rose with every lift of Kit's bow. By the day's end it all felt so right she didn't want it to end. She could have gone on playing till the next day's dawn. Later in the evening, as she came by Kit's room, there'd been sounds; human, almost a moan, but softer. She'd turned to the door, till something stopped her and she knew beyond certainty there were two people in the room. The other couldn't be Tulloch. Could only be …

Before her thought could finish, Kit's ecstatic cries blasted her back along the corridor, her feet tripping to stumble till she reached the foot of the stair and the question in Heather's face.

Heather wondered what came next; she hadn't thought through what might follow from what she'd done, trusting that somewhere between Marchmont Crescent and Dunpark House, the right words would come to her. So far they hadn't, and now they were less than ten miles away. Sitting in the car beside Luce was different from planning it out in her mind safely back in Edinburgh. She couldn't simply turn in her seat and say "Why don't we give Dunpark House a visit?" Heather had never asked Luce why she'd decided there wasn't a band any longer, that day Luce had near tripped over her feet coming down the staircase. There was no need to. Almost since they'd arrived, Heather had guessed what was likely to happen at some point. Seeing Charlie Cameron step so carefully around the edges, being watchful his watching wasn't observed would have been comic if it hadn't had the seed of a tragedy about it. Heather had never betted on anything in her life;

she knew fine how it was with Kit and Tulloch, but Kit was aye Kit, and there were things it was as well Tulloch never heard of. When she'd found herself alone in Dunpark's eerily empty drawing room and kitchen, she'd not thought that much of it. Then Luce came down the stairs with a look on her face that told her what she'd been afraid Luce would discover. So Luce announcing there wasn't a "G Strings" anymore hadn't been that surprising. One thing that *had* surprised Heather was that Luce had never picked up a fiddle in her presence from that day on. A sin Heather wasn't going to put up with any longer. All the same, Heather was canny enough to realise that whatever you do, people still do whatever they damn well want to, and that if you stand in their way they've every right to run you down.

Those were the kind of thoughts that made Heather nervous. You could plan and plot as much as you liked and still make a botch of it. When Luce's godfather, Roddy MacLennan had told her of his scheme, to tell Luce that there was a lost Neil Gow manuscript to be found in Dunpark House, she'd wanted at first to talk him out of it. Heather wasn't as convinced as MacLennan that advancing musical scholarship would be enough of an inducement. In fact, she was damn sure it wouldn't be. It was also a con.

Heather would say she never lied, and that was almost true, but what MacLennan had proposed was a pure confidence trick, and once Luce discovered it was, the situation could be even worse. No, her own plan might be clumsy and badly thought out, but at least it was honest. The problem was that very soon, Heather was going to have to be honest about what she'd done, and she wasn't looking forward to that one little bit.

Loch Tay

If you were to tell anyone how you got here, they'd never believe you. You didn't believe it yourself. How many miles had "Republica" covered, and in how many hours? You'd no idea, but this was where wind and chance had brought you. You'd no idea where Tam Linton and Archie Cameron had got to. Tam had told you once that his uncle was a man called Neil Gow, who lived somewhere nearby. The man was scarcely a name to you, and in any case the folk of the place had their own concerns – there was some kind of protest against the Militia Act going on. Hundreds of people were making their way, so you were told, to Blair Atholl. They had a petition of some sort they wanted the Duke of Atholl to sign, making him promise not to support the Militia Act. The crowd would have taken you along with them, had you let them, but you gave them the slip. It was Tam and Archie you were after, and you doubted they'd get themselves mixed up with the protesters if they could help it. You needed to find somewhere to hide in the meantime, though. Walking along the shore of the Loch you found somewhere. An old run-down place built of stone and shaped like a beehive. It was near enough ideal, for want of anything better. You could see it had once been a Masonic temple, the square and compass over the door told you that. Abandoned long ago, so no one likely to trouble you. The ones protesting, as far as you can tell, are nothing more than tired and angry souls that don't want themselves or their bairns put into any militia, keeping their failing spirits up with boasts and songs and illicit whisky. Folk desperate enough to talk endlessly about what they'd do if the French landed or the people from the next village rose up themselves were to be found all over Ireland. No surprise the same sort sit on the hills around Loch Tay waiting for something to happen without them having to do a thing to bring that about. You have to get away, only you don't know how you can; you've not a clue where Tam and Archie are to be found, and you don't know how to manage the balloon by yourself. Some of the hotter heads have left the camps on the hillsides to lay siege to one of the great houses round about. Exactly the sort of thing that will fetch soldiers and God knows what else faster than you care to think about it. Give people that have nothing to lose the chance to burden themselves with this world's goods and watch them turn into as great slaves of property as the folk they've stolen it from. You keep close to the old building, only venturing out to see if you can find Tam or Archie, living like a dog for over a week, until, on the morning of the tenth day since you landed, you see someone you never thought to see again. Mattie. How she got from Edinburgh to the Loch you haven't a notion, but there she is, bright as the morning and clear as the day itself. It's luck she doesn't see you, and so you follow her. It's not long before Mattie turns away from the main path and down a track to a cottage. Someone must have told her Tam and Archie have been hiding here, for they're out of the cottage and dancing round her before they all quickly move off toward some bushes near the shore of the Loch. It's only then you notice how many folk are lining the road, and see the soldiers on their horses and a carriage coming down it. Tam and Archie have "Republica" out of the bushes by now, and are trying to fire up the brazier, but it's a poor fire they set going. They go back toward the bushes. They must be looking for drier kindling, you reckon, but in any case this will be your best, maybe your only chance. You decide to take it, though what you'll do and how you'll manage to get "Republica" into the air, you haven't the least idea. For all that, you're up and running across the open ground toward the balloon. You take a tumble but you're quickly back on your feet and running again, only now Tam and Archie have seen you. You up your pace but they keep after you.

Fearnan

Luce settled back in her seat. Dunpark was miles away, but the thought still nagged in her brain that round a bend in the road, out the corner of her eye, she'd ... Luce shook herself. Pigs might fly or sheep might swim, but the chances of either were almost as remote as encountering the people she'd least want to meet.

Had Tulloch really set off for Dunpark, kept his promise? She'd heard nothing from him, not that she'd expected to. She hadn't fully considered the irony till after she'd got his agreement. Tulloch had been Kit's man. When he'd taken to walking them home after playing in The Forest, she'd wondered how long his move might take, and in whose direction. She'd not been that interested in him then. Now? She wasn't ready to answer that. One night Kit and Tulloch had said they were off to a party. No invitation to tag along. They'd not been seen for three days after that, until Kit sailed through the door of The Forest, the triumphant smile on her face enough preparation for Tulloch shambling in after her. Time and too much lay between her and those days. Other faces, different names flashed in and out of her mind. That was then and this was now and none of them had been Tulloch.

Was she in love with him? She wasn't ready to answer that question and wasn't sure what her answer might be. Not at the moment, at least. What about simply loving him? More time to think about that one too, please. She was still rediscovering somewhere she'd not been since …

She shook herself again, then began to wonder how she could explain what had happened in the last few days. Not that there was really much to explain. A one-night stand, less than that, and here she was fantasising about slapping someone she hadn't seen for years in the face with a relationship which might never be more than a couple of ships on a stormy night. Stop drifting and dreaming, Luce. Enough to think about in the here and now, never mind the future and a maybe. Then again, she mused, that's all the future is, a maybe which might never happen. Whatever we dream or hope for, plan and struggle and save toward isn't always what we get. So much of her life had been chance, and if she'd been born somewhere else, gone to another school, never learnt the fiddle, met Kit and Heather, well, she'd have had another life. Maybe better, maybe worse, but certainly different.

She'd not thought this way in a long time. Until the "G Strings" came to an end, everything felt as if it were part of a plan and her knowing the way each step would lead to the next. After, she'd no such illusion, but having lost her plan she'd lost her way. Lost it till she couldn't find a way back, didn't know one. She'd lived on scraps too long. Modeling at the Art College, being a tour guide, filling her days with work that did nothing but put food in her mouth and a roof over her head. There were plenty, she knew, content with that, but not her. There had to be more. She'd shriveled. Grown small among her stash of memories, which couldn't give her what playing could, if she'd had the guts or the will or whatever it took to begin again. Oh, she'd bring out her fiddle every now and then, go through a couple of tunes and put it back in its case, an old friend she visited out of duty, not love. That was what she'd banished, of course, ever since she'd run from it. Knowing that didn't make her any happier.

'Is this the place you meant?' Heather's voice broke in on her dreaming.

Luce nodded. It wasn't quite as she remembered it, but it would have to do.

Edinburgh, the underground city

There was no one to be seen on the great approach to Blair Castle now; the bonfires continued to burn on hills on the Loch sides, and groups of people moved up and down the valley, while lairds and gentry watched anxiously and wrote to Perth and Edinburgh demanding soldiers be brought in to quell the disturbances. The schoolmaster at Dull had been set backward on a horse and paraded through the village until he had let go of the session book clutched in his hands. The parish minister was said to have been treated near as bad, the pair of them pushed and bullied in the open street until they agreed not to take down anyone's name or do anything else to help put the Militia Act in force. Another rumour came across the hills from a place called Tranent, a village not far from Edinburgh. "Eight or twelve" were said to have been killed. Or maybe not, depending whose tale of what happened you believed. The troopers had drawn their swords; the protesters had ripped the tiles from the roof of the local inn and pelted the Volunteers with them; the soldiers had got out of hand, or their officers had turned a blind eye to what they did; the rioters had run wild. Whatever the truth might have been, it was lost among the standing corn in the fields around Tranent. It was hard to know what effect such news had on Angus Cameron or other bold spirits, but the day after the demonstration at Blair Castle, Sir William Stewart of Gath and his brother were forced to agree not to implement the Act. John Maclaggan and his cronies had extracted the promise from the two men before moving on to Castle Menzies. Although some had gone back to their homes, in the belief that the Duke of Atholl would make sure the Act had no effect on them, others behaved as if the demonstrations gave them licence to do as they pleased. Sir John Menzies was, in his turn, forced to sign a declaration that he opposed the Act and would not ask Government to bring soldiers among the people. There was scarce a laird or gentleman that was not forced to make such a declaration. Although most of those who signed or swore had no intention of keeping their word, the people believed that they would. Very soon letters were being sent to Perth and Edinburgh, calling for soldiers to come and bring order with them. The Provost of Perth, having heard the news from Strathtay, was anxious that as many soldiers as possible stayed near at hand. Although there were musters of Volunteers with marchings and counter-marchings, colours flying and drums beating, not a solitary soldier stirred for over a week. Meanwhile, although Maclaggan and his band had disappeared into the hills, neither His Grace the Duke nor any other gentleman felt safe even on his own property. Cameron and Menzies continued to be seen in the company of those who had delivered petitions to one landowner or another, and it was said that the two men had been seen at an inn near Aberfeldy, talking to a stranger. Rumours ran like wildfire of unknown men administering oaths and talking of revolution, but no one was ever found who matched the imaginative descriptions of the rumour-mongers. For all the oaths that were demanded, all the stravaiging up and down the shores of the Loch, and the rough handling of one or two, but one soul came to grief, and that, it was said, by accident. Nonetheless, both lairds and gentry remained nervous, writing letter after letter, pleading for soldiers, which they thought the only means by which order would be restored. The Omnivore paid as little heed as he could to what went on. The less he saw, the less he could tell those in Edinburgh who imagined they knew what was going on. The Omnivore had discovered that those who imagined they knew most were usually those who knew least. What he did know was that soldiers would arrive sooner than later and when they did nothing would be the same.

Fearnan

An hour later than they'd hoped, they found the spot that Luce had spoken of. Heather struggled the big plate camera from the back of the car.

'Give me a hand, will you?'

Luce was pulled back to the present. She'd been a wee lassie again, making her way across the countryside, roots cracking above the thin cover of soil, parched and yellowing needles crunching under her feet.

'Tripod.' Heather was trying to be professional, as she grabbed hold of the item, with its three gleamingly varnished wooden legs from Luce's hands. Setting off along the bed of the burn, Heather scouted for somewhere which looked as close as might be found to the setting of her treasured image. Luce followed Heather at what felt like a safe distance. Muddy pools challenged them every few steps; when rain came, this would become a trickle of a stream, though now its best was a handful of miniature bogs. Luce reckoned she had stepped in every one of them, and by now the tripod Heather had placed once again in her hands was an uncomfortable weight as well as difficult to grasp.

'Here.'

At the decisiveness in Heather's voice Luce let the tripod slip to the ground.

Heather was opening the canvas bag she'd slung over her shoulder so as to leave two hands free for the bulky plate camera. Luce expected lens cases, light meters, and the general paraphernalia of photography. Instead Heather produced a shift that wouldn't have looked out of place at a pre-teen disco.

The same cut and style as the one on the photograph they'd pored over; reality once again slapped her hard against previous naïveté. I'm going to look completely ridiculous, she thought.

Luce took the proffered garment and held it at arms length, as if it was something picked from a bargain rack, only fit to be instantaneously put back. Heather was busily arranging tripod legs.

As she tramped back to the car to change, the realisation of how cold she was going to be dressed in the stupid little shift that might pass without comment in a dodgy disco but certainly wasn't designed for Perthshire weather did little to lift her already flagging spirits. She was still feeling uncomfortable as she stumbled back out of the car and negotiated her way toward where Heather was setting up the plate camera.

'How do I look?' she asked, feeling stupid about seeking approval for something she wouldn't otherwise be seen dead in.

'The bra's got to go' Heather announced, turning to check the light levels.

'Not in this weather.'

'It'll show. Ruin the photograph.'

Luce flashed a look at Heather.

'I thought this photograph was for your exhibition, not *Playboy*!'

'It *is* for my exhibition! Come on Luce, it's only for a minute.'

'I know how long one of these photographs takes you. It won't be just for a minute. You'll probably want to take more than one as well.'

'I'll be as quick as I can, promise.'

'I'll freeze!'

Back in the car again, Luce unhooked her bra. She really wasn't comfortable doing this, but Heather was clearly going for the authentic look, and pleading modesty wasn't going to make her relent. Luce felt ridiculous, self-conscious and sure she was going to be deeply embarrassed once Heather had an actual photograph to show. She wasn't at all sure how she was going to feel about other people seeing it either. At least they were far enough away from any sort of road for no one else to see anything of their foolish nonsense. She only hoped she could get through the next few minutes without any more embarrassments.

the ice house, Dunpark

It was slow work, with no way of making it any quicker, but compared with the first hinge, McIlwraith reckoned he'd struck lucky. For all that, although some of the mortar had loosened, there was still a lot that hadn't. Using the spike, he'd chiseled a fair bit away, but it took a long time even to break a small piece off. He'd noticed he was still getting less food every time the tin plate was left for him. The guy's food stocks had to be getting pretty low by now. Which didn't help when you were trying to escape. You needed all your strength for something like that. How long had he been here now? He wasn't rightly sure, but it had to be days. If that was right, the sooner he was out of here, the better. McIlwraith pushed the spike harder into the mortar.

'It was luck that near where the balloon had come down was a cottage where Tam and Archie could shelter while we worked out what to do next. The very next day, it became clear that the demonstration at Blair Castle wasn't the end of the matter; a crowd at least as big went to Farquharson of Persie's house, its bonny gardens trampled by near as many feet as had walked from the Kirk at Dull to Blair Atholl, and they made Farquharson promise to oppose the Militia Act. Other gentlemen in the area found that they had to receive the same sort of visitors. Sir John Menzies was one, and after the crowd had got his promise to oppose the Act, they walked back close to Blair Atholl, hoping, I suppose, to persuade the Duke to do the same. The Duke had got about four hundred together to defend his castle, though I doubt they could have withstood an onslaught by such numbers. The crowd waited on the hills around Blair for hours, only melting away once darkness fell. Yet even that wasn't the end of the disturbances, though the days that followed were in the main quiet enough, with folk trying to get back to the kind of life they'd known before lists were posted on kirk doors. I tried hard not to get taigled up in any of the things that went on, Nathaniel, though I knew fine that there were letters going to Perth and to Edinburgh and that they would be taken heed of before long. On Tuesday the eleventh, soldiers came from Perth. That same day, Matilda Tytler arrived in the valley, searching for Archie and Tam. It must have been about that time that soldiers came to arrest Angus Cameron. Although he told them he had done no wrong or committed any crime, he was quickly taken into custody, along with the man Menzies. A post chaise carriage at the inn was commandeered to take both men to Perth. It was clear that Tam and Archie had to leave as soon as they could. There had been talk already of "strange faces" being seen in the Strath, and two strangers with something as outlandish as a balloon in their possession would likely be arrested as Cameron and Menzies had been. The balloon still lay undisturbed where Tam and Archie had left it, and with the excitement the arrests had caused, they likely thought it the best chance they had of leaving without being stopped by soldiers or anyone else. By now, folk had begun to move toward the Perth road, *in the hope that they could stop the soldiers taking the two men, Cameron and Menzies, away to Perth. I caught a glimpse of Tam and Archie, carrying what Tam cried the burner between them. It was clear they were making for where the balloon was hid, for with everyone's attention on the carriage taking Angus Cameron and James Menzies to Perth, Tam and Archie would have no better chance of escape than in those very moments.'*

Meall Grieach, Perthshire

The drizzle was turning to short, sharp bursts of rain. The small birch, under which Luce was trying to shelter, was struggling valiantly against the blasts of wind throwing its branches in one direction then another. Shivering, she hugged the voluminous rain cape she'd insisted on taking. She'd pulled it from the car before Heather and she had set off up the gully, and yanked it on the moment Heather had spotted the man lurking at the edge of the trees as they'd tried to set up the photograph. Her mind traced back along the journey that ended with her shivering under a tree.

Uncle Roddy with his pleading face and last request. That madness with Tulloch, her crying into his chest as her fists beat against it, then afterward persuading him to go and find the Gow manuscript, because she was too proud or too stupid to go home. Impulsively agreeing to pose for Heather's stupid photograph because anything was better than sitting in her flat listening to lawyers and undertakers talk at her all day.

So they'd gone north, at the sunshine start of what was now a miserable day. She'd never imagined there'd be some sort of peeping tom lurking around. As soon as he'd been spotted, she'd snatched up the rain cape and run, not thinking what she was doing or where she was going. She knew it had been a stupid thing to do, for now it seemed she'd run so far she couldn't find her way back to Heather and the car. In a better frame of mind Luce might almost have laughed at yet another example of her ability to run away without thinking of the consequences, but she was cold, tired and frightened and seemed to have lost her sense of humour. Suddenly she stiffened, aware of something, uncertain what it was or might be. Then a twig snapped, the sound as loud to her as an echo across a valley.

III

FAREWELL TO
THE CREEKS

Meall Grieach

He'd lost track of time, but it had to be after noon by now, with the sun hovering a little lower in the sky than it had been an hour or so before. Then he heard a noise, scarcely more than a bird might make, but enough to draw him away from the track, toward a scrawny birch standing in the lea of the hill. Tulloch couldn't quite believe it, but the figure cowering beneath it looked like someone who ought to be in Edinburgh, not out on the Perthshire hills. He looked again, and was sure it was she. He struggled up the slope and they collapsed into one another. Tulloch drew her to him, as if holding onto her was all that allowed him to stay on feet that would have buckled beneath him otherwise. Looking into her eyes he saw relief and release mingled with a wariness the last few hours had brought.

'I'm not even going to ask how you got here. I managed to find you, that's enough to be going on with.'

Luce gave him a wee ghost smile, pulling the cape closer to her. The rain was thinning again, but the temperature wasn't rising by much.

'Can't stay here all day' Tulloch announced, taking her hand and leading her back onto the path he hoped was going to lead them somewhere there might be shelter. Tulloch noticed Luce begin to shiver; it wasn't simply the cold. The only advice he could remember for dealing with shock involved cups of tea and warm blankets. Small chance of either of those.

Still a wee bit smile on her face, and that had to be something. They stumbled back to the track, Luce's steps painful and slow at first, then gradually picking up Tulloch's quicker ones, until they found a way of walking together that was as near comfortable as they could be where they didn't know the way. They walked on in companionable silence for what seemed long enough, till in a moment, it was as if they'd turned a corner and banged into what they'd hoped for but least expected, near taking both their breath away.

Glimmering in the gathering sunlight, Loch Tay's water seemed almost to wink at them, as though the Loch itself was in on the conspiracy. They stood without moving for what felt an age, before beginning to climb the path skirting the Loch's edge. They made a strange pair, Tulloch reckoned as they stumbled along, loose stones beneath their feet lurching them in first one direction, then the other. Tulloch slipped his arm under Luce's shoulder, but this meant that if she stumbled, his own weight thrust them both further in any direction she might suddenly take. As one foot stubbornly thrust past the other, Luce scarcely realised where they were heading. Then in a moment she lost her footing completely, and her arm pulled him after her in a precipitate lurch that took them off the path and onto a steep slope, setting the pair of them stumbling toward the shore of the Loch.

Between them and the Loch lay the road; Tulloch watched the ribbon of tarmac broaden the nearer they got. There was enough of it to slow their helter-skelter pace before they would topple into the water. He felt a sharp pull on his arm as Luce's rump hit the bracken and he landed beside her. Tulloch followed her gaze down toward a car snaking its way beside the Loch side. Was it friend or foe? The last couple of days had made any vehicle an object of suspicion to Tulloch, who decided that they were not in a position to be as suspicious as they perhaps ought to be, and watched as it slowed to a halt.

Dawn had been watching the speedometer since they'd set off from Perth, ready to smack Eddie's wrist if it inched above forty, so Eddie was driving slowly enough to clock something moving on the hillside above them.

'Something's moving up there.'

'Rabbits' Dawn replied, trying not to encourage interest.

'Bollocks.'

Eddie drew the car to halt.

'If those are rabbits, they're big enough to feed the pair of us for a fortnight.'

Eddie opened the car door and stepped onto the tarmac, his eyes flicking in as many directions as possible before scrambling ponderously up the slope. Dawn watched uncertain and nervous as Eddie pulled something – which she quickly realised was someone – upright. The figure looked as if it had spent the night under a bush. More than one night, in fact. Then another figure emerged, and Dawn realised that the second one was female, and looking even more lost than her companion.

Tulloch drifted from dozing to wakefulness and back to almost sleep, oblivious to Eddie driving as if he had crates of eggs on the back seat instead of two exhausted human beings. How Eddie had managed to be so very much in the right place at the right time, Tulloch could no more have explained than how he had found Luce. He tried the shadow of a smile on her. Her eyes lifted toward him a little, unsure; Luce couldn't quite believe she was where she was, or whom she was with. Tulloch's hand closed into hers; squeezed. She smiled then, squeezing his hand in return.

Shaking himself once more back to wakefulness, Tulloch found that his hand was still holding Luce's and let out a sigh. A warm fuzz of thankful relief and a curious happiness was bringing water to his eyes. He'd never been near the place in his life, but he knew that a few more miles and they'd be at Dunpark. He turned – Luce's head had rested in the crook of his arm a moment ago, now she was leaning forward, turning right, then left, searching the braes for ... What? Who? He didn't know.

He doesn't know, Luce thought to herself. He never asked, and I never said. She wondered if she ought to, even yet. For a short space, Luce had felt a comfort watching places she'd explored as a child go past the car window, as if she were watching film rewinding. Sparsely grassed hummocks and dusty tracks down which burns had long ceased to course were part of her childhood. Then the film running in her head rushed forward, till she was at Dunpark again, grown, the band shaken by Belfast but still together, looking to her for shelter from the storm around them. It had seemed so obvious, so simple.

Dunpark was where she'd been happiest. Take them all there, let them chill, practise, play together the way they had in the beginning, before they needed every gig they could get and agents hadn't hassled for a new CD every year. Each turn of the car's wheels was taking them closer. Three years, she thought, as another involuntary shiver ran through her body. Almost. Not a word in all that time. She'd never mentioned the place to anyone after she'd left. If where she was born came up in conversation, she'd say 'Perthshire' and nothing more. Sometimes they would probe, and she'd evade with a change of subject, as if being more precise would become a boring lesson in geography. Humour often saved her; when it failed, she lapsed into silence till they gave up or moved on.

Now she was almost in sight of the place, memory becoming more vivid with every turn of the wheel. Chill seized her again. Tulloch had his arm around her, pulling a rug around her with the other; she needed shelter, a warm fire and a bed to sleep away the worries she was making for herself. Warmth. Sleep. Please. Now. Her thoughts reduced to such simplicities as Eddie announced.

'Here we are.'

Edinburgh, the underground city

It was late on Tuesday morning, ten days after Angus Cameron had addressed the crowd that had gathered outside Dull's Parish Kirk, before The Omnivore saw any of the soldiers that had been promised. Then a column of horsemen came cantering along the road from Perth. The man who led them was, he learned later, Captain Samuel Colberg, and the soldiers he led were from a Volunteer regiment called the Windsor Foresters. They had orders to arrest Angus Cameron, along with James Menzies and John Maclaggan. By then Maclaggan had disappeared into the hills, as had a number of others. Even supposing the soldiers had set out in pursuit, it was clear Maclaggan was unlikely to be caught. Cameron and Menzies were another matter, however. They were found at

Cameron's cottage, calmly waiting for the soldiers to arrest them. They claimed to have done nothing wrong, and were surprised when Captain Colberg fetched a carriage from somewhere and bundled them into it. At that point, dozens appeared as if out of nowhere and would have surrounded the carriage if the soldiers had let them. Baulked of their prize, they and many more rushed to line the road leading to Perth, calling out Cameron's name and words in Gaelic The Omnivore didn't recognise. What followed were a series of blurred pictures he was never able to piece together afterward. The carriage began to move off, but as it did The Omnivore could feel the wind begin to rise and saw the crowd lining the road turned toward the Loch. The water had begun to rise in waves, with two currents seeming to rush toward each other. As they did so, the carriage sped on, till it halted in front of a group that stood in the road. The escort of soldiers halted, and one who looked as if he might be Captain Colberg rode forward toward one of the men in the road, who might have been Maclaggan. The Captain stretched out his hand, and the carriage horses were urged forward. Taking their pace to a gallop, the horses and carriage brushed aside anyone foolish enough to try and halt them, and pressed on at a furious pace. There was a roar from the crowd, which instantly began to pursue the soldiers and their prisoners. They had no chance of catching up with fast horses, of course, and before long both the soldiers and the carriage were less than specks in the distance. The Omnivore, however, continued to watch as the waters of the Loch grew more tidal, or so it seemed. From either end of the Loch water moved, slowly at first, then with greater and greater force, until two huge waves met in the middle, as if contending against one another. The waves receded then grew once more in strength and intensity, rolling forward toward each other again, to batter against one another, only to fall back once more till whatever force was behind them impelled them forward once again. Suddenly The Omnivore saw an object appear in the sky, rising from the shore of the Loch. At first he couldn't make out what it was, but as it rose in the air, he recognised its shape as the same kind he had seen when his coach had stopped outside Edinburgh. The winds that drove the water across the surface of the Loch sent the balloon scurrying first in one direction then another. His eye was drawn to something that seemed to dangle from underneath the basket of the balloon. It was several seconds before he realised it was a human figure, clutching a rope which it was trying to climb. The Omnivore couldn't believe what he saw, nor that anyone could achieve the feat it seemed to be attempting. Yet it appeared to be making some sort of progress upward, when suddenly the rope fell from the basket and the figure with it, disappearing into the waters below. The Omnivore continued to stare, scarcely believing what he had seen. As he watched, the balloon grew smaller against the horizon before it disappeared completely. Turning back to look at the road to Perth, he realised the coach and its escort were also nowhere to be seen.

Dunpark House

Luce shivered again, then lay still. Tulloch looked around the room. He'd helped her up the stairs and down a corridor and now they were here. A bed, simple chest of drawers, a chintzily out-of -place dressing table, a stool and near it the chair he was sitting on, watching her drift in and out of sleep almost as frequently as he did. She was shivering again. He got up, went over to the bed. He tried remembering the last time he'd done this; it felt like, but wasn't, that long ago. The techies he offered to help, especially the female ones, tended to be suspicious; till one or two, grudging and dubious, let him "have a go" and work on them. The word spread, and "Doctor Bones" began dreaming a career move, a brass plate at a smart address, about manipulating horse-faced women who'd fallen off hunters (or that was what they told him). But he wasn't trained, and getting the right letters after his name would have come expensive at the time.

Drawing back the cover, slipping a hand on each shoulder, pressing firmly downward, Tulloch gently worked the flesh, willing it to relax. He was tired, but he'd always been better when he was tired, till complete exhaustion finally collapsed him. He pushed on, gentling her muscles as cramps sent complaints running from fingertips to forearms. Ignoring them, he moved down her upper arms, coaxing, prodding, determined to produce the relaxation that would bring her the untroubled sleep she so clearly needed.

Her position told him to move her onto her chest, so as to let his hands begin their work down the almost-perfect column of her spine. The way she lay prevented them pressing into the sides of each vertebra easily. Tulloch slid his hands under her hips; a quick, gentle yet firm movement and she was lying with her back to him. She gave a small whispered protest as he began again. Hands travelled the length of her back, to travel upward again, fingers pushing firmly, willing the tension downward and out of her, and whatever held her in thrall beyond its power over her. Her skin was warming. He could feel that, as he let the electricity pass from her flesh to his, upward along his arms until it seemed as if he could feel her pulse explode softly inside his chest.

He only became aware of the change after his hands had taken their own wayward licence, moving slowly over her buttocks, now more firmly and insistent, building rhythm, feeling her response, slow at first, gradually becoming stronger, each downward thrust of his fingers meeting and matched by her body's own thrusts.

Little gasps from her now, her buttocks arching against his hands as they moved across the flanks of her muscles, down toward her thighs. Instinct was driving her now; no thought of where she was, on which bed she lay, or even of how exhausted her body felt. The pain she felt as she thrust against teasing fingertips became exquisite. She could hear herself, a long way away, until suddenly, like a terror dreamt of yet somehow wished, it came in a rush, filling all her flesh then slipping away into incoherence. When she returned to full consciousness, Tulloch was lying beside her, fast asleep.

'Tulloch?'

No response.

She tugged at him. Still none.

'Tulloch?'

The body beside her scarcely moved.

She tucked as much as she could of the duvet around herself, curling into the small of Tulloch's unresponsive back. Had he been awake enough to hear her last words before sleep claimed her, they would have sounded remarkably like

'Fuck you, Ninian Tulloch.'

the ice house, Dunpark

He'd been lucky again; so lucky he'd almost fallen over the length of timber lying a couple of paces the chest he'd found the diamonds in. Why he hadn't fallen over it before now, McIlwraith had no idea, but he reckoned as soon as he picked it up that it was solid enough to do the door some serious damage. He swung it toward the side where the hinges still hung, though they were barely in place now. The lock side is always stronger, he'd been told. The first couple of blows didn't seem to do that much, but a third swing of the timber against the door thrust it free of the lock, to hang yawning on what was left of its grip of one of the hinges. A kick was all it took. Free at flaming last, McIlwraith thought to himself, though he knew fine this wasn't the end of his troubles. The fresh air in his lungs felt good, all right, but he'd more than enough to think about before he could finally leave the place. He went over to the chest with the diamonds and pulled out a bag of stones. Not the biggest, maybe, but enough in it to last him long enough, even supposing he wasn't canny or had to barter the price with whoever was daft enough to fence them for him. On the way back to the door, he near tripped over something. Bending down, he discovered it was what was left of the padlock and staple off the chest. He picked up the remains and put them in his pocket. You never knew when something might come in handy. He was still in that frame of mind when he spotted the pages lying beside the other chest. Wherever the shapes of dust had gone to, McIlwraith neither knew nor cared. Good riddance to the pair of them. He picked up the loose sheets of paper and stuffed them in his other pocket, not knowing what he was going to do with them, but loath to let them lie. He walked carefully toward the open door, still wondering who might be out there and what they might want, and with no notion what he was going to do now, except that the daft old fool that put him in here was going to suffer. He'd not decided what he'd do with him yet, but it would be very painful, and very slow.

'The balloon was the only means of escape for Tam and Archie. If they'd stayed, there were enough folk that had seen "strange faces" in the valley to

cause them trouble, especially after everything else that had gone on. The Irish fellow, Oliver Corcoran, as Tam and Archie told me he was called, that had forced them to take him in the balloon, was still around somewhere. By now the soldiers were swarming around like bees in a byke. I'd seen Tam and Archie carrying the burner, so I was sure they must have been making for the balloon. A great crowd had turned out, having heard that Angus Cameron and James Menzies had been arrested. Some were following the carriage with Cameron and Menzies inside, while others were lining the road along the bank of the Loch. Then the carriage began to slow, and I could see a group of folk standing in the road, ready to stop it. The officer in charge rode up to the people and held out his hand. One of them took it, and that must have been some kind of a signal, for of a sudden the carriage and the soldiers around it galloped through and were on their way in an instant. I couldn't watch any longer, for I still had to catch up Tam and Archie. It was a while before I found the pair of them, lying behind a clump of whin and only then coming to, for Oliver Corcoran had overpowered them while they'd been searching for sticks to feed the fire that gets the balloon off the ground. They told me they'd come upon Mattie, as they cried her, and that she was minding the balloon. Archie and Tam ran toward where the balloon had been secured to the ground, only to see it lifting away from the place. I heard Archie cry out, for Matilda was in the basket that hung beneath the balloon, and we saw Oliver Corcoran clinging to the rope that still held it to the ground. The peg that held the rope was slowly coming free, and we watched helpless as Matilda tried to loosen its other end, to free the balloon before Corcoran could pull himself up into the basket. The wind that had been fresh when we set out in search of Tam and Archie was whipping into a storm and as we looked toward the Loch we could see great waves lashing first one way and then the other across its surface. Then the wind changed and played a good turn and an ill one – the balloon was caught squarely in its blast and pulled in a different direction so the peg that held its mooring rope came away. Sucked by the wind, the balloon began moving away from us. Oliver Corcoran was still struggling to reach the basket when of a sudden the rope he clung to fell free toward the water. Matilda had cut it, and as Corcoran's foot was still wrapped firmly around the rope, he and it disappeared beneath the water. The balloon was free again but it was still a prisoner of the wind. Archie and Tam ran along the shore trying to catch it up but it was no use. The balloon was climbing higher by now, and drifting further and further toward the other end of the Loch. Soon it was no more than a speck. The two lads didn't know what to do then, but I knew they had to be got away somehow. The Laird of Dunpark was the only one I could ask. Whether that was the right thing to do, I still don't know. All the same, I went to The Laird and he gave me his word he'd do what was best. Only you, Nathaniel, can tell me if what he did was the right thing also.'

Dean Terrace, Edinburgh

The sunset, Magnus Macdonald decided, was a really splendid one, as he watched yellow turn to orange verging on crimson. He'd have fished his camera from its case, bolted downstairs and tried to get a couple of photos, but the conversation he was having on his mobile was preventing him.

'Alys, you're supposed to be on Phandroupos to study Byzantine mosaics, not to buy houses! I'm sure it is lovely, but what's the asking price? So that's roughly … yes, that'd be about right … What do I think? My love, I haven't a clue! … You want me to come out and take a look? Brother Marcus would have a fit if I told him I was going to Greece to look at a house, especially if I said I was advising you … I'm not being unreasonable, but I think you're being unrealistic. Look, d' you think you can keep them sweet for a couple of weeks till I can come out? … That's my girl. I'll speak to you very soon.'

Magnus was on the point of switching his phone off and avoiding any telephone calls from his brother when a troubling recollection began to perturb him. He'd not heard from Luce Cameron since their conversations earlier in the week. Magnus dialed her number and waited while it repeatedly rang out. Eventually the voicemail message kicked in. Magnus tapped the "end call" button, rose and reached for his coat.

He had pressed the bell for Luce's Marchmont Crescent flat three times when a voice at his ear asked, in the purest of Morningside accents, if he was looking for Miss Cameron.

'As a matter of fact I am' Magnus replied, turning to face a lady whose bright, eager face might once have beamed on Miss Jean Brodie.

'She went away with her friend this morning.' the woman replied, adding 'They said something about going to Perthshire and not being back till late.'

Magnus digested the information and wondered, since the evening was already veering toward "late", what might have delayed Luce Cameron in Perthshire. He knew from MacLennan that Luce and her father had had some sort of falling out, though MacLennan hadn't confided what it was about. Magnus smiled and nodded at the woman before walking back to his car. All the way home he could hear a small voice he wasn't at all sure was his own, telling him 'You have to go to Perthshire'. Whatever the voice had to say about it, Magnus was sure the last place he wanted to go was there. Apart from the inadvisability of tracking down someone who quite possibly didn't want virtual strangers enquiring after her welfare, Magnus remembered a news report that an escaped and possibly armed criminal was on the loose in that part of the world. Paper targets were the only things Magnus had ever fired a gun at, and that had been over twenty years previously. Even if he had still been in touch with anyone from that time in his life, they were very unlikely to let him have a weapon on the off chance he bumped into some escaped potential killer. Unarmed and not very dangerous it would have to be. Not much change there, then.

Home once more, he glanced out of the window, where streetlights now shone down on passing traffic. He rang Luce's number and waited till the voicemail message asked him again to please leave his message after the tone. He went over to his laptop lying on the coffee table. He switched it on and waited for the email programme to open. Two messages from his brother, one titled "Urgent", the other "Important". They could wait. He hit 'new message' and began to type.

From: marcus.macdonald@ram.co.uk
To: ajmackenzie@sms.ed.ac.uk
Subject: In case

Heartsbeat,

I'm off to Dunpark House up in Perthshire. There's a Charles Cameron living there, whose daughter has been looking after the arrangements for Roddy MacLennan's funeral, but I can't get hold of her here in Edinburgh. Have this feeling she's at Dunpark, but can't explain why. In case I get lost or stolen by gypsies or something, please call The Forest on Friday (usual time), and if I'm not there, get them to organise a search party.

Amare te aeterno
M

Loch Tay

You're that close to the balloon you can almost touch it, but Tam is still a step ahead of you. A blow to his head and he goes down, then you turn and give Archie one under the chin. He reels back and you give him another and he's down too. You turn and you can see there's less than a couple of hundred yards between you and "Republica". You see too that the burner has its fire lit and the bag is already inflating. All you have to do is get in her, cut the mooring and you're away. You look up, and there's folk lining the road, watching as a coach makes its way along the loch shore. Get to the balloon and into the air, Oliver. Get away while you still have a chance. Never mind what else is happening that you can't do a damn thing about anyway. You feel the wind rise, quickening faster than you can quicken your pace, so that soon it has near enough the force of a storm behind it. You can see the water of the Loch begin to move, becoming waves as the wind sweeps across it. The waters on the Loch seem to build into one huge billow, getting bigger and bigger with every movement of the water, until each wave is almost as high as a house, and the water at the other end of the Loch begins to move as well. You know it's now nigh impossible to get the balloon into the air, but there's no chance for you on land. You struggle toward the balloon, and your eyes discover that Mattie is already in the basket. You've no idea how she's got here, never mind that she's sitting in the basket and glowering at you like you're the devil himself, but you don't have time to think about any of that. There's still a chance, so long as the mooring rope holds, but Mattie's there before you. Though the wind is by now buffeting "Republica" this way and that, Mattie still tries to pull the rope free of its fixing in the earth. She hardly needs to, for the gale takes a turn, spinning the balloon in an almost complete circle. It only needs to do this a couple more times, you reckon, and the mooring rope will be out of its fastening and "Republica" free. So you try the only thing you can and twist the rope around your leg and begin trying to pull yourself up toward the basket. It's hard, for every twist and turn of the wind is almost enough to knock you loose and land you back on the ground. You keep your grip, all the same, going hand over hand up the rope, but you can feel yourself being pulled back every time you manage to get one hand above the other. Each small movement is a great battle against the wind, "Republica" and Mattie herself, who pulls on the rope, in one direction, then another, till you're nearly seasick. If you look up you can see Mattie, staring daggers at you, still pulling as hard as she can on the rope, hoping with every twist of it to shake you from the hold you have on it. There's a real storm brewing in the sky by now, and the waves on the Loch are even higher, if that's possible. The trouble is you're not quite as young as you once were. You're putting every atom of strength you have into this climb, but each pull on the rope is harder than the last one, and the winds batter you this way and that and backwards if they can. Then, in a second, you feel the rope go slack beneath you, and you know without looking that "Republica" has pulled its mooring rope free of the ground. Then you look up, and watch with disbelief as the other end falls free of the balloon, going past you toward the Loch. You hear yourself scream as you start to fall backward into the Loch below you. In seconds you feel your body hit the water before you can put yourself in a position that would let you swim clear. It's no good. You can feel your body sinking under the water, as the rope around your leg is being pulled further and further beneath the waves. By now you're fighting for breath and it's not coming easy.

The same as you're fighting the exhaustion that seems to fill every atom that's in you, and you sense you won't win that struggle either.

Dunpark House

Looking into one of the full-length mirrors that marched along either wall, Luce watched a gangly-tall figure step away from a much smaller one, pacing out the room's length to its further end. Tulloch slowly turned and looked, as if he had only become aware of her in that moment, and broke the silence

'Great space.'

Luce nodded. This was her space, though. The one she hadn't thought to be in again, certainly not in these circumstances. She still wasn't sure how she felt about that, no matter how sure she had begun to feel about the man she was with, his eyes offering a shy, self-deprecating smile as he began to move toward her.

Eddie's fingers ran along the tops of spines, and then came to a halt. Thumb flicking against ring finger, he tried banishing the dust to the further end of the shelf. He had heard a few horror stories concerning the libraries of stately homes – boards hanging off mildewed first editions, their pages uncut, or pages loose and plates missing where an impecunious heir had sold them or some sub-literate scion of the house thought they'd look rather fine in the billiard room.

The library at Dunpark wasn't bad, but some thought about what can happen to books in damp rooms wouldn't have gone amiss. What made Eddie think he was going to find the answer here to the strange disappearance of Oliver Corcoran, he couldn't have begun to explain. There had to be an answer; no-one disappears off the face of planet Earth without leaving some clue leading to a reason, provided you look long enough and hard enough for it and aren't willing to take "no" for an answer. Eddie had never liked the word "no". "No" meant accepting what other people told you, giving up or giving in. He hadn't come all this way to do that.

"*A True Relation of the Kirk in Perthshire*"

No relation Eddie wanted anything to do with.

"*With Gun and Rod in Grandtully*"

Not today, thank you.

He was being stupid; it felt for a second as if the rows of leather-backed oblong items were laughing their spines off at him. Wherever Oliver Corcoran was hiding, the answer surely wasn't going to be bound in Morocco leather. He'd come to learn that in this paper chase he'd embarked on, the primary sources were rarely printed ones. He should be looking for letters, or a diary or any damn thing that wasn't a book. But where the hell was he going to find anything like that?

Luce watched Tulloch's feet pace across the polished floor. When he did reach her, his hand slipped easily to her waist, while he led her the length of the room, past the wide gilt-framed mirror in which she could see... well, not a handsome couple. How could they be? After all that had happened yesterday, and only an hour or two of rest, neither of then could be said to be looking their best, but somehow they were managing to look a couple for all that. Or was that only what she wanted to see? Still, she let her head half-rest against his shoulder, till she caught a sound she wasn't, for a moment, quite sure she'd heard.

Tulloch, wishing he had more confidence in himself than he really felt, struggled to ignore what lay between them, what they hadn't yet spoken of, had scarcely acknowledged, yet was quietly bedding down in their conscious selves. The closeness felt perfect and somehow strangely familiar, for all of its newness. He scrambled to find the right one among all the words he used to know. We're all too clever, or too stupid, to say "forever" and mean it anymore, he thought, terrified at the same time by a reality he recognised but hadn't known before. They were near as close as their skins. They might have stayed that way, if another sound hadn't broken their stillness.

Charlie was crossing the front hall when he heard it. It was only when he did that he remembered he'd not checked the ice house since Lucette and the others had arrived. He'd been busy making sure Lucette was all right, that they'd clean sheets for all the beds and how he was going to manage to stretch what little food was left to six people. There was Katherine to think of as well, and all the complicated tangle he'd no idea how to untangle, though it seemed it was unraveling without help from him ... Since last night he'd not thought what he was going to do or say. He'd pushed the questions that might be asked, the answers he wasn't sure he had, to the back of his mind. There was Lucette, and the bedraggled stranger who'd brought her home. He knew about Tulloch, of course, but he'd never asked Katherine about him. Now he wondered if he ought to have. He stood as the past and present circled in his mind. When the big fellow, Eddie, had parked the car outside the house, Charlie felt as if the cavalry had arrived. He'd been worried sick all week, less for himself than for Katherine. Now there were four other people in the house, and he ought to have felt safer because of that. He listened again for the noise he'd heard, while he chided himself that telling what he could have told them was what he ought to have done, but there had been so much else he'd needed to think about. Only the day before he'd dreamed of strangers at the door, of being able to tell them he was barely in control of a maniac he suspected might also be a murderer.

'Roderick MacLellan was Luce's god-father, wasn't he?'

They had been sitting in the drawing room, a couple of hours after Lucette had arrived. Charlie had a whisky in his outstretched hand, but the words he was about to speak in offering it to Tulloch were silenced by his guest's question.

'He's dead.' Tulloch continued. 'Sorry to be the one to tell you. Before he died, he got Luce to promise to fetch some manuscript from here. She didn't want to come back. I didn't ask her why, but it was a thing she wanted done, and I promised to do it.'

'Roddy MacLennan's dead?'

'I'm sorry you had to find out through me. Luce was the one who told me. She was fairly upset about it, so I didn't pry.'

'Did she tell you why she didn't want to tell me herself?'

'No. I didn't think it was my place to ask that. Nor to ask you either.'

Charlie rocked slowly in his chair. Had he believed in karma, in getting what the gods let you pay for, he might have managed to smile at this potentially explosive reward for his previous sins, if that was how he ought to regard the past three years. It didn't feel the least bit amusing, though.

'You must be very tired.' Charlie spoke quietly, as if turning something over in his mind. 'Speak to you in the morning, eh?'

That was all he'd said, knowing that when the next day dawned his silence would likely be a source of some scorn, that at least one of them would demand to know why he hadn't spoken the simple truth. Truth was never simple, and now he might never have a chance to tell his daughter, or anyone else … His body tensed as he heard the noise again, only louder this time.

Edinburgh, the underground city

Ten years since that time around Loch Tay. The Omnivore was still eating in other people's houses, but not so often. Fate had been kinder to him since then. He wondered, at times, what had really happened all those years ago, around Loch Tay? He remembered everything he had seen, though he knew he hadn't seen everything. There were still questions for which he had no answers. Angus Cameron, for instance, had vanished. Due to stand trial at Perth, he had been granted bail, only to disappear and had never been seen since. Neither had young Archibald Cameron, the heir to Dunpark. No one had ever been able to tell him what had happened to the lad. These things troubled him. The country around Loch Tay was quiet. Great Britain was still at war with France, but France had a dictator leading it, for all it called itself a republic, and had precious few friends in Scotland. Then one day The Omnivore received an invitation to dine. The man who had once employed him, the one who called himself Laird of Dunpark these days, was to be of the party. The Omnivore wondered what the laird might have to say about Archibald Cameron, and whether he could tell where the young man was now. After the ladies had retired, there was talk for a time of events in Spain, where a band of what were called Guerillas had recently forced a French army to surrender. The Omnivore said he wondered if these Spaniards were anything like the folk he remembered holding the hills around Loch Tay. He watched the

Laird of Dunpark react. The Laird thundered that patriots acting to save their country were nothing like the upstarts who had tried to prevent the King's laws being acted on. It was then The Omnivore decided to ask his question, the one that he'd wanted to ask for so long. He had heard that young Archibald Cameron had been seen near the Loch all those years ago, but nothing had been heard of him since that time. Did the Laird of Dunpark know where the lad might be?

The Laird stared at him, with a look that would have frozen stone. The Omnivore could feel the silence as much as hear it. He knew the company thought he had gone too far, though they probably didn't understand why he had asked such a question. The Omnivore hardly ever asked a question, but this, he said to reassure his host and the other guests, was an innocent one, surely? It was clear, however, that he was the only one to think it so. The Laird was still glowering at him. The Omnivore cleared his throat and tried again to put his question. He'd scarcely spoken a word when the Laird rose from his chair and walked toward him. His face close to The Omnivore's, he said he had not seen Archibald Cameron since that day and hoped he never saw him again. Then, sinking his mouth as close to The Omnivore's ear as he could, the Laird, whispered that he had to thank The Omnivore. His work had given the Laird exactly what he had needed. A place that was both a prison and a tomb. The Laird was walking back to his seat as what had been done, what he had done, slowly dawned on The Omnivore. At first he couldn't believe what the Laird had said, still less what he meant by it. Then it came to him in a rush. There could only be one explanation, and The Omnivore was appalled by it. He had to say something, wanted to say it very much, but felt his chest shrinking, and a pain like a stone pressing hard against his heart. He struggled for breath and could tell by the expressions on the faces of the other gentlemen that something was wrong. As he attempted to rise from his chair, the shock of knowing the work he'd done had helped a monstrous crime and great injustice broke in on him. Darkness was swallowing him and the Laird's guilt would remain unknown. He could do no more about it than ...

Dunpark House

Kit put one foot in front of the other. It felt almost as if she were learning to walk again. It must be nearly a week since she had the accident, she thought, although she had little recollection of any of it, except how it had hurt. Thankful enough to lie in bed, feel glad when she was told that Sugar Puff was all right then drift back to sleep. Now she was awake and on her feet again, wondering how long she might manage to stay on them. It took her what seemed like an age to reach the door, turn the handle and step out onto the landing.

Eddie could hear something. He walked to the door. There was no sign of anyone in the corridor. Stepping beyond the door, he walked until the corridor turned. As he rounded the corner he discovered he was staring into a pair of eyes, the maliciousness of which made him flinch. Belfast. The gig, the sudden noise, turning to watch brains spill on top of blood, standing frozen, a voice yelling 'Get after him!' He'd been running ever since. Oliver Corcoran, Archibald Cameron and the rest something to keep him busily not doing what he ought to have been doing; asking the right questions, the ones that kept him awake for hours while two orphans probably slept through the night. Now the answer was staring him in the face.

Eddie was trying hard to find his voice, think of the right question and get his lungs and larynx into a fit enough state to ask it. The man's eyes were slowly registering Eddie, trying to remember where they'd last seen him. Eddie's gaze swung first right and then left, searching rapidly for a way of escape.

He almost gasped aloud as the woman he remembered as "Kit" from the Belfast gig appeared on the other side of the landing. Eddie wanted to call something out to her, but whatever the right word was, neither his brain nor his lips could find it. As he struggled to form sounds, Eddie saw that the man in front of him had something in his hand that he was gripping fiercely. The man finally gave out a tremendous yell, as the flash of steel rose upward. Eddie flinched to avoid it, as another flash of metal, attached to a hand appeared as if from nowhere and swept across the man's face, leaving a thin line of red from eyebrow to jaw. With a scream, the man swayed backward. Eddie swung round and launched a fist at his mouth. The figure began to crumple, then recovered and stumbled toward the staircase, missing its footing and tumbling noisily toward the floor. Eddie looked at the man now at the foot of the staircase. He hadn't hit anyone since school days. He'd thought he'd feel a bit of satisfaction in finally coming to grips with the man who'd ruined more of his sleep and waking hours than he cared to count. He hadn't bargained on it making him feel rather queasy.

'You all right, Eddie?' Dawn watched Eddie sway a little, press his hand against the nearest door frame then turn to her with a self-deprecating smile.

'Yeah. Bit out of condition, that's all.'

Dawn was inspecting her ring. It had been an impulse purchase at an art college show. She'd liked the sweeping crescent of silver, but had never thought of it as offensive weaponry before. She looked down to where McIlwraith lay moaning on the floor. Charlie Cameron glanced across at McIlwraith, gripping his arms firmly behind his back in case an impulse led him to continue what Eddie had started. He turned away at the sound of a car in the drive.

Maurice Macquarie despite a night and a day on the Perthshire hills still managed a bit of the old Service swagger as he got out of the car and walked toward Charlie at the door.

'Inspector Maurice Macquarie, Special Branch.' he announced.

'Do come in, Inspector.' Charlie found himself saying, as if he were a minor character in a third-rate mystery.

Macquarie breezed past Charlie and was standing in the middle of the hall surveying a slowly recovering McIlwraith struggling to his knees. So the numpty-heid had finally got here, McIlwraith thought. He was consoled by noticing that Macquarie looked like he'd spent last night in a jungle and been mugged by the chimpanzees.

'You are under arrest, pal!' Macquarie yelled, as if to assure McIlwraith and anyone else who happened to be listening, that whatever torments the past few hours might have inflicted, he was still a force to be reckoned with.

Rob couldn't believe his eyes as Heather drove them close to the door of Dunpark House. Macquarie was emerging, handcuffed to a guy with a piercing stare that Rob found disconcertingly familiar. McIlwraith.

'This man has escaped from prison in Northern Ireland.' Macquarie announced too no one in particular, as he bundled McIlwraith onto the back seat. 'He is a dangerous convicted criminal and I'm returning him to custody. Thank you for your co-operation.'

Macquarie slammed the rear door of the car and gave a cursory wave before a burst of acceleration took the car and its contents away down the drive. Mouth still open in disbelief, Rob clambered out of the car and watched Macquarie and his prisoner became a receding speck. Charlie moved toward them, a smile on his face, hand outstretched.

Back inside Dunpark House, Eddie was examining a sheaf of papers lying near where McIlwraith had fallen. He picked them up. They looked, felt old. The hand was cramped and spidery. Something about the brittle, crumbling sheets of paper intrigued him. It was likely going to be a struggle, but he decided to read them. He had a sense that for some reason he ought to.

Charlie had recognised Heather at once, but wondered who the big fellow in the tracksuit might be.

'Hello, Heather, long time no see.' he said, as cheerfully non-committal as he could manage, considering he'd had a potential murderer under his roof moments before.

'Hello.' Heather smiled.

'Come in.' Charlie gestured them inside, unsure himself what might follow.

The house was almost as Heather remembered it from the last time she'd been there, almost three years before. Small changes, but not, she decided, ones that Charlie would have made. Kit and Luce were in the drawing room, sitting on the sofa. They turned at the sound of footsteps and Heather let her arms stretch wide to embrace them both.

Charlie looked at Rob. 'Cup of tea?' he enquired.

Rob nodded.

'Come through to the kitchen and I'll make us both one.' Charlie steered Rob past the drawing room and toward relative safety.

They'd drunk their tea in the kind of silence more usual at funerals than reunions. Charlie had made a few remarks about the weather, asked Rob what he did for a living, a question that made Rob feel uncomfortable as he had to become evasive, but the less anyone knew about his connection to Macquarie the better, as far as Rob was concerned. Eventually Charlie said something about needing to get on, but why didn't he take a walk round the place? So that was what Rob had done. Out by the kitchen door, down a path that had turned out to be muddier than it had looked until he caught sight of Charlie Cameron's prize Jerseys.

Rob wandered over to the fence at the field's edge. He needed space in his head, lots of it. He decided to forget Macquarie and McIlwraith and concentrate on the cows. It was almost as good as the holiday he'd not had in a long time, watching the beasts. He looked round. The guy that owned the place didn't seem to have anyone giving him a hand. He knew fine there wasn't as much need for farm workers these days, but the beasts must take a bit of looking after. Daft idea, but why didn't he ask yon Charlie Cameron if he could use another pair of hands? You don't ask, you don't get, that was what he'd aye been told. So that's what he'd do. Ask him straight out.

Tulloch decided the only thing he could do was wait. He'd no idea how long it might take Luce and Kit to talk through all the things they needed to. Truth to tell, he needed time himself. Why hadn't one of them told him? Women and men. Complete mysteries to each other.

Charlie Cameron came shambling into the drawing room, where Lucette and Katherine were still on the big sofa and Heather was leaning forward from one of the armchairs. A bit strange, after all this time, to see the three of them together again, stranger to think how they'd come together, or been brought together. His gaze fixed on Lucette, and he watched the trace of a smile flicker, fade and light her face again. He wanted to carry on watching her for the rest of his life. He hoped she was going to let him.

'There's precious little food left in the house, I'm afraid. Still some whisky, though. Fancy a dram?'

Katherine smiled at him and nodded. 'I think we could all use one, Charlie.'

'Whiskies all round, then?'

Charlie attempted an ingratiating grin as he made the suggestion, but thought better of it, adjusting to a slight smile as he made for the door, heading once more for the comparative safety of the kitchen.

the ice house, Dunpark

Macquarie decided he had to be plain daft to be doing this, and to have agreed to it in the first place. Having got McIlwraith out of Dunpark in one piece, the daft bugger wanted them both to go straight back there. As soon as they were safely away, McIlwraith starts blethering that there's diamonds stashed in the ice house where the old fellow had locked him up. It dawned on Macquarie then what Cameron had been up to. He'd heard about diamonds being found on some Russian sailor and that Vialysov was supposed to be mixed up with that somehow. Cameron had hidden them in the ice house, or more likely got someone to do that for him, but in any case, that's where a substantial contribution to Macquarie's retirement fund was to be found. So he'd turned the car round and headed back they way they'd come, with McIlwraith staring straight ahead, a dangerous grin starting to spread across his face. There was plenty that could still go wrong, Macquarie admitted to himself. For one thing McIlwraith was adamant he wasn't going to go back in the ice house even if Macquarie had a loaded pistol to point at his head. Apart from that, Macquarie had a feeling that something was about to go badly wrong. Exactly what, he wasn't sure, but the looming clouds overhead echoed his mood. No point telling this to McIlwraith, determined to get his mitts on what he'd been sent for. Macquarie could see Dunpark ahead of them. Time to get off the main road, and on to the track leading to the ice house. McIlwraith was still grinning like a maniac. Macquarie let the car nose forward, the sun extending the shadows of the trees across the windscreen, as if he was part of a film he couldn't stop and re-wind till he was safe again, on the road to Perth and not, as he imagined, en route to a bit part in a disaster movie. Something was going to happen. He was sure of it; same as he was sure he was going to get the hell away from whatever impending fate there might be as fast as possible.

Dunpark House

Luce found Tulloch, sitting by the Loch side, a few yards from the old ice house. As she sat down beside him, their fingers fumbled into one another's, though their eyes pretended to be more intent on the view than the person they were with.

'Well?'

Luce turned slightly, not sure what to tell him, not sure what his question implied. His response was to let his hand slide gently across her face, probing cautiously for the mystery behind those eyes, that mouth. He jerked his head toward the water.

'It looks more than bonny' he mused. 'but deep. A man could drown, if he didn't take care. If he wasn't wise enough to work out that he'll never really know what's there. Maybe that's our failing; we spend time trying to know, when we ought simply to appreciate what we have.'

'Do you, Tulloch?'

'I don't think I've an option.'

Luce's face lit with the smile he'd walk over coals for. They stood watching as glints of light chased the Loch's waters. She scared him rigid. But then the only things that ought to scare a grown man, in Tulloch's view, were unopened bank statements or a grown woman. Luce was fully grown all right. You're going to be a handful, Lucette Ginevra, he mused to himself.

Suddenly, she was out of his arms.

'My foot's gone to sleep!'

Trying to stamp the ground with it, gyring on one leg, she'd have fallen if he hadn't caught her.

'Damn cramp!' Luce muttered between her teeth.

Forty odd kilograms is a fair weight, but Tulloch caught and held her.

'If you're up early the morn, time you were in your bed.'

As they turned up by the side of the ice house, Tulloch noticed a car parked a few yards away. He suddenly wanted to hold her tighter, but she was moving in his arms, recognition and alarm mixing in the look she gave to the man standing in front of her.

'Hello, Lucette.'

'Uncle James.'

Tulloch didn't like the grin on the man's face, any more than he liked the way his feet were planted firmly between them and the house.

'Who's the young man?' James Cameron demanded.

The grin scarcely broke when the words were spoken, though Cameron's charm couldn't disguise how irrelevant any answer might be to him.

'Ninian Tulloch.'

Luce, her feet now back on the ground, made the introduction, although her words seemed to make no impression on Cameron's polished and imperturbable exterior, his smile as sharp and calculating as before. Cameron came straight to the point. Nothing to be gained by beating about the bush.

'A little bird tells me your Papa has plans for the old ice house here.'

'Has he? Does he?'

Luce's question searched Cameron's urbanity, and found a chink. He realised his mouth had dropped open.

'Something about ice cream, or so I've been reading in the papers.'

'I don't read them very often. I didn't know you were going to pay a visit.'

'Neither did I till today.'

Eddie lifted his head and took a break from reading the manuscript. He'd nearly finished. When he'd begun he knew it would take him a while, and stepping outside for a bit of peace and quiet had seemed like the best way to get some. The script looked like a spider had been slipped a dose of speed and then careered across one page after another. From the moment Eddie's eyes had lighted on the first page, he'd known this was it. Whatever Anne Enderby had to say to him when he got back, this would trump any charge of wasting time and money. He'd not been prepared for what followed, all the same. He certainly hadn't expected his presumptions and imaginings about his supposed ancestor, Oliver Corcoran, to be completely overturned, or to discover that Archibald Cameron was simply another one of history's hapless victims. He wished he didn't have to wrestle so hard with questions that could only lead to half the "real" truth, whatever that might be. Behind every fact are questions no-one has the guts to admit they don't have answers to. Real questions don't care who gets in the way, only stand straight up demanding an answer, their obviousness a challenge to the bland darkness of smug certitude, and the only hope of honest doubters everywhere.

Eddie considered briefly all the tedious tomes lining the walls of his Vauxhall Bridge flat. Not one of the clever buggers who had written them could tell him any more about Archibald Cameron than Neil Gow, not that he'd told Eddie much. Eddie thought he knew a tiny atom more about what had really happened, but gaps remained, wide enough to drive an artic through. He sighed.

Maybe that was all history was and could ever be. A vague approximation of the smoke and mirrors we laughingly call ' real life'. Oliver Corcoran? He'd no answers to Oliver Corcoran's behaviour, any more than he had to any other part of the mystery that still surrounded the whole affair.

'So now I've told you all I can, Nathaniel, of what happened around Loch Tay. I've given Archie this letter, to be brought back with them when it's safe to return.'

Eddie turned the sheet of paper over, hoping that there would be more, though he sensed there wasn't going to be. Instead, Eddie was staring at several bars of music. The speed-addicted spider had been at work again. Picking a way through the devil's gallop of notes cascading after one another across the page stopped any attempt to hum along after the first bar. Whoever had scribbled these phrases was either stark mad or as near genius as God allowed. Eddie turned from the manuscript, defeated but still fascinated, his eyes lingering over the tune he couldn't imagine how to play. It hadn't been what he'd hoped to find, but there was something here, though Eddie couldn't fathom what that might be.

He was about to lay the manuscript to one side, then decided it would be safer in his pocket. Looking toward the Loch, he made out two figures beside the ice house, talking to someone. Two together were privy council in Eddie's book, but three were possibly open court. He decided to walk in their direction, when suddenly what he could see on the Loch made him pause.

From the far end, which he could barely make out in the gathering gloom, it seemed as if water was being sucked into the middle of the Loch, forming a huge wave, gradually building in its height and power. The wave was now at least a metre high, maybe more. It was crashing against water being driven from the opposite end of the Loch, causing another wave to form, till the two waves joined and became one, higher than before, speeding toward the shore beside the ice house. Eddie watched with shock, and then began to run toward the figures, who appeared to be oblivious of the potential danger they were exposed to.

'Have you come to see my dad about something?' Luce's question hung in the air till Cameron flashed a smile.

'Your father always was the stubborn one of the family. He has a tendency not to realise what's in his best interests. Which is where you come in, my dear. You're going to help me persuade him to start being sensible.'

The pistol seemed to appear from nowhere, but Cameron's grip around its trigger was as firm as his tone had become threatening. Years ago, when it had become clear to James he wasn't going to be left much, he'd helped himself to the odd thing from the house, his father's service revolver among them.

Tulloch thought he had calculated the odds of landing an effective blow pretty well before he lunged, but he found he was lying on the ground, from where he very slowly inched his way to a semi-upright position till a kick from Cameron floored him again.

'No you don't sonny! We'll have no heroics, thank you!'

Cameron pushed the gun against Luce's head, his other hand twisting her arm around her back.

'Now let's you and I go and say hello to your father, eh?'

Cameron turned, only to find his path blocked by a small, bedraggled man wearing the remains of what had once been a black tracksuit.

'Drop the gun, Cameron.'

Cameron stared at McIlwraith, his mouth moving without uttering a coherent sound.

'Thought you'd got it aa worked out, eh? Set me up tae get your stuff an your pal Macquarie tae take it aff me, then blow ma heid aff, so's there's naebody tae incriminate the pair o yous. Clever stuff, Mister Cameron, real clever stuff.'

'I can explain ... '

'Och, we can aa dae that, Mister Cameron. I'm sure you can explain. Only trouble is, I'm no listenin.'

Cameron didn't even have time to aim the pistol before the object collided against his wrist. McIlwraith silently congratulated himself on picking up the padlock back in the ice house and remembering he had the thing in his pocket. Its weight had been enough to make Cameron drop the revolver, and before he could retrieve it, McIlwraith had pounced, thrusting Luce to one side in the process. In another second, McIlwraith had Cameron in a grip that made him scream in pain. By that time Tulloch had stumbled upright, and catching hold of Luce, pulled her out of the way as McIlwraith's free hand landed a blow to Cameron's head. Cameron yelled and tried to strike back. No-one noticed a large figure in a caftan running toward them till Eddie loudly roared 'Behind you!'

Thundering across the grass, Rob Ainslie barely had time to ask himself what the hell he thought he was getting himself into, bar more trouble. He could see the water building up across the Loch, and something was telling him if the folk standing around didn't get out the road fast, they were in for a nasty shock.

Luce turned at the sound of Eddie's voice, which also made Cameron and McIlwraith look toward the Loch, in time to see the wave sweep over the tiny ribbon of strand till it reached the grass beyond. Tulloch and Luce tried to gain the shelter of the ice house. Luce turned to look back; she could see the water sweep up and over Cameron and McIlwraith, now wrestling with each other by the Loch's edge, the water now so high she could barely see them.

The wave receded, leaving two drenched figures struggling at its edge. Eddie moved toward them, but the water was rising again, another wave already building in height and speed as it made toward the shore. Rob couldn't believe what he was seeing, but he was seeing it right enough. He slowed, watching as the wave struck against the shore.

Almost as the wave hit, McIlwraith's foot slid and carried him to the wave's edge, with Cameron, locked in his grasp, sliding with him. The full force of the wave engulfed them and McIlwraith slipped again, the weight of Cameron's bulk taking them both further into the Loch. McIlwraith's feet went from under him as he stumbled, dragging Cameron down. Eddie advanced as far as he dared into the still-boiling water of the Loch, his hands outstretched. McIlwraith still held Cameron firmly, despite Cameron lashing out against him. Yet another wave seemed to be building. Eddie turned to the shore and yelled

'Tulloch, come on! I'll never get hold of them on my own!'

Rob gave himself a shake and hurried on to the water's edge. Before Tulloch had reached the water, Eddie had managed to get Cameron under the armpits and was pulling with as much effort as his body had left. McIlwraith was struggling to keep hold of Cameron, and a mad tug-of-war ensued with Cameron pulled between them, first one way, then the other. Another wave came on, its spray drenching Tulloch as he came up beside Eddie.

'Get me round the waist.' Eddie ordered. Tulloch slid his hands as far round Eddie's ample girth as they would stretch.

By now, Rob was standing with them in the water.

'Pull as if I'm a bad tooth and you're a dentist.'

They began pulling. Nothing seemed to be happening. Luce was in the water by now, and then Eddie began yelling as though about to give birth to a baby elephant while his feet traced a backward path up the bank at a rate more rapid than Tulloch or Rob could keep up with. As the bank leveled and Eddie slowed, Tulloch managed to catch him up and slip his arm under Cameron's. Eddie collapsed on the bank, Cameron lying between them. Eddie fought air into his lungs, chest heaving till he wondered if a blood vessel was going to burst. He rolled onto one side, then struggled to his feet.

'You're never going back out there, are you?'

Eddie nodded his head in response to Tulloch's question. 'No mate, I'm knackered. Down to you two.'

Luce watched as Tulloch waded cautiously into the water. Rob followed at a distance, wishing he didn't feel that he had to. McIlwraith's struggles were feebler now, his hands fending off the receding wave as a fretful child might push away what it didn't want but couldn't avoid.

Macquarie, hidden behind the ice house door, had watched Cameron and McIlwraith struggle themselves first one way, then another. He'd had a good look round the place and decided which of the two chests he should take. McIlwraith had told him they both looked the same, but it was obvious, when you thought about it. The one that weighed the most had to be the one with Cameron's diamonds in it. So he'd tried them both for weight and near ricked his back in the process. He'd barely managed to drag the one he'd selected out of the ice house and then heave it into the boot of the car when he turned, in time to see the skinny bastard that had lamped him twice, alongside Rob Ainslie, the pair of them wading out into the foaming water of the Loch. Time, he decided, to get away while he still could. Get the hell out of it, now, Maurice, and to hell with what might happen to McIlwraith. There should be enough here to see you set up for the rest of your life. No sense being a damn fool over people who never gave a damn about you.

As the water continued to foam, and rise with every wave, McIlwraith swung at Tulloch, his energy returning with the prospect of capture; Tulloch went down, and Luce gasped as he fought himself upright against the waves.

Beyond where Rob stood, the waters were gathering again, less high and strong than before, but strong enough, she was sure, to knock down and drown anyone in their path. Eddie was signaling, gesturing for Rob to grab McIlwraith from behind, but his signals only alerted the drenched figure to the man now behind him. McIlwraith let out a roar and stumbled toward Rob.

Then he was down, head beneath the water as the wave came on fast. Eddie waved impatiently at Tulloch and Rob to get back to the shore. The water was nearly up to their waists, their clothes soaked, making it hard to move. Rob struggled to get alongside Tulloch so they could support each other. Hands about each other's necks, they trod water like a pair of heavy horse stamping their way across a muddy park, feeling the water try to suck them down.

It took both Luce and Eddie's combined strength to draw two pairs of leaden feet toward shore. Tulloch could feel the wave crash somewhere behind him as his feet came out of the muddy sand of the Loch and onto the bank. Luce was hugging him tightly, as if he were somehow going to break.

A rasping. prolonged coughing, like someone being sick, came from behind him. Eddie turned his head in the direction of James Cameron.

'Bloody hell,' he announced, to no-one in particular. 'He's still alive and breathing.'

Dunpark House

Tulloch had stopped shivering; it had started as Luce and he were walking back to the house, beginning at his feet and racking its way up through his whole body with a will he couldn't control or stop.

He lay easier on the bed now, Luce's arms still round him. She was talking, but it was as if her voice came from another room; as if what she was saying to him was about other people, not the two of them lying cosy under a deeply layered duvet.

Once they'd got Tulloch back to the house, Charlie and Heather had gone for the police, one of whom was now sitting downstairs sipping tea and waiting for James to regain consciousness before asking questions very few of which the Honourable James Cameron was likely to want to answer. Tulloch's own question about why the tide on the Loch had turned as wild as it had was only partly answered by Luce. According to her father, it had done the same thing about two hundred years before, though no-one, then or now, had ever come up with an explanation.

Perhaps it was some form of delayed shock, perhaps only that the events at the side of the Loch remained uppermost in his mind, but it was some time before Eddie felt something damp and heavy in the pocket of his caftan. He realised at once what it had to be. Neil Gow. If he'd had any energy left, he'd have burst into tears. He'd fished in his pocket and dragged a fistful of dripping sludge from where he'd stashed the manuscript. Lines of black ink merged into one another, creating images for a dozen Rorschach tests. There never would be a "great discovery" story in the papers, and any dream he'd had of a glittering career on the back of it was turning to pulp along with the sheets of paper. Laughter or tears, Edward, laughter or tears? Eddie heard his Dad's grim question, but had had no answer.

He was still pondering the question when he noticed a small group by the edge of the now calm Loch. Moving closer, he could see they were looking at something that lay on a tarpaulin on the ground. One of the policemen nodded at Eddie's approach.

'Found a body in the Loch' was his terse remark. 'It was probably that storm brought it tae the surface.'

'Only it's no the one we're lookin for' his colleague went on. 'This guy's been dead a hell of a long time.'

Eddie stared down at what might have been a skeleton, supposing there had been enough left to call it one.

'Funny, though.' the first policeman commented. 'Looks as if he's got a rope wrapped roon his leg.'

'Suicide?' asked the other, without curiosity.

'Why no tie it on right, then?'

Eddie wanted to say because he was trying to get into a balloon, but realised he'd likely be dismissed as a nutter if he made such a suggestion, as he would be if he demanded a test to establish if the remains were those of his long-lost (literally, it seemed) relation, Oliver Corcoran. Oh well, Eddie, decided, at least they'll give the poor sod a decent burial. He paused a moment as the two policemen pulled the tarpaulin over the heap of bones. Someone ought to give Oliver Corcoran some respect.

Eddie found Dawn seated on the steps of the house. He settled himself beside her and wondered how to begin to tell her what had happened to the best chance he was ever likely to have to become more than "almost famous".

'What d' you do, Dawn, when you realise you've been a complete idiot?'

'What did you do, Eddie?'

'Put a piece of real history in my pocket and clean forgot it was there. Waded into the middle of the Loch and let it get that wet there's nothing left. Nothing readable, at any rate.'

'You saved a life, Eddie.'

'I know the manuscript was important. I thought ... '

'Thought what?'

'That maybe it was a way out of doing one damn gig after another, coming up with jokes and routines when I don't feel funny – at least not funny ha-ha. Chance to branch out, do something different. Might even have become a sort of academic ...'

'Eddie, do you remember what *The Observer* said about you?'

'What was that?'

'You do remember! "One of Britain's sharpest musical satirists"'.

'I don't feel very sharp at the moment.'

'Eddie, you're a comedian. That isn't why I love you, but that's what you are. You'd hate being any sort of academic! I don't know that much about you, but I'm sure of that. Always having to defend your budget, worrying about who gets to pass and who's failed. Depressed students throwing themselves off the top of the tower block ...'

Dawn's description of the everyday lives of academic folk struck Eddie as a bit melodramatic, but it did little to lighten his mood.

'Maybe. But to find something really important, then discover you're the one who's managed to destroy it ... '

'Life is what's important, Eddie. Isn't there a saying somewhere that if you save a life you save the whole world? Doesn't matter what you think of the person, life is what matters.'

Eddie looked at Dawn. She was right, of course. Life was what mattered, and he ought to stop feeling sorry for himself. He was going to have to get used to Dawn being right about most things, though there would be times when he'd not understand why. Maybe that was life too.

Charlie Cameron was beginning to get used to unexpected visitors turning up unannounced, but the most recent arrival had managed to surprise him, nonetheless.

'Always glad to see you, of course, Magnus, but what brings you to Dunpark?'

Magnus Macdonald sighed inwardly. That was a question he'd hoped Charlie Cameron wouldn't ask.

'Like Joan of Arc, I heard voices. Or in my case, a voice.'

Magnus let the enigmatic statement hang in the air for a moment before adding a more down-to-earth reason that Charlie might accept.

'I needed to talk to your daughter about Roddy MacLennan's funeral ... You had heard he died? It came as a shock, of course, when she told me, as I'm sure it does to you.'

'Poor Roddy. I knew his health wasn't that good. He'll be missed, not least by me.'

'Lucette is one of the executors of his will. So when I couldn't get in touch with her in Edinburgh, I though I'd see if perhaps she'd come to tell you about you about Roddy's death herself ...'

Charlie digested Magnus' explanation slowly. He was gradually coming to terms with his uncomfortable reactions when questions arose about the gap between Lucette's last visit to Dunpark and the present. He decided to move on to practical matters, where he felt safer.

'It was lucky Heather turning up like that. After the storm on the Loch subsided, I persuaded her to drive us both to fetch the police. Well, after we'd done that I managed to get Tam Robertson to open up his store, and there's tea, milk, a tub of marge, corned beef and a couple of family-size loaves of bread. Even managed to get some eggs, so we'd have something for tomorrow's breakfast ... '

In another part of the house, Tulloch drifted in and out of sleep. Exhaustion had drained what sense he'd ever had out of him and even Luce couldn't hold his attention for long. It was good to be here, lying with Luce's arms holding him. He minded one of the lads in The Forest, the kind of bloke you wouldn't think capable of coming out with one of the great truths. 'There's nothin nicer than lyin in bed wi one you really love. Nothin nicer in the whole world.'

Settled in one of the chairs in the kitchen, Magnus MacDonald's curiosity got the better of him.

'Any idea why the Loch should do that? Was it a freak tide or something?' He asked Charlie.

'There was a storm like that in 1797. Someone around at the time wrote it up. The tide started building at one end of the Loch, then the other, till there were two great waves meeting in the middle. What we had this evening matches the description almost exactly.'

'I don't suppose there'd be any way of predicting it could happen?'

'When something happens once in two hundred years or so, it's a bit difficult to know what we ought to be looking for.'

Magnus nodded. There was an irony about the whole business of McIlwraith, whose appearance he'd been unaware of until he was told of his re-appearance. He ventured the name as Charlie rose to switch off the boiling kettle.

'They're still searching the Loch for that man McIlwraith, the constable told me.'

Charlie answered with a nod, careful not to spill the tea he was pouring into two cups. McIlwraith drowned in a freak storm that had nearly killed his brother James as well. He didn't really understand any of it. That James might have been contemplating murder to get whatever he was after was more than he could get his head around. They'd never got on, but this … All the same, he couldn't deny the solid reality of a constable seated in the hallway, ready to call headquarters whenever Cameron regained consciousness and could "help with enquiries" as the phrase went.

None of it seemed to make sense. James could surely have lived comfortably on a few directorships. Why get mixed up with criminals? As inexplicable as why McIlwraith returned to Dunpark when he could have put as much distance as possible between himself and the place.

A sound behind him caused Magnus to turn. A small figure had slid onto the nearest chair. Kit Barber flashed a shy smile at Magnus before twisting her head in Charlie's direction.

'I think they're asleep.'

Charlie's returned smile questioned her.

'She's fine' Kit reassured him. 'They both are.'

Magnus sensed the awkwardness of his presence. Besides, he'd have an early start in the morning. Nor was it the time to mention the very generous provision in MacLennan's will for Ms Lucette Cameron. He couldn't help noticing Kit, all the same. He remembered her from his visits to The Forest after Jenny had died, when he'd sought any company sooner than his own and music had been all that had made any sense to him. You'd have needed to be deaf not to have known when Kit Barber was playing, even when he couldn't quite manage to see her. Sometimes sex crawls up your nostrils and hammers on the door of whatever the right hormones are till you can't but help take notice. That was what was happening now, even though Alys was all he really wanted or ever would. You're a canny lass, for all that, was Magnus's thought as he rose and made for the door.

Safe in the silence of the hall, Magnus reluctantly decided his brother ought to know what was going on, as far as Magnus himself could tell him that. Stepping out onto the porch, he pulled out his mobile and tapped in a number. There was a lengthy wait before he got a response.

'Magnus, what the hell do you want at this time of night?'

'To tell you the Honourable James Cameron is in police custody awaiting arrest.'

'Some sort of driving charge is it?'

'Marcus, he's lucky it isn't murder.'

There was a long pause at the other end before Magnus heard his brother's voice again.

'Must be a bad line. For a moment I thought you'd said something about murder.'

'I did. The Hon. James Cameron is facing a charge of attempted murder.'

'Good Lord!'

'Very likely on two counts, at least.'

The ensuing pause was long enough for Magnus to check his phone battery and hope Marcus wasn't going to carry on doing this.

'What sort of proof?'

'Two very reliable witnesses. Charlie Cameron's daughter, for one.'

'Magnus, you are sure James Cameron is mixed up in whatever this is all about?'

'I'm on the spot, Marcus. Dunpark House, where James is being detained until the Perth constabulary decide what to do with him next. We can trade pleasantries till my battery runs out, but that won't help James Cameron.'

'I didn't think you'd want to help him.'

'I loathe and despise James Cameron both personally and politically, but he is your – I perhaps ought to say our – client, and we should therefore be doing whatever we can for him. Such as finding him a decent defence lawyer.'

'D' you have anyone in mind?'

'Hari Patel.'

'What's wrong with Jimmy Strathearn?'

'Strathearn's no match for most of the prosecutors around. No, Marcus. No golfing buddies, if you please. This is going to be too important a case to leave to old pals.'

'Have a word with Harry Krishna if you must. If this is going to get nasty, Magnus, I'm probably best kept out of it anyway.'

The line went dead. How like my dear brother, Magnus thought to himself. Yet the fact Marcus had let him have his way gave him a deep sense of satisfaction. It was always a contest – had been since they were toddlers – and keeping Marcus out of mischief took up more of Magnus's time and effort than he often had to spare, but every now and again there was the vicarious pleasure of a small victory.

Forth Road Bridge Approach

Magnus MacDonald was humming quietly to himself, eyes on the road ahead, when a yawn caught him unawares; he'd got used to sleeping alone, ever since Alys had left to study in Greece for three months, but last night had been a particularly wakeful one. Waiting for Luce and Tulloch to rouse and organise themselves had given him time to begin puzzling through the last few days. The Honourable James Cameron would likely need all the help he could get to explain how he'd come to be brandishing a firearm in the face of his niece and a man with whom she appeared to be quite intimate. It probably was best, Magnus decided, if he could keep his brother as far away as possible from what seemed a very complicated case. He'd wheedled a bit of the story from the policeman stationed in the hall last night. About the same time Professor Roderick MacLennan had died, a body had been fished out of Leith docks. A Russian seaman, making his way back to his ship the worse for drink, had fallen into one of the docks, his cries unheard. No suspicious circumstances as such, the man had been drinking and probably took a wrong turning; the stone he had in his pocket was a different matter. It had turned out to be an uncut diamond. The ship was searched and the haul had proved on inspection to have been of high quality, the constable had told him, though how he could have known that, Magnus had no idea.

'Smuggled?' he'd enquired, innocent as a schoolboy.

'I've told you more than enough already, Sir.'

Magnus had always wondered about Oleg Vialysov. He knew he shared a prejudice with several that when the word "Russian" was followed by "businessman", it implied "unconvicted criminal". Cameron certainly knew Vialysov, though. Hadn't he been the one to wine and dine Vialysov when he'd first arrived in Scotland? If there was some kind of diamond smuggling going on, how deeply implicated was he? Let the courts sort that lot out, Magnus, he told himself.

On the back seat, Tulloch and Luce were as near asleep as made no difference. He resisted a temptation to ask if they were all right, which they clearly were, and found his mind returning to the problem of James Cameron and Oleg Vialysov. Where did McIlwraith, whoever he'd been, fit in? He remembered there was also a mysterious Inspector Macquarie, who'd conveniently turned up to arrest McIlwraith and had then presumably managed to lose him, unless McIlwraith had himself somehow managed to dispose of Macquarie ... Leave it, Magnus, leave it. You've a funeral to go to and these two people to get there. They were approaching the far side of the bridge, and MacDonald scrabbled to find the coins on the dashboard, before passing them into the hand outstretched from the little cabin. They'd soon be in Edinburgh; just as well, since he needed to change his suit and he imagined Luce and probably Tulloch would want time to prepare for the funeral.

Luce was trying to put any thought of her Uncle Roddy's funeral as far out of her head as it could go. The past few days were more than enough to think about. The closer they got to Edinburgh, though, the harder it became to hide from what was to come.

'You'll do it. You'll not enjoy it, but you will do it.'

Tulloch's voice was quiet in her ear. Matter-of-fact, confident but unassuming. Luce liked that in him, that self-assurance she'd seen in very few of the men she'd ever spent time with.

It always felt strange, though, when someone knew enough about you to know what was on your mind, the things that made you worried or scared or both.

'Have to, won't I?'

She drew away from him, wanting more space than there was. It would be expected, that was the thing. Professor Roderick MacLennan had no church connection and showed no sign of ever wanting one. So it was down to brief words from those who had known him, rough sketches of the presence that was no longer among them. When it had come to her that the task of comforting the living was likely hers alone, she'd wanted to run away; in truth she had. Strange that running away led where she was now, that it had maybe been Uncle Roddy's last real gift to her. It had brought her Tulloch, after all.

Lying was a thing Tulloch had never got the hang of. He could tell her it would be fine, she would be fine and in any case most of the folk there would forget her small part in the funeral almost as soon as they'd got the first whisky down them. Likely true, but it would be a fool who'd prattle nonsense like that to her and Tulloch was trying hard not to be a fool.

Luce could hear the voice of Shug, manager at The Forest, reminding anyone in hearing distance that 'The dead don't care, but they aye matter.'

Ay, Shug, right. It was what she would do because not to would be not only to deny what Roddy MacLennan was to her, but also what she was to herself. Shug would have put it rightly in the nutshell that it belonged. It was what was really meant when folk said death is for the living. You can box up the dead but you can't neatly put all the things we feel in that box and bury them along with the dead. If people are angry or resentful or confused or frightened because someone they love has died, they need someone to lead them through those feelings. She hoped she might be able to help them.

Magnus wondered how Lucette Cameron was going to react when she discovered quite how wealthy an heiress she was about to become. She was undeniably very pretty. With more than a few hundred thousand in her account, she'd be one of the most eligible women in Scotland. If he were ten years younger ... Magnus, if you were ten years younger, you'd have recently buried both your mother and your wife, with less then two months between the funerals. If you hadn't been rescued, you'd quite possibly be a pathetic drunk, and Alys Mackenzie, apart from anyone else, wouldn't have given you a second look, far less ... Magnus turned the car onto Melville Drive, and tried to remember the turn-off for Marchmont Crescent. He decided to tell them he'd go back to his flat and change, calling back for them when it was time to set off for the funeral. He'd call the office once he was home, and see what Marcus had been up to since their last conversation. The last thing James Cameron needed was Marcus putting his foot where it was likely to do the most harm to his own client.

Edinburgh, the underground city

It was the perfect hiding place, Macquarie decided. All he had to do was get the muckle thing out the car, down and along the passage, then wait until he had enough time to find someone to fence the stones for him. Then again, he could aye get a safe deposit in the Royal Bank of Caledonia, then take them out one at a time and sell them off quiet like. There had to be enough in the chest to give him a decent pension. Soon as he tried lifting the box, he decided one thing he might splash out on was likely to be a hernia operation. It weighed a ton, and felt like near enough two ton, by the time he'd lugged and dragged and peched the chest down the passage. Here it was, Maurice Macquarie's personal pension plan, waiting for the covers to be taken off. Macquarie could see there was no padlock where there might once have been one. McIlwraith, of course. He's saved you a bit of work, Maurice. Slowly opening the lid, Macquarie could see what looked like steam begin seeping from under the lid, till it became more solid, like dust. Something seemed to be inside the dust, rising up until it slowly began to take on a shape. Then the shape began to separate into two shapes and Macquarie could feel a noise begin deep within himself, struggle its way into his lungs till at last he could hear himself scream. He screamed again, because both shapes were moving toward him. It was then he sensed the smell; sickly-sweet, strong enough to almost choke him. He remembered chemistry classes when he was a laddie, the teacher aye making him sniff the results of experiments. This one seemed to have gone very wrong indeed. It smelt of rotten eggs or fruit, but worse then that. It was making his eyes water, whatever it was, and then through his tears he saw ... Them. They were moving slowly. Like puppets without strings, they moved jerkily as bairns might, or ones not used to being on their feet. Macquarie could feel hands grip him, hard as steel. He struggled against the bony grips but they weren't letting go. He had to get out of their grasp, but it was a long way to the cellar's mouth. Beyond the figures, the cellar floor sloped upward toward its roof at the further end. Macquarie struggled out of the grips that were holding him, howling and yelling as he ran toward the far end of the cellar and his fingers began to scrabble against the stone. He could feel the bony fingers again, gripping his ankles this time and could smell the fetid stench behind him. Get one stone loose, Maurice, that's all it'll take to make a beginning. One stone. He felt a grip round his leg, another round his waist and a scream started once more in his lungs. Kicking with his feet, he scrabbled the harder with his hands. Somewhere above him he was sure he could hear voices and music. No, he wasn't kidding himself. The sounds he could surely hear were human. If only he could get to them he'd be safe. His hands tore at the stones and the stour, ignoring the trickles of blood already running down his fingers. A stone did come loose, a tiny one, then another, and a third followed. His hands were covered in blood by now, but he didn't care. Grabbing and pulling and tearing at the bits of mortar around the stones became all consuming as he attempted to block the shapes and their bony grips from his mind. He tried to focus solely on tearing away the next stone and the next as he heard them clatter behind him, hoping they were dunting the heads of whatever it was he could still feel clutching at his ankles. The sounds above his head became louder, clearer, till he thought he could hear singing. He began to pull at the stones even harder, but as he did so, he could feel himself gripped ever more firmly. Once again, he heard himself scream.

The Forest, Edinburgh

The last notes faded as the coffin was carried out to the waiting hearse. Luce allowed herself a moment before making her way back to her seat. She'd not played a slow air in a long time, and she'd been fearful her playing wouldn't match the ambition of 'Farewell to Whisky', Neil Gow's response to the failure of the barley crop in 1799. More than a farewell to whisky, it had been written as an elegy for the loss of comfort of any sort till another harvest would lift dearth from the land. A huge cry in sound against the loss of what we cherish. There'd been a moment, when she'd thought she wouldn't reach the tune's end but she'd somehow managed to carry on, and now it was done. As she walked back to her seat, Tulloch gave her a nod and discreet thumbs up. Not that she really needed anyone's approval, not even his. She'd not played, after all, for anyone in the otherwise silent church. And after the last few days, smiling and shaking hands with Uncle Roddy's tearful, drink-reeking cronies was going to feel the transitory thing it would be.

Luce and Tulloch found themselves practically wedged against the door of The Forest. Luce shyly began to acknowledge the greetings of folk whose faces she knew even if she'd never known their names. It had been long enough since she'd been in, but there were still folk who recognised her, and knew her well enough to be glad to see her among them again.

Magnus MacDonald had explained it to her before she'd gone north with Heather.

'Professor MacLennan also left two hundred and fifty pounds to be spent at The Forest so everyone attending his funeral could drink to his memory.'

Tulloch nudged his way to the bar, already throng with early Friday drinkers. Turning, Luce saw other faces, ones that she'd seen at the funeral, entering the bar in twos, threes, and larger numbers, till the crowded corridor that was The Forest seemed packed with them.

'There.'

She turned to face a tall glass and pint tumbler, delicately held between Tulloch's fingers. Taking the glass from him, Luce carefully placed it as far from the nearest table's edge as space allowed. A large figure was trying to get past the drinkers crowded by the door whose comfortable positions he was disturbing. Dawn smiled uncertainly as Eddie waved a newspaper in Tulloch's direction.

'Wondered if we might find you here' Eddie nodded toward Luce.

'Thought you two were playing cricket?' came Tulloch's response.

'Dawn took three wickets, then the match was abandoned 'cause of rain.'

'Seen a paper?' Eddie continued.

Luce and Tulloch might think news was the last thing they

wanted; the headline Eddie had already read was one they ought to know about, all the same. He felt uncomfortable now he and Dawn were in the pub, among the mourners. Eyes questioned their presence, though Eddie had no intention of explaining. He'd had to watch Dawn's match. Not his fault it was the same time as MacLennan's funeral. If the buggers wanted to stare that was their problem. No, he wasn't going to say "their funeral". Luce glanced at the newspaper in Eddie's hand and shook her head. He flicked the paper over to reveal its front page.

'James Cameron arrested. MSP charged after diamond smuggling "sting" operation. The Hon. James Cameron was arrested in Perthshire yesterday as part of a police investigation into East European diamond smugglers ... '

Eddie's words were drowned by a sharp bang on the table. Heads turned in the direction of Magnus MacDonald, standing as close to the bar as the crowd permitted.

'Ladies and Gentlemen, as most of you are aware, we're here to offer our last act of respect to Professor Roderick MacLennan, in a place where he was known to many. We ask you to charge your glasses and drink to his memory.'

It took a minute or two for Shug and his staff to fill the glasses that suddenly came at them from all parts of the bar. When no more glasses appeared for re-filling, Magnus took the silence firmly where he wanted it to go.

'Each of us will have our own memory of the man, ours to keep in time to come. However you remember him, I invite you to join us in drinking to the memory of Professor Roderick MacLennan.'

'Roderick MacLennan' and 'Roddy MacLennan' echoed round the bar. Then, from nowhere Luce could at first discover, came a voice, soft at first but piercing clear. Recognising the words, she thought at first the singer must be drunk or daft, then realised this was the perfect last thing that could be offered.

'Should auld acquaintance be forgot,

And never brought to mind ...'

The sound travelled the length of the high, narrow room, coming from somewhere up by the bar. Magnus moved closer to the sound, his voice baritoning out the words. Other voices came in and Luce pressed forward to catch sight of the first singer. Perched on a bar stool that was surely her accustomed spot, a woman whose face carried her disappointments lightly but clearly, known to Luce only by sight, sang on.

'An shairly I'll be your pint stoup

An shairly you'll be mine,

An we'll tak a cup o kindness yet

For auld lang syne'

Luce had promised herself she wouldn't till it was over and she could be alone. It was the smoke, the harsh light, the stale smell of the place that made her eyes water. Don't fool yourself, Luce. Tears were stinging her face now and she didn't care who saw them or who or what they thought they were for. A shocked voice whispered;

'It is a funeral, after all.'

Yes it is, Luce thought, but it's not only an end, it's a beginning as well.

'And there's a hand my trusty fiere

And gie's a hand o thine

And we'll tak a right guid willie waught

For auld lang syne

For auld lang syne, my jo,

For auld lang syne ...'

Tulloch gripped Luce's right hand as if it was in danger of

dropping off; Eddie's grasp of her other hand was near as firm. The bewildered faces of newly arrived Friday evening drinkers slid to defensive grins as the last lines rang into the gathering dusk.

'Thank you' Luce murmured in the singer's ear, surrounded as she was by three large men. The woman was off her bar stool and into the crowd before Luce could think of anything more to say. Tulloch watched Luce move toward the huddle of musicians around the corner table. The band was rattling into "The Mason's Apron". Luce stood listening, and the weight of the week and the day, where she'd been and had come back from might have held her longer, only the musicians had segued into "Big John McNeil", which a twenty-something in a bad suit was using to demonstrate his version of the Highland Fling to his giggling friends. Bad Suit's smile froze as the space he'd been putting his feet was taken over by a large figure in a caftan.

'Gentleman's Excuse-Me.'

Eddie's own particular excuse was that the music deserved something better. His feet took steps that left Bad Suit's mouth hanging open. Not what was expected at a funeral, Eddie admitted, but this clearly wasn't any funeral and he'd already paid more respect than pimple-face in chain-store nastiest was ever likely to. The set left John McNeil behind as it went for "The High Drive". Eddie found enough space to step-dance into.

It was in Catterick he'd come across Ailidh MacBride. They were both about nine, and Ailidh had wanted a partner in between step-dancing classes. The only way to get one had been to teach Eddie, who had since forgotten neither Ailidh nor the steps she'd taught him.

He'd long got used to folk calling him "Inappropriate Eddie". If he thought something was the right thing to do, that was what he did. If other people had a problem with that, it was their problem as far as he was concerned. He danced over to Luce and watched a puzzled smile spread slowly over her face. He beckoned with his head as he danced away from her to the other side of the circle that had formed.

Luce couldn't quite believe what she was doing, but somehow it had a rightness to it. A punctuation mark to all that had happened, and Eddie was giving her an opportunity to put her own kind of ending to all of it. The tune changed again, and Eddie's feet pounded the tiles of The Forest, drumming their own tattoo in time with the beat.

Then came another drumming, louder and not at all in tune. The sound grew louder, and people began to move away from the old trap-door opposite the bar. A noise like that of straining timber became very audible as the wooden slats of the disused trap door began to split. Then came the scream. It was like nothing any of them could have heard before; the kind of sound that might come from a soul tortured to madness, till what was left was nothing but the scream itself. A dirt-crusted human hand edged onto the Forest floor, fingers cautiously exploring the surface. A human head followed and someone else screamed.

There was something familiar in the face Tulloch realised, one hand on Luce's shoulder, the other ready for whatever trouble the sudden appearance was going to bring. He'd seen the man before, for sure. Even the way his mouth opened and closed like a fish's out of water ought to have rung an instant alarm bell, but it took several seconds to identify Maurice Macquarie underneath the stour and glaur that caked him. A couple of men had pulled Macquarie out by now, and he rocked like a frightened bairn between their supporting arms. The sound coming from his mouth wasn't canny; a low, persisting keen of a whine that made you wonder if he'd some internal injury. His eyes, though, told you it was his mind the wound was in. He might have been in a hospital or at the gates of hell; it would have made no difference. Tulloch knew whatever they got out of Macquarie's mouth wasn't going to be sense, not for a long time, maybe never.

Now something else felt as if it was pushing its way out from the hole; something or someone or more than one, jostling the bystanding crowd, sending a shiver through it fierce as an electric charge, barging doorwards and out into the covering night. The door hung open, fixed in place as surely as the folk staring toward it, till one voice, with more courage or foolishness than the rest yelled

'Hi, shut the bloody door behind you!'

The door obligingly swung to, its punctuating bang echoing in silence.

Eddie felt the cold leave him slowly. He didn't believe in ghosts or anything like them, but if he had, then maybe they would have felt and smelt a little like whatever it was had swept into the night. He shook himself. Don't add credulity to your list of crimes. Own up to getting carried away before they carry you away and chuck the key in the Forth.

Tulloch turned to Magnus MacDonald and said, as quietly as he could

'That's the fellow Macquarie we were telling you about.'

Magnus gestured to Shug to let him use the phone sitting on the bar. Taking a look at Macquarie, shivering like a scared greyhound in the corner, he knew he wasn't going to enjoy making this call one little bit, but it seemed it had to be done. He punched a number and waited for a response.

It was Shug's fist banging on the bar counter that drew the attention of the remaining drinkers.

'Ladies an Gentlemen, apologies for the inconvenience. Seein as we've aa had a bit fleg, your next drink's on the house.'

Taken by surprise the customers might have been, but not so much that the next few minutes at the bar were not as busy as any Hogmanay. Eddie considered getting himself and Dawn another drink, but he was tired, in shock and more than a little inebriated already.

Eddie had negotiated an extra week's stay in the flat he'd rented for the Festival; he couldn't really afford it, but it meant he and Dawn had a roof over their heads tonight and time to themselves before a London train tomorrow. He clocked Luce and Tulloch, who looked as if they too might be passing on the free drink and were nearly ready to leave. They looked quite good as a couple, Eddie acknowledged to himself. Maybe better than he did alongside Dawn, though he did make Dawn seem particularly petite in comparison.

Does it ever make sense, he wondered, outside the delicate shell couples build around themselves? The only truth lay in the moment. What you feel, when you feel it. Anything else is a make-do excuse for when you're asked what you don't know. Eddie couldn't have told even his much-missed father why he reckoned he and Dawn were going to work out. The life of a comedian was never going to be easy or secure. Considered rationally, they oughtn't to have a cat's chance in hell. Who's rational, though, when every bit tells us this is what we want and where we want to be?

'Dawn?'

'Eddie?'

'I'm tired. The train's at ten tomorrow and I could use a bit of sleep.'

He listened to himself. Thirty-four-year old packs it in. Early bath for Corcoran. Then another thought struck him and he brightened.

'But I'm also hungry and I'll bet you two are as well. Let's get something to eat.'

Luce glanced at Dawn. She's probably had as much as she can take in one day, Luce thought, as she drew Tulloch's hand toward hers.

'Thanks, Eddie, that'd be lovely, but I think we ought to make a move.'

Before Luce could specify where, the phone on the bar began to ring. Shug lifted the receiver.

'Hello, The Forest Bar. Can I help you?' A pause. 'Is that you phonin aa the way frae Greece? Ay well, he's no been in. Only kiddin, Doll. Haud on a wee minute.' Shug cupped his hand over the receiver and called: 'Magnus, it's Alys. Frae Greece. Says it's important.'

Magnus MacDonald all but ripped the phone from Shug's hand. Luce found herself amused by his performance. It wasn't the kind of behaviour she expected from a middle-aged lawyer a little worn at the edges.

Watching Magnus talk animatedly into the receiver, Luce shook her head, thinking how little anyone knows and how much everyone assumes. She slipped from her chair, then her eye caught a young woman seated in the corner, playing her fiddle as if the events of the past minutes had never taken place, and were no concern of hers. Luce stopped a moment and listened, wondering what she might say to this younger version of herself. That it was all written out for her if only she'd take the time to read the signs? That what might be for her wouldn't go by her? That sometimes the hardest thing was realising the thing you'd run away from was what you had to go back to?

Luce formed a wish that whatever this one wanted was given her. Tulloch's hands were slipping her jacket over her shoulders. Eddie and Dawn were almost at the door by now, while Magnus was still deep in his telephone conversation. He waved at them and signaled Luce to telephone him. She glanced back as the band in the corner began developing a version of "Coilsfield House" that involved massive reconstruction. Tulloch noticed the look on her face.

'Never the same tune twice. You know that better than I do.'

"Coilsfield House" had been the tune that opened every concert by "John Knox's G Strings". But it was only a tune, to be played, played with, syncopated, decorated, massacred or murdered according to the player's preference and potential. And truly that was all. No-one owns a tune, not even a pair of sentimental lovers.

Her jacket now on, Luce made for the door and Tulloch followed, Eddie and Dawn, already there, were waiting for them. Shug called out something about being pleased to see her.

They were going their separate ways in a mixture of regret and relief. Eddie and Dawn watched Luce and Tulloch head toward Middle Meadow Walk and Marchmont. As she watched them go, Dawn sensed Eddie's eyes weren't looking in the same direction.

He could see them clear as day, in the basket of the balloon sweeping across the Meadows. The balloon moved further and further away, till it seemed to enter a bank of cloud and was gone. He didn't believe it had anything to do with what might, if he believed in such things, have been a pair of ghosts escaping at last from a lengthy imprisonment and into the night via the door of The

Forest bar. That was all some sort of fantasy and so it couldn't have been him, Edward Osnabruck Corcoran, who had no truck with any such nonsense, who'd murmured 'God's speed' as if he might have meant it.

'What did you just say, Eddie?'

'Oh, nothing, Love. Only clearing my throat. Lovely night, isn't it?'

Dawn nodded. She wasn't sure what had happened, but was sure something had.

'Let's decide where we're going to eat, eh? Then what about a nightcap?'

'Don't think one would suit you, Eddie' Dawn confided, as she slipped her arm through his.

Marchmont Terrace, Edinburgh

Luce watched as Tulloch put the brown bag on the table in front of her.

'That smells good' she smiled up at Tulloch as he eased himself onto the futon.

'Luce, this wouldn't be here if I hadn't borrowed a tenner off Magnus Macdonald in the pub. I'm skint till the bank opens on Monday. D' you think you can put up with me till then?'

'Oh,' Luce said, trying hard not to smile 'I might manage to.'

Tulloch unwrapped the parcel and placed its contents on a waiting plate

'You ought to give Heather a call. She was pretty serious about the two of you getting together and playing again.'

'A band isn't only playing together. It's all the other stuff. We'd need a manager or someone like that.'

'I'm not doing anything at the moment. C'mon missus. Gie's a job.'

'How does ten per cent sound?'

Tulloch gazed at her with a mock-aggrieved expression

'I was hoping for something more than that' he murmured.

'Were you, now?' Luce enquired with a mischievous smile, drawing Tulloch toward her.

Dunpark, Perthshire

Rob Ainslie opened the door of the cottage and stepped out. He'd been nervous asking Mister Cameron if there was any chance of a job at Dunpark. Now here he was installed in the cottage by the gate, with the prospect of paying work as soon as the ice cream making started. He set his mug down on the step and looked across to where the cattle were beginning to settle for the night. He could hear birds calling, though he'd no idea what they were. He'd find out, though, given time. Charlie Cameron had said to Rob they'd go into Perth next week and get some stuff for the cottage. He'd manage fine till then. He could get used to this, he thought to himself, as he watched the last rays of sun slip away behind the hills. He'd no felt this way in a long time. It felt a bit strange, to be honest, but he'd get used to it, given a chance. Ay, he would. Grand feeling, peace.

Although the usual disclaimer that no character is other than a recombination and projection of the author's imagination applies to the 'contemporary' narrative, the following individuals and events are part of what is called history –

Angus Cameron (?) There is no direct evidence that Angus Cameron was involved in the United Scotsmen movement. A timber merchant residing in Dull, Cameron read the Militia Act (translating it into Gaelic) to a large crowd outside Dull Parish Kirk, and subsequently participated in the march on Blair Castle. His arrest and transport to Perth are also on record, as is his escape whilst on bail. Nothing more seems to be known of his story.

Julia Margaret Cameron (1815-1879) began her career as a photographer at the age of 48, when her daughter gave her a camera as a present. She joined the London Photographic Society within a year, and is now regarded as one of the most significant British photographers of the mid 19th century. As well as photographing well-known individuals, such as Charles Darwin, Lord Tennyson and others, Cameron also photographed scenes from legend and history, using these as moral allegories. She was recognised as important by Helmut Gernsheim in a book published in 1948, since when her work has been increasingly appreciated.

Neil Gow (1727-1807) was unquestionably the finest eighteenth century composer of fiddle music in Scotland. His slow airs in particular continue to be played as part of the traditional repertoire. Of these, *"Farewell to Whisky"*, *"Lament for the Death of his Second Wife"* and *"Hector the Hero"* are among the best known. Gow was born at Inver, in Perthshire and trained as a plaid weaver, but the Duke of

Atholl became his musical patron, and ensured his employment as fiddler at local gatherings. Neil Gow married twice, having five sons with his first wife, Margaret Wiseman, – William, John, Andrew, Nathaniel, and Daniel, as well as three daughters. Nathaniel is the best known, with nearly two hundred tunes of his own to his credit. After being widowed, Neil married Margaret Urquhart in 1768. She died in 1805. Neil was deeply affected by her death and his first tune on resuming composition was the celebrated *"Lament for the Death of his Second Wife"*. He died at Inver on 1st March 1807, aged 80. Aged 70 at the time of the Perthshire militia riots, and reliant on aristocratic patronage, there is no evidence he was involved in the disturbances.

Nathanial Gow (1766-1831) The fourth son of Neil Gow, born at Inver, he chose to follow his father into the musical profession. He was involved with performing at many assemblies throughout Scotland, notably at the Caledonian Hunt Balls. He was also King's Trumpeter in Scotland. Nathaniel went into partnership with William Shepherd, with whom he established a music publishing business, and it is as a prolific publisher of Scottish music, particularly the repertoire and compositions of his father, that he is remembered. His own tunes are still widely played today, including *"The Fairy Dance"*, *"Coilsfield House"* and *"The Miller of Drone"*, among many others.

Loch Tay The Loch did indeed exhibit an "agitation of the waters" much as described, but annoyingly for this narrative, on 12 September 1784 rather than 12 September 1797. No subsequent similar event appears to have occurred.

John Maclaggan 'The Duke of Lennox' (?) is known to have had an alehouse close to Loch Tay at the time of the militia riots and to have taken part in them, much in the way described. He appears to have left the area shortly after, and nothing more is heard of him.

Henry Melville, Viscount Dundas (1742-1811) A member of the Faculty of Advocates by 1763, he became Solicitor General for Scotland in 1766; after his appointment as Lord Advocate in 1775, he relinquished his legal practice to devote himself to a political career. In 1774 he was returned as M. P. for Midlothian and subsequently entered the Cabinet as Secretary of State for the Home Department (Office) and served as Secretary of State for War from 1794 to 1801. Fear of French invasion or home-grown insurrection led him to foster the network of informers glimpsed in the novel. Suspicion arose about the financial management of the Board of Admiralty, of which he was Treasurer from 1792 till 1800. He was impeached in 1806, facing the last impeachment trial conducted by the House of Lords. Although negligence was the only charge proved against him, he never again held office.

James Menzies, 'The East Indian' (?) A small merchant in the Loch Tay area at the time of the militia riots, he also appears to have been an active participant along with John Maclaggan. He was arrested at the same time as Angus Cameron, but no records of either a trial or of his subsequent release appear to exist.

Thomas Muir of Huntershill (1765-1799) Possibly the best known of the "Radicals" active in the 1790's, Muir was arrested and tried for promoting "seditious material" (i.e., Thomas Paine's *"The Rights of Man"*). Sentenced to transportation to Botany Bay in Australia, Muir subsequently escaped from there, making his way across the Pacific to California, whose Spanish Governor secured his passage to France, where he was given shelter by the revolutionary government. The privations he had endured in Australia and during his escape took their toll and he died in France in 1799.

Perthshire Militia Disturbances The riot at Tranent and its aftermath (below) may have contributed to disturbances in Strathtay. Arising also from opposition to the Militia Act, the disturbances arose when lists of those eligible to be balloted for service in the militia were posted on kirk doors. Although both Angus Cameron and James Menzies are credited as agents of the United Scotsmen, the spontaneous nature of both the protests, the appeals to the protection of feudal superiors and the rapid waning of resistance in the face of armed intervention by authority suggest little if any external involvement or support.

Tranent On August 28 1797, a large crowd gathered at Prestonpans and agreed a series of resolutions against the Militia Act. The crowd sacked the schoolmaster's house and destroyed the militia list. The ballot for those eligible to serve in the militia was to be made the next day. The Deputy-Lieutenants, backed by troops from the Cinque Port and the Pembrokeshire Cavalry, as well as local yeomanry, advanced on Tranent. The crowd asserted the Militia Act was "against the Union" (i.e., that of 1707) and stones were thrown, leading to the soldiers being forced into a public house that was then surrounded by the crowd. The soldiers fired blank rounds to disperse the crowd, but then resorted to live ammunition. Managing to clear the streets, volunteer cavalry then chased the people out into the open fields where for a half-hour they set about "shooting, spearing, slashing and riding down a populace armed only with stones". Twelve men, women and children were killed, and many more injured. The Lord Advocate, Robert Dundas, refused to indict the troops for murdering unarmed civilians and justified their actions in the face of "such a dangerous mob as deserved more properly the name of an insurrection".

James Tytler (1745-1804) Possibly the most interesting of the Scottish Radicals, Tytler was born the son of a Presbyterian minister in Angus. After training for the ministry, he studied medicine at Edinburgh before becoming a ship's surgeon and subsequently a pharmacist. He edited both the second and third editions of the "*Encyclopaedia Britannica*", then published in Edinburgh. He was also the author of a number of political pamphlets. Always close to bankruptcy, he was nevertheless the first person in the British Isles to attempt manned balloon flight, although after initial successes, his experiments became overshadowed by those of Vincenti Lunardi. His politics led to his being outlawed in his absence by the High Court, and he fled Scotland first for Belfast and subsequently the United States, where he died as a result of an accident.